TALES OF THE SLAYER

Buffy the Vampire Slayer

TALES OF THE SLAYER

Includes stories from *Tales of the Slayer Vol. I* and *Vol. II*

SIMON PULSE

NEW YORK   LONDON   TORONTO   SYDNEY   NEW DELHI

This book is a work of fiction. Any references to historical events, real people, or real places are used fictitiously. Other names, characters, places, and events are products of the author's imagination, and any resemblance to actual events or places or persons, living or dead, is entirely coincidental.

SIMON PULSE
An imprint of Simon & Schuster Children's Publishing Division
1230 Avenue of the Americas, New York, New York 10020
This Simon Pulse paperback edition December 2018
™ and © 2018 by Twentieth Century Fox Film Corporation. All rights reserved.
"A Good Run," "Die Blutgräfin," and "Mornglom Dreaming" ™ and © 2001
by Twentieth Century Fox Film Corporation. All rights reserved.
"Again," "The War Between the States," "House of the Vampire," and "Abomination" ™ and © 2003
by Twentieth Century Fox Film Corporation. All rights reserved.
Cover illustrations by Neal Williams
All rights reserved, including the right of reproduction in whole or in part in any form.
SIMON PULSE and colophon are registered trademarks of Simon & Schuster, Inc.
For information about special discounts for bulk purchases, please contact
Simon & Schuster Special Sales at 1-866-506-1949 or business@simonandschuster.com.
The Simon & Schuster Speakers Bureau can bring authors to your live event.
For more information or to book an event contact the Simon & Schuster Speakers Bureau
at 1-866-248-3049 or visit our website at www.simonspeakers.com.
Cover designed by Sarah Creech
Interior designed by Mike Rosamilia
The text of this book was set in ITC Berkeley Oldstyle.
Manufactured in the United States of America
2 4 6 8 10 9 7 5 3 1
Library of Congress Control Number 2018957432
ISBN 9781534443600 (pbk)
These stories were previously published in *Tales of the Slayer Vol. 1* and *Tales of the Slayer Vol. 2*.

· CONTENTS ·

Again   1
Sunnydale, California, 1999
   Jane Espenson

The War Between the States   39
New York City, New York, 1922
   Rebecca Rand Kirshner

A Good Run   79
Greece, 490 B.C.E.
   Greg Rucka

House of the Vampire   101
London, England, 1897
   Michael Reaves

Abomination   143
Beauport, Brittany, France, 1320
   Laura J. Burns and Melinda Metz

Die Blutgräfin   177
Hungary, 1609
   Yvonne Navarro

Mornglom Dreaming   221
Kentucky, 1886
   Doranna Durgin

AGAIN
Jane Espenson

Sunnydale, California, 1999

"Anya? Anya, what's going on?"

Xander was mumbling, still half-asleep. Maybe even three-quarters. But not entirely. And he absolutely knew something was wrong.

Part of it was the light. Even face-down, face smooshed in to the pillow, blankets up around his ears, he could sense it was wrong. The light was too bright, and even stranger, it was coming from the wrong side. "Anya?" She was probably responsible somehow, like maybe she moved the bed while he was asleep. Some bizarre prewedding preparation? Everything she did these days was about the wedding. The very thought of that made him want to bury himself even deeper in to the bed. *Warm, warm delightful bed . . .*

Except something was still wrong. *The light. Right.* And more than the light. Like . . . where *was* Anya? Still face-down, eyes still closed, he sent one sleepy hand out on a reconnaissance mission. Anya wasn't in her half of the bed. And, in fact, her half of the bed was missing entirely. That didn't normally happen.

He flipped over and sat up in one panicked motion. His heart kicked in his chest. He looked around the room with suddenly clear eyes. He found himself in a twin bed, narrow and too soft and extremely familiar. In fact the whole place was familiar. He was in his old room. Not the basement, but the room upstairs, the room that was his from first grade through twelfth grade. It had never really been a great place to be, but now, now it was positively alarming.

He took it in quickly. Everything was there. The olive-colored shag carpet. The poster of Tyra Banks in unlikely swimwear. His skateboard, leaned against the wall next to a pile of untended laundry. His old bulletin board with his name doodled messily across the cork. On the dusty bookshelf, next to an abandoned pizza box, his Spider-Man action figure recoiled from an imminent attack from G. I. Joe. "Whoa . . ." It was all Xander could manage. "I was pathetic."

It was obvious that something supernatural was going on. In Sunnydale it was almost always easiest to just start with that assumption. *Time travel. Gotta be. Someone sent me back, years back, probably because they're evil and somehow this is part of their plan, which probably ends with me all eviscerated and dead.* It wasn't a comforting thought. He got up and went to the dresser. He might end up eviscerated and dead, but he wasn't gonna be eviscerated and dead and naked. Not in front of Tyra. The top dresser drawer was full of comic books. *Right.* He sighed and turned to the pile of laundry. *Oh yeah, this routine.*

Willow's hair was tangled: Her eyes were squinty and they had little crusty bits at the corners. Her cheek was imprinted with a diagonal crease from her pillow. And she wore flannel PJ's with pictures of tiny purple pigs on them. She wasn't at her sharpest. She was, in fact, at her unsharpest.

Willow's bedroom was on the ground floor of her parents' house. So the knocking on the front door had awakened her right away. She stumbled out of bed, ran into an unexpected wall, ricocheted, then finally careened to the door, which was in entirely the wrong place, and opened it. And found Oz. Absurdly, the first thing she registered was that his T-shirt read "Robot Baby Cat."

"Hey," he said.

When Willow imagined the human brain at work, she always pictured it as a kind of machine. Not a computer, but a sort of H. G. Wells steam-powered cogs-and-gears kind of machine. And right now the gears were locked up and the steam valves were backing up. She couldn't fathom how she'd come to be here, in the doorway of her parents' house, in purple pig pajamas, looking at her high school boyfriend-slash-werewolf.

"Um. Maybe I should come back when you're less . . . comatose," Oz suggested.

Willow blinked at him, which made her aware of the crusty things at the corners of her eyes. She rubbed at them while she stumbled through, "Um . . . Oz . . . what the heck's going on?"

"Willow?" Suddenly Oz didn't even sound so sure she was really herself. Which was understandable, since she was a little vague on that very same point.

The phone rang. The laboring machine of Willow's brain recognized that sound right away.

"How 'bout I go ahead?" Oz volunteered.

The phone rang again as Willow nodded at him blankly. Oz turned to walk away. Willow closed the door and stepped to the phone. She picked it up cautiously. "Hello?"

It was Xander.

+ + +

They walked toward the high school as they talked.

"It's just so weird. And why'd we get our old bodies back, anyway? I mean, what kind of time travel is this? It seems all non-standard if you ask me," said Willow. She felt better just having Xander to talk to.

"Gimme a sec to look it up my *Big Book of Time Travel*—oh yeah, don't have one."

"Right. Sorry, Xander. Hey, what's the last thing you remember?"

"Me and Anya, going to bed. Like every night."

"Me too." She hesitated. "Only, you know, not with Anya, obviously. Alone."

"Oh. So when do you think we are, Will? Exactly, I mean."

Willow watched as Xander idly kicked at a rock on the sidewalk. She answered slowly.

"Three years ago. Senior year. A couple months before . . . you know, graduation. I saw my calendar at home. I forgot I used to cross off the days. Neat little Xs and small notes about papers being due. Then I'd go back and write down what grade I got on each one."

Xander looked at her. "Wow. I'm glad I didn't know that then. New heights of teasing would have been scaled."

Willow glanced at Xander. "It's weird how weird you look."

"I didn't realize how much the construction work kinda changed me. I mean, look at this arm. It's all scrawny. How'd I live like this?"

"I don't know. Oh, Xander, watch this. I noticed right before you came by." Willow pointed at a passing dog-walker and muttered something Xander couldn't hear. Obviously a spell. Xander looked at her.

"What did you do?"

"I turned the dog into a turnip."

Xander looked at the dog. It was small and fluffy and not very much like a turnip.

"Xander, I can't do magick, I mean, not *well*. It's like *that* went back to how it used to be too! I don't even get how that happened! Isn't that creepy?"

"Oooh. Yeah. That's by far the creepiest part of unexplained nonstandard time travel."

"Shut up. I think it's plenty creepy." She instantly regretted that. "Sorry. Little bit cranky."

"'S'Okay. Maybe it's like jet lag. Losing three years probably does that. Or maybe it's gaining three years, depends how you look at it, I guess."

They walked in silence for a few steps, deep in thought.

"You tried reaching her?" Willow asked.

"I told you. Only like a dozen times. There's no answer. Maybe she's still in the present—I mean, the future."

"Wait, that doesn't make sense. Xander, even if she's still in the . . . even if she wasn't sent back like us, she still exists in this time. I mean, it would just be, like, high school Buffy. She's got to be around."

"So where is she, Will?"

"I dunno. Let's hurry up."

Xander and Willow moved along the residential Sunnydale street. They walked fast, as if something was on their trail. Which maybe it was. When magick happens and the world goes wonky, it was often good to make oneself into a moving target. Because sometimes something evil was watching.

+ + +

A tree stood in front of the Summers house. And stretching away from the foot of the tree was its dark shadow. Other things in the yard had shadows too. The mailbox had a shadow. So did the tennis ball abandoned there by the neighbor's spaniel; it had a little shadow. But if you looked close, you might notice that these weren't quite as dark as the tree-shadow. The tree-shadow was very dark. When the wind moved the branches of the tree, the shadow moved too. At exactly the same time. Until it didn't. Until it twitched. Until it shifted on its own. Until it turned its attention to the house. Until it thought, *Now. I will move now.*

Buffy was vaguely aware that she'd been sleeping through the ringing of the phone. And some part of her mind was a little pissed off that no one had been picking it up. *House full to burstin' with people, after all, Willow and Dawn and Giles.* The place was a commune. Then it registered that it didn't *feel* like a house full of people. Not this morning. Maybe it was slayer-sharp senses picking up different acoustics from different furniture, or a different pattern of air moving through the halls, or a different scent from different human bodies. Or maybe it was just because she knew really well what it felt like to be alone.

Then there was a sound. *Outside. The front porch.* Someone or something was at the front door.

Buffy was on her feet immediately, lunging for her weapons in one smooth motion. But her weapons chest wasn't where she left it and she ended up slamming her hand into the nightstand. *Crappity-crap!*

She found the weapons chest, unable to take the time even to wonder why it was there, against the opposite wall, where she used to keep it. She grabbed a stake and flew for the bedroom door, down the stairs, even as the front door began to swing inward. Out of time.

Buffy launched herself down the stairs, stake braced in front of her.

She came to a rest with the tip of the stake pressed against her mother's chest.

Joyce looked frightened and startled. Buffy looked back. At her mother. Who was obviously completely alive.

There were a thousand things Buffy wanted to say to her, to ask her. *Are you real? Will this last? Can I tell you how much I love you?* She opened her mouth, half-wondering which of them she was going to hear.

"Were you at the gallery?" That wasn't one of the ones she was expecting to pick.

Frowning, Joyce moved the stake away from her heart. "Yes, I was. The alarm went off and the company called me. False alarm. We don't open till ten, so I figured I'd head back here, grab a shower, and maybe get impaled by my teenage slayer daughter."

Unsure what else to do, Buffy nodded, wondering if she looked as freaked out as she felt.

Willow was still aware of a pressing instinct to hurry, but right now that was out of the question. Right now there was more of a need to do this. To stand next to Xander and stare open-mouthed.

"There it is," she heard him say, very softly. "Then. Now. You know . . . before it blew up."

Sunnydale High. Not an unsafe charred hulk left damaged by a mayor-snake, then devastated by a mayor-snake-killing explosion, but a solid building that looked like it would stand forever. They stood and looked up toward the main entrance. Around them students crowded and swarmed, hurrying to get inside before the bell.

"It looks smaller," he continued. The building, the parking lot, the bike racks. "Even the buses."

Willow turned to look. "Xander, that's the special education bus. It *is* smaller."

"Oh . . . right."

"Oh my God! Look! Over there." Willow jabbed him in the ribs hard and pointed, picking one figure out of the crowd. A blond head shone among the rest. Not Buffy, someone else.

"Ow! Who? Oh, Harmony." Xander squinted at the girl who would be turned into a vampire. Soon. She was bitten during the graduation melee. It felt strange seeing her, knowing what was going to happen.

"In the sunshine. How strange is that? She has no idea . . ."

Xander looked blankly at Willow. "So, do we, what? Do we warn her? Are we here to, like, keep that whole thing from happening? Like a *Quantum Leap*y thing? Or, you know, not?"

Willow turned and headed for the main entrance. "I don't know. But I bet Giles will. Maybe he's even like us, you know, from the future or whatever, and he can help us figure this out."

Willow and Xander walked through the halls, making their way to the school library. Xander kept being distracted. His old locker. The flyers on the walls. The display case in the hallway, the one with that cheerleading trophy that always gave him a funny creepy feeling. The halls were emptying as students made their way into their homerooms. That's what Larry was doing when Xander saw him. Larry was a football star, and he was one of the many students who would die at the upcoming graduation ceremony. Xander got the strangest feeling watching Larry disappear into a room and close the door behind him, like he was watching Larry die right then. He shuddered.

"This is really weird, Will. I don't like this. It's like we can see what's gonna happen to everybody."

"I know. I used to think I'd love to be able to see the future, know all that stuff. But not if it's like this."

"You there!" A familiar voice rang out behind them. "Why aren't you in homeroom, you nasty little vagrants?"

Willow looked back, knowing already who it was. Principal Snyder, every scant inch of him. He would also die soon, swallowed whole in front of the entire student body. Willow and Xander stopped and gave in to the unique and sad experience of being lectured by a ghost.

"Let me see your hall passes!"

Buffy looked at the waffle iron and tried to figure out if the waffles were done. She was pretty sure the light was supposed to go on. Or maybe it was supposed to go off. It was definitely one or the other. She tried to remember if the light had been on when she poured the batter on. Maybe it was and then the light went off and she didn't see it. Or maybe not. "Mom?"

Joyce entered the kitchen. "What? Haven't you left for school? Oh, Buffy."

Buffy looked at what her mother was looking at: bowls and spoons on the counter, some spilled waffle batter, and the uncooperative waffle iron, which was starting to smoke a little around the edges. No matter what Mister Light said, they were probably done. Really, really done.

Joyce hurried to rescue the waffles while Buffy tried to explain.

"I was trying to make you something nice for breakfast. You know, for us to have together before you have to go back to the gallery. And I knew waffles were your favorites. *Are* your favorites. I promise, I promise so much that I'll clean up the mess."

Joyce was using a fork to try to scrape a half-raw, half-scorched waffle off the surface of the waffle iron. "Buffy, you really should've asked me about this. Did you even grease this thing at all?"

"Um . . . grease it?"

Joyce sighed, exasperated. "Sit down over there, out of my way, and let me fix this."

Buffy sat.

"Aren't you going to be late for school?" Joyce asked.

"There's lots of time. They pushed first period back a half-hour this week." The lie came easily, and it made Buffy feel like a criminal. So few sentences, a finite number of sentences she'd ever spoken to her mother. How many of them had been lies?

She watched in silence as her mother moved around the kitchen. Cleaning up Buffy's mess, making food for the two of them to share, humming softly. The humming wasn't a song. Anyone else might call it tuneless. But, with a jolt, Buffy recognized it as her mother's own *particular* tunelessness, the same little nonsong she always hummed to herself. When she died, the nonsong would go with her. Buffy let the tears fill her eyes. She wasn't going to lie about that, about the tears. If Mom saw, she saw.

Buffy knew there were things she should do. She should call Giles and say "Hey, I've been sent careening three years backward in time. How 'bout you?" She should round up Willow and Xander and Anya and Tara. *No, no, Anya and Tara aren't my friends yet*. But she *should* round up Willow and Xander and they should figure this out—find out why it happened, what the threat was. Kill it. And go back to the right time.

The right present. When Mom is dead.

Joyce was making omelets. Buffy watched, marveling at how easy she made it look. Where did her mother get that grace, the ability to make things look easy? Back in the present, Buffy was running a household now—trying to, anyway. She never felt graceful, never felt able. She'd had her mom in her life for such a short time, and she'd never really appreciated her, not this part of her anyway. Maybe this was a gift. A chance to do it again, do it right.

A thought occurred to Buffy. "Um . . . Mom? Where's Dawn? Did she go to school?"

Joyce looked up from the omelet. "Dawn? Who's Dawn?"

A bird flew over Sunnydale. Its small shadow hopped and glided along the ground. Over streets and sidewalks. Over lawns. For a fraction of a second it crossed the Summers' front yard. The shadow flicked from a corner of the driveway to a corner of the house before it leaped to the roof and on over the town. And while it crossed, almost too fast to be seen, something rode with it, skittering along the ground to the deep shade of the bushes at that corner, near the front door. The something dark was moving closer.

Finally free of Snyder, Willow and Xander burst into the library, startling Giles, who was just crossing the room with a thick book in one hand and a cup of tea in the other.

Xander slumped with disappointment. "It didn't happen to him."

"How can you tell?" Willow asked.

"Well, just look at him. Look how young he looks. His skin is much tighter. This is Giles from three years ago."

"Xander, we all look young. If our skin was as old as his we'd be tighter too! These are our bodies from three years ago, remember?"

"Oh yeah. So maybe it is him."

They both turned and stared at Giles. After a second Willow realized something.

"If it happened to him, he would've said something by now."

"Mmm." Xander nodded in agreement.

Giles cleared his throat impatiently, which made them both jump.

He spoke. "Oh yes, absolutely. If it had happened to me I would undoubtedly know what in the bloody hell you two were on about and then perhaps I wouldn't be watching you stare at me like an exhibit in a bloody wax museum."

Willow blushed. "Oh."

"Sorry," Xander mumbled.

"It's possible we're not thinking too clearly right now, Giles. I mean, I was asleep and then I woke up and there were pajamas and my old house and Oz was there . . ."

Giles shifted his weight to the other foot, taking it all in. "Hmmm. Yes. Again, I'm sure I'd be extremely understanding if I, well, understood. One of you, for God's sake, tell me what's going on."

"Time travel," Xander explained. "For us, last night was November 8, 2001. And today we're partying like it's 1999."

"Extraordinary." Giles took off his glasses and cleaned them as he sat down at the library's central table.

Willow and Xander followed him to the table.

"You believe us, right?" Xander asked, anxiously.

Giles met his eyes. "Yes, yes, I do, actually."

"Um . . . can I ask . . . why?" Xander asked.

Giles thought a second, then said, "If you live on a Hellmouth and you question the unlikely, I find that it just slows everything down."

"We thought maybe it happened to you, too," Willow volunteered. "But I guess not."

"No, no, it certainly did not. What . . . have you talked to Buffy?"

"No." Xander turned a chair around and straddled it backward. "We tried to call, but there's no answer."

"We walked past her homeroom on the way here and she wasn't there either. So I guess we know a little more . . . nothing. We know nothing." Willow had tugged the ends of her long sleeves over her hands, twisting them nervously.

"Hmm, yes."

"But we're okay," Xander said hopefully. "I mean, we're not injured, and, you know . . ." He shot a glance at a nearby patch of floor, "The Hellmouth looks like it's neatly shut. It could be worse."

Giles was startled, and his nerves were thin. "Xander! Time has been disrupted! Something very powerful did this for motives we can hardly begin to guess. The Slayer hasn't been located. She may be in danger. We all may be in danger. And on top of this it's starting to look like the mayor is up to something—"

"Giant snake on graduation day," Willow said simply.

"What?"

"It's okay. We kill it." Xander supplied. "Blow up the school in the process."

"So you might want to start getting your favorite books out of here."

"Stop it!" Giles was on his feet now, almost shaking with alarm. "Stop! It's vitally important that you not tell me any more about the future!"

"Oh. Okay." Willow nodded. "You don't want to influence it. I get that."

Xander nodded too. Then stopped. "Wait. I *don't* get that. I mean, we know stuff that could really help you right now. And it's not like, oh no, if we influence the past we change our present, because, frankly, there's a lot of problems in our present and a little changing might be, you know, just what we need."

"No." Giles was firm. "It's too risky."

"Um, Giles? I'm kinda with Xander on this one. I mean, I don't get the what's-so-risky."

Giles cleaned his glasses again. "Well, any knowledge of the future could affect me in unforeseen ways, my choices and emotions. For example, if I know that we will defeat the mayor, then perhaps I don't work as hard to make it happen."

"You might take it for granted," Willow supplied.

"Yes. Just knowing the outcome might make the outcome fail to happen, you see? And, for another thing, we have no way of knowing if you're from *this* future."

Xander thought he was following along pretty well, but that part threw him. "What?" he asked. "Which future?"

"The events you remember, they might have happened on a different time line from this one, making your information dangerously misleading. Or they may not have happened at all. Perhaps someone has magickally implanted three years of false memories into your brains, although that's a stretch."

"Ooh. Not really a stretch," Willow said, thinking it through. "It's kinda like what the monks did with Dawn."

Giles looked at her. "What monks? Who's Dawn?"

Willow and Xander exchanged a look.

Xander cleared his throat. "Um . . . I guess that's one of the things, one of the things we're not supposed to tell you about."

Giles looked at the two of them searchingly. Obviously curious, but resisting. After a moment he went on: "Well, one thing is certain. We have to find Buffy. We need her, and she may be in some kind of danger. If something sentient did this, then it did it with a purpose."

The darkness at the corner of Buffy's house lay flat against the ground. Sometimes it rippled at the edges, agitated by the closeness of its goal. She was in the house, on the other side of the door. It didn't know her name. It didn't even know she was the Slayer, although it sensed the power. All it knew was that it had to do this. It had to clean it all up. Put things right. Others would clean up the rest of the Violators. They were probably closing in on them now. But that wasn't its concern. It just had to get rid of her. To start to put things right.

The knowledge of its closeness to its goal made it hold. It rippled itself forward, creating a shadow where none could he, on the unshaded stoop—a deep stain of shade. It pushed forward, elongating, reaching for the door. It inched itself forward, slowly.

It was paper thin. Thinner. It slipped under the door without effort. It did not know what effort was.

It was inside the house.

+ + +

Buffy stood at the bathroom sink. She stared at her own reflection, the reflection of how she'd looked three years ago. Her hair had been lighter that year, and her face a little younger, more unformed, still half child. It was distracting, leading her mind down paths of choice and regrets. She shook her head, looked down, and gripped the edge of the sink, trying to force herself to think.

She had her mother back. Alive. Buffy wanted to cry with joy at the very thought. She had her mother.

But she lost her sister.

But she had her mother.

Buffy heard her mother downstairs now, crossing the entryway from dining room to living room, probably looking for her purse, her keys, getting ready to head out to the gallery again. And Buffy knew she should go to school. She'd ducked her mother's question earlier with a lie, but now it was clearly time to leave. She needed to seek out her friends anyway, talk to Giles, start working on making her way back into the future . . . except that the future wasn't necessarily where she wanted to be.

Here, she had no sister. She had a mother.

I could take her to the hospital, Buffy thought. *It's so early. If they caught it now, caught the tumor now, they could fight it maybe, cut it out of her. There'd be no fatal hemorrhage.* Maybe it wasn't over after all. Maybe the last three years were best forgotten, discarded. But Dawn—*How do you weigh a sister against a mother?*

The phone rang. Phones rang for a lot of reasons. It could be anyone on the other end of that line. But what were the chances . . . what were the chances that it was Giles calling, or Willow? Someone who would make her do the "right" thing? Someone who would say, *You can't do this. Can't step out of time this way, accept the mistake, take back the three years.*

Buffy ran from the bathroom, back into her bedroom. She picked up the receiver and immediately dropped it down onto the cradle again, severing the connection. Then she reached under and behind the bed, groped for the phone cord, where it snaked into the jack. With a violent wrenching pull, she unplugged the phone from the wall. She'd have to disconnect them all, all the extensions. But that was easy. And it was the right thing to do. She needed time to think. Time to spend with her mother.

Buffy stepped out onto the landing. Joyce was in the doorway, hand on the knob. Heading out. She looked up the stairs toward Buffy.

"Buffy? Did you get the phone?"

"Yeah. Wrong number."

"Oh, all right. You want me to drop you at school, or—"

"Mom?"

Joyce paused and looked at her daughter. Buffy continued, "I think I'm sick. I suddenly feel terrible."

Joyce frowned, concerned. "Terrible how?"

Buffy looked away as she answered. "Kinda hot. You know, fevery. And my skin hurts. Not serious sick but still . . ."

"Oh, Buffy. Well, I suppose you can stay home, if you—"

"No. Mom. I really . . . do you think you could stay with me? For a while?"

Joyce hesitated.

The something dark was curled around the bottom post of the banister at the bottom of the stairs, a round black shadow that listened and waited. It was content to wait now. Now that she was in sight. It needed to be done, but it needed to be done neatly. If the other one stayed, that would be all right for now. Because at some point the Violator would be alone and then she could be taken away. And the others would be gone too. It could be clean again. Everything could be put right.

Willow waved her hand and pointed. She knew without even looking that nothing had happened. When you did magick, really *did* it, there was a kind of surge. It started as a kind of surfacy thing, a crackle in the fingertips and a sort of carbonated feeling that sizzled up your arm. And then, right after, as the magick took hold, you could feel something deeper in your chest and belly—a feeling, just for a moment, that felt a little like panic and a little like joy and little like anger. And it felt as good and clean and strong the hundredth time you felt it as it did the first time. There was no feeling like that now.

Xander leaned over and asked, "What did you try to do?" They were sitting together at the central table in the library. Willow inclined her head toward where Giles was standing in the stacks, looking for texts that might help them understand what was happening. She spoke softly to Xander, respecting Giles's desire to be kept uninformed about their current lives. She figured that included her improved magickal abilities. "If it worked, all the books that mention time travel would have turned red. Then we could only worry about the red ones." She glared absently at her hand as if the lack of magick was somehow its fault.

Giles returned to the table, carrying a book. He handed it to Xander. "I think this one may be helpful." The book was red. Xander looked Willow, his eyes wide.

"Hey! Maybe it worked!"

Willow glanced at the book. "I've looked at that one before. It was always red."

"Oh." Xander sounded defeated.

Willow had a sudden thought. She looked to Giles. "Xander and I, we need to go to class."

Giles was surprised. "Surely you—we have research to do."

Willow realized that this Giles wasn't used to her being so forceful. She explained: "We're not getting anywhere here. I think we should go try to figure out if we're on the right time line or not, by, you know, *living* here . . . just till we can tell."

Giles hesitated. Xander didn't look that certain either. "Exactly how can we tell that?"

Willow closed the book on her lap. "We want to know if we've lived this day before, right?"

Giles, clearly picking up on the idea, answered, "You'll want to look for independent events, things that aren't influenced by the different ways you're going to interact with them—a science exam, a lecture or class project, or a fire drill . . . something."

Xander nodded, thinking that it was a pretty impossible job. Who remembered a fire drill from three years ago? But it was better than sitting here feeling helpless. He nodded and said, "Giles, while we're doing that, maybe you should try to find Buffy. I think we've let this go too long without her."

Giles nodded. Xander was right. This Xander and this Willow both seemed more confident, less likely to be led. Stronger. A part of him felt very proud.

Buffy was propped on the living room sofa, a blanket draped over her. She smiled as Mom handed her a bowl of Chicken and Stars soup, then adjusted the blanket as she sat down by Buffy's feet. "Thanks, Mom."

"Oh, honey. You're welcome. I know how it is to suddenly feel yucky."

Buffy felt a shiver of alarm. "Do you? I mean, have you been feeling sick?"

"What? No, of course not! I just mean that when you feel sick, it's just such a helpless feeling, like you're young again and you just want your mother to take care of you."

Buffy looked into the soup, moving stars with the tip of her spoon, hiding her emotion. "Yeah, that's it. That's exactly how I feel."

Willow slipped into History class, late. It had taken her some minutes of walking the halls, peeking into classrooms, for her to recall her senior schedule. But this was right—Mr. Harten at the front of the class, Oz in a desk to her left.

"Miss Rosenberg, nice of you to join us." Willow remembered that Mr. Harten had never been an original guy. He'd decided, years ago, on an appropriate quip to address tardiness, and he saw no reason to change that habit.

"Sorry, Mr. Harten. Couldn't be helped," she said back to him as she took her seat. She noticed a few heads turning toward her in surprise, including Oz. It took her a moment to realize what they were reacting to. She was out of character. High school Willow didn't have that confident offhand voice. She wouldn't ever have shown up late for class, and certainly not without a notebook, and if for some reason she did, she would have been blushing like a radish from having the eyes of all the students on her.

After a moment Mr. Harten started talking again. Willow listened hard, trying to remember if she'd heard this lecture before, a discussion of the role of accident in history. It was interesting, and some of the facts sounded familiar, but she wasn't sure. Maybe this part—

"Pssssst!"

Willow looked around to see who was hissing. Oz, in that desk to her left. Probably worried about her after her strangeness this morning, and now . . . *He probably thinks I'm ignoring him. Which I kind of am.*

She looked at him, met his eyes. He smiled at her, one of the little smiles he reserved just for her, the faintest twitch of his lips. To her surprise she *felt* that smile, felt the warmth that it caused. She smiled back at him, almost involuntarily. A connection. She felt her pulse speed up, blood rush to her face. She looked away, fast.

Whoo. She was one confused little kitty. At first this world had felt terribly foreign. But there were parts of it that were beyond familiar. She had just been patting herself on the back for having moved beyond the scared, radishy teenager that she had been, and suddenly here she was, scared and red-faced—radish deluxe.

And desperately homesick. She didn't want to be here any longer. Her world in 2002 was kinda screwed up, with Tara getting so strange on her, moving out . . .

And now with this reaction to Oz . . .

What do I want?

Tara.

She knew she'd rather be there with Tara, even an angry Tara, than anywhere in this old landscape where she felt herself losing ground, slipping back into what she used to be. She still loved Oz, and she'd never lied to herself about that, but not like how she loved Tara. And she didn't want to be back in the life that Oz-love belonged to.

She slumped a little lower in her seat and tried to concentrate on the lecture. Maybe she'd remember this section on scientific accidents. She didn't look toward Oz again. She didn't notice his confused frown. Or the dark, dark shadow that his desk made—darker than the other shadows.

Xander looked at the parallelogram on the blackboard. Geometry. It suddenly occurred to him that perhaps this wasn't time travel, perhaps it was one of those hell dimensions, and he was going to be enrolled in remedial ninth-grade geometry forever. But it didn't matter, he supposed, if he understood anything now. He was just here to play "Do I remember this?"

Mrs. Holland was drawing a rectangle on the board. She labeled one vertical side *A* and the top *B*. "So who can tell me the area of the rectangle?"

Xander knew that. *A* times *B*. He nodded to himself, a little self-satisfied. A person didn't take geometry twice without learning something. Someone else in the class gave the answer and Mrs. Holland continued. She pointed at the parallelogram. Its top was *Y* units long and it was *X* units tall. And the length of its oh-so-slanty side was *Z*. What was its area?

Xander started looking around the room at the other students, no sense in even listening to this. Then he looked back. Something had suddenly struck him. What if that parallelogram was made of wood? What if it was part of a carpentry project? He imagined sawing off triangles from both sides, leaving a square. Then you could put those triangles together . . . another square, put them next to the first square. He could see it in his mind. It was a rectangle. A Y-by-X rectangle. And he knew how to do that.

"The area is X times Y!" He stood up and shouted it. Everyone turned to stare at him.

He sat back down, smiling sheepishly, while the teacher, obviously startled, explained to the class why Xander's answer was right.

They went on, discussing areas of circles, volumes of pyramids . . . Xander wielded a mental saw, rearranging the shapes, building huge structures in his mind. It was simple. Could it really have been this easy all along? All the torture, all the years of feeling stupid . . . unnecessary. Well, that was just terrific.

Xander was having a breakthrough about cutting the area under a curve into infinitely small rectangular slices when he saw a shadow flit across the floor, but he barely noticed it. He was moments away from understanding the basic principle behind all of calculus.

Willow and Xander sat, heads together, at lunch. They discussed the total absence of any progress, except that Xander was now convinced he was a misunderstood geometrical genius.

There weren't two shadows following them anymore. They had merged into one. It lay, spread like a manta ray, under their table. It didn't care who they were or what they were talking about. It just needed to clean them. They didn't belong there.

Willow was talking over the babble and rumble of the cafeteria. "But, Xander, I told you all that! Every time I tutored you I talked about cutting up that parallelogram!"

"But you didn't say it was made of wood!"

"*Wood?* For God's sake, Xander, how does that make any diff—"

She broke off and Xander stared at her.

Then she screamed.

She slumped in her chair, silent now, and started to slide to the ground. Xander, scared and confused, jumped up and hurried to grab her. He picked her up in his arms, ignoring the stares from the students in the crowded lunchroom.

There was something on her leg. It was clinging to her shin. A dark film. Xander had never seen anything like it. And whatever it was, it was clearly hurting Willow. She whimpered, semiconscious. Xander carried her out of the lunchroom, toward the library. Giles would know what to do. *He has to.*

Giles stood on Buffy's front stoop. He knocked again, getting impatient. Finally Joyce opened the door.

"Oh! Mr. Giles . . . Rupert."

"Um . . . Joyce. Hello."

The two of them had been awkward with each other ever since a candy-addled encounter on the hood of a police car the previous year. He cleared his throat, willing himself to soldier through the tense moment.

"Is, um . . . is Buffy here?"

"Well, she is, but the thing is, I'm afraid she's not feeling very well today. Unless the world is at stake, I think it would be best if you waited to see her tomorrow, or, you know, whenever she feels better."

Giles met Joyce's eye and set his jaw. "I'm afraid the world might be at stake, at least a bit."

Startled by his determination, Joyce took a step backward and Giles brushed past her, turning left into the living room.

Buffy was on the sofa, feet up, blanket to her chin. A can of soda with a bendy-straw protruding from it sat on the floor next to a celebrity tabloid. She blinked up at Giles.

"Giles? What's going on? Is it Faith and the mayor?"

Faith and the mayor. Giles hesitated, thrown off balance. Was it possible that the time phenomenon affecting Willow and Xander had left Buffy untouched? But there was something about Buffy's open, guiltless face. Strikingly unblinking. It wasn't ringing true.

"When you're really innocent, your eyes aren't quite that wide. You're not telling the truth. I know what's happened, Buffy. I know where you're from."

Joyce was in the doorway. "What do you mean? Where she's from?"

Buffy sat up and pushed the blanket aside. "Mom, I have to talk to Giles, if it's okay."

"Oh, well, all right, if it's slaying business. I'll be upstairs." Joyce reluctantly turned toward the stairs.

Giles sat heavily on the sofa next to Buffy. He didn't know how to begin this conversation. Directly, he supposed, was best.

"You have to go back to where you belong, Buffy."

"I don't know what you're talking about. Go back where?"

"Buffy, please. This is serious. I know what's happened."

She looked at him sharply, genuinely curious. "How? Did it happen to you too?"

"No, but Xander and Willow were affected. They're at the school, trying to figure out what happened. We were all quite concerned when we couldn't reach you."

Buffy tossed the blanket aside and walked to the fireplace. She leaned her forehead against the mantelpiece. She took a deep breath. With her head still down, she said, "I don't want to go back."

The shadow on the mantelpiece fluttered. She was so close.

Giles wanted to come closer, to stand near Buffy, but something told him not to get too close, that her composure couldn't take it. He gave her a moment, then he asked softly, "I understand that your life in the future isn't perfect, but it is your life, and you have to go—"

Her head snapped up and she fixed on him angrily. "It isn't perfect?" she mocked. "What I'm dealing with is way beyond 'isn't perfect.' You want to hear about it? The fabulous parade that is my future?"

"I can't." He hastened to stop her. "It's important that I not know what's going to happen."

She took a step toward him and he backed up involuntarily. Buffy never used her superior strength to intimidate him, and he was alarmed and frightened, frightened for her. What had happened to her to harden her this way? He was afraid he was about to find out.

"Here's my life, Giles. My lovely, miraculous life. First, Angel leaves me. Then I meet a new man, Riley. But he leaves me too. Oh, and I get a little sister, did they tell you about that one? I get the little sister I've always had but who never existed. And then my mother dies."

Giles took another step backward and steadied himself with a hand against the wall. Joyce was going to die?

"That's right, Watcher. She dies. A brain tumor. It's probably in there now, cooking away."

"Buffy, please, don't go on. I can't—"

"Can't what? Can't hear it or can't take it? Because it's not over. We're not even at the part where I die again to save the world. But I go to heaven, until Willow brings me back, pulls me out of paradise. Then you leave forever, which, by the way, thanks oh so much in advance. And I'm so alone, Giles. You can't image how alone I am. I'm so alone I'm having sex with Spike just because it's the only way I can feel anything."

Giles's face was a frozen mask, incapable of registering the amount of shock he was feeling. Could this really be the future? How could Xander and Willow have kept this to themselves? And how could Joyce be dead? How could Willow bring Buffy back from the dead? And could he leave Buffy alone in such a state? It didn't make sense.

"I'm so sorry." It was all he could manage, and he was deeply aware of how ridiculously inadequate it was.

"So that's why I don't want to go back. I know it's wrong and selfish, but God help me, Giles, it's what I want. I think . . ."

"What? What do you think?"

"I think maybe someone gave me a do-over."

Giles sat down, polished his glasses, and thought about that.

Xander burst into the library, Willow a slight weight in his arms. "Giles! Damn it, Giles, you have to be here!"

Willow was gasping for air, fighting obvious pain. "He's not here, Xander. Put me down."

On the verge of a screaming panic, Xander decided instead

to listen to his friend. He set her gingerly onto a chair. "Maybe I should take you to the hospital."

Willow winced and closed her eyes. "Right, because they're so good with killer shadow demons."

Xander knelt in front of her and looked at her leg. "Is that what this is, Will? A shadow demon?"

"I dunno. Maybe."

It looked to him more like a sheet of dark thick plastic that had been burned onto her. Where it had touched the skin of her ankle it had clung and seared itself right to her. Where it had touched pant leg, she'd had some protection, but it had still worked through in places and adhered to her. He tugged at the cuff of her jeans, trying to pull the substance or demon or whatever it was away from her. But he could feel it resist, pulling tighter against the pressure he was exerting.

"Xander! Stop that! It hurts!"

He pulled away and sat back on his heels. "I don't know what this thing is, Will. I think it's probably good that a lot of it's just touching the fabric. But I don't know how to fix it."

"I do."

He looked up at her, confused. Her eyes were open now, bright with pain but very focused. She continued, "We have to get back home."

"But Giles isn't here. And he said we'd need to know more so we could figure out what spell did this."

"This thing is doing something inside me, like it's put in little roots or something. It's spreading and we don't have time to do this Giles's way."

Xander blanched. Willow was making it sound like she was dying or something. "What other way is there?"

"My way. Can you . . . um . . . push me over to the table . . . or . . ."

Xander didn't like the sound of trying to maneuver her across the room, not with her in such pain. He pushed the table to her. She continued talking as she paged through one of the books Giles had piled on the table. "A spell sent us here, right? What Giles wanted to do was find out what spell it was and then undo it. Like untying a knot. What I'm talking about is stronger. I want to cancel any hold that any magick has over us. It's more like . . . like breaking a chain."

"Is it harder?"

"It takes more force, yeah."

"But, Will, you're already weak, and we've seen that your magick isn't exactly working its best here—"

"That's why . . ." She paused, and Xander realized she was fighting constant pain. "That's why you'll have to help me."

Xander shifted his weight from one foot to another. He was getting impatient, watching Willow read.

Something was killing Willow, and he had no idea where Giles and Buffy were.

Buffy watched Giles as he polished his glasses and thought. She'd missed him terribly since he'd returned to England, and she found herself absurdly grateful to have him here again. Even if she wasn't going to like what he was going to say.

Finally he took a deep breath and put his glasses back on. "You've put me in a difficult position, Buffy. And the truth is that I can't know for certain that the right answer is to send you back to your time. But I cannot help but feel that something is terribly—"

Buffy felt something hit her bare right arm. Something heavy and very, very painful. At first she thought she was being burned. Then it was worse than that. She screamed.

Giles leaped to his feet and ran to her. "Buffy! What is it? What is that thing?"

Buffy spared a fraction of a second to look at her arm. The thick dark film looked like it was grafted over her skin. And now . . . now it felt like something was burrowing in, digging its way into her flesh. She leaned heavily against the mantel again. The pain was making it hard to remain standing.

Willow felt terrible. The pain in her leg was fresh and sharp, and it was spreading. She had this mental image of tiny vines growing from a seed. The tiny vines were pain, and they were working their way up inside her leg. She found herself closing her eyes for longer and longer stretches of time, and it was getting harder and harder to pull herself back to the task at hand: getting home.

She was jolted back one more time when Xander plonked something onto the table in front of her: a small plastic bag full of herbs.

"I found this one in Giles's desk too. Bottom drawer behind a bunch of other stuff."

Willow forced herself to lean forward and examine the contents. The first bag Xander had brought to her had turned out to be Giles's stash of English tea. Useless for performing spells. But with any luck . . .

"This is it," she declared. The cured leaf of a rare tropical plant, it had one very valuable trait: whatever magick she and Xander might manage to conjure up, this herb would make it stronger.

Now there was nothing left to do but try to give it something to act on.

Xander asked, "So what do we do with it? Burn it or . . ." Willow looked at him and managed a smile. Xander was doing great, especially at not asking constantly if she was okay. The dark thing had spread, was halfway up her thigh, but Xander was being very cool about it.

"Just scatter it around. Make a circle around us."

So Xander pushed the table away again and scattered the chopped and wilted leaves around Willow's chair in a circle. When he finished he knelt in front of her. "What now?"

"Hold my hands. That'll focus my energy too."

Xander held her hands. Willow closed her eyes and leaned her head back. She concentrated on bringing the power of the universe around her, to use it to pull her back into her real time. If it worked, she and Xander, and anyone else nearby who was in the wrong time, would all be returned to where they belong.

She felt the power. Felt it building. She visualized it like a tower, growing from the ground up within the circle of her and Xander's arms. It grew, strong and bright. But the pain in her leg was strong too.

She opened her eyes. "Xander? I don't think it's gonna work."

Buffy held her arm out away from her body. Whatever this thing was, she didn't want it spreading to her torso through her own carelessness.

Giles was standing beside her now. Steadying her with one hand on her opposite shoulder, bending over the arm, examining it. Taking too long.

"Stop looking at it." She gasped. "Get me a knife."

Giles hesitated. Buffy locked eyes with him. She gave him a look that said, *Don't argue.*

Giles hurried to the weapons chest and within a second he was handing her a wicked-looking hunting knife.

"What are you going to do, Buffy? Try to peel it away—"

Buffy plunged the knife through the clinging entity and into her inside arm, halfway between wrist and elbow.

Stunned and horrified, Giles jumped back.

The dark thing on Buffy's arm had a three-inch slit right through its middle. It loosened its grip as Buffy's blood coursed through and splattered on the floor, leaving fat red circles.

"Buffy! What have you done?!"

"I don't know. I just . . . I needed to cut it. I thought maybe it would let go."

"I don't think it's that kind of—"

"Wait. Look!"

The dark thing was moving, contracting and thickening on Buffy's arm. Over the wound. Over the blood.

It tasted the blood. It was dirty—foreign blood from the future. It had to go. It all had to go. The person. The blood. But there was more blood. Blood got away. The foreign body was scattering. That couldn't be allowed. Where was the blood?

On the floor.

The dark thing let itself gather, contract, and drop.

Buffy and Giles watched in amazement as the dark thing dropped to the floor. It flattened out to a shadowy skin and moved to the spots of blood. It moved over them, moved on.... Two spots gone. It moved on.

"Giles, look. It's drinking the blood. What is it? Some kind of horizontal vampire?" Buffy was almost dizzy from the sudden lack of pain. Blood continued to run down her arm from the knife wound.

Giles was staring with sudden realization. "It's... cleaning. I think it's getting rid of you."

"What?"

"You don't belong in this time line. This... thing... it's cleaning up the time line by getting rid of you. All of you, including the spilled blood. I've read of such a thing, but I disregarded it." He looked sharply at Buffy. "We're not done. When it's done with your blood it has to take you out."

Buffy still held the knife. She fell to her knees by the shadowy creature. Stabbing it hadn't worked, but years of being the Slayer had taught Buffy something very important: Almost nothing could survive being cut into a hundred tiny pieces. It was a remarkably consistent law.

She hacked at it. Making deep cuts one way, then the other. It was in five pieces, then eight, then a dozen. She kept going.

Finally she felt Giles's hand on her shoulder. She looked up, a little dazed from what she'd been doing, and weak from loss of blood.

"You're done, Buffy. It's dead."

She kept her eyes on his face. She knew she was pleading, but she hoped it didn't sound that way. "If it's dead, can I stay? Can I please stay here?"

Xander lifted Willow into his arms. She'd finally passed out from the pain, and he'd decided it was time for the hospital. Willow might not think it could help, but he had to do something.

He lifted a foot to step over the patchy ring of dried herb. His foot hit something that felt like . . . all he could think of was . . . an electric sponge. He stepped back. And, as he looked, a glowing cylinder formed around him.

"Man, I hope this is a good thing."

The world seemed to fade around him. "Oh my God, we built a transporter. No, wait, I mean a time ma—" And before he finished the thought, he was gone.

As Giles looked into Buffy's face, he was searching for a way to say yes to her, a way to tell her it was okay to stay here. Then she began to fade.

Sunnydale, 2002

Buffy, Willow, and Xander were in the Magic Box. It was one day after they all materialized back into their beds. Willow had no evidence of ever having been attacked. Buffy bore a thin silver scar from her own knife.

They hadn't talked to Giles yet. Buffy thought he probably had ended up with no memory of their visit to the past. How could he possibly have known everything she'd told him and not let it show, all this time? Willow wasn't so sure. Giles could be very strong.

Willow asked a question, though, that they *should* know, one that had been bothering Buffy. "So who did it?"

Xander looked confused. "I thought it was that shadow monster thing. Right?"

"No." Buffy'd thought about it a lot. "They were just doing what they do—cleaning up. Something else actually sent us back there."

"So who?" Xander asked. "I mean, who would do something that, like, weird?"

Warren looked at Jonathan and Andrew. "Wait. Say that again?"

Jonathan cleared his throat nervously. "It didn't work." Andrew piped up. "Well, dude, not true exactly. It did work. *Bam*, time displacement. But then, *Bam*. They're back."

Warren nodded. "That's okay. It's a good start. And we've got lots of other surprises for 'em."

Buffy sat alone in the training room and thought about what had happened. Willow and Xander's spell had worked just in time. They'd done it again. She'd seen Giles's face as she'd faded back into this world and faded out of the world in which her mother was alive. *Go Xander. Go Willow.* They'd pulled her out of heaven.

Again.

THE WAR BETWEEN THE STATES

Rebecca Rand Kirshner

New York City, 1922

Through the window of the train, a transformation had been taking place. The lazy flats of Carolina marsh had dried away and swollen into rolling green hills, then stretched long into great gapes of land rooted with unfamiliar, proud-looking trees, and now had metamorphosed into ancient towns made of brick and shutters and copper steeples gone green with time and weather. Now she was only a few hours away from New York City. Time passed as the train chugged forward, and she watched as the sky began to color, brightening into pinks and yellows like fireworks set off in slow motion, and then without ever seeming to reach its apex began to fade away into shades of gray and then blacks, until Sally Jean was left with nothing to watch but her own reflection.

She was a very pretty girl, eighteen last February, with soft brown eyes and soft blond hair that she wore piled on her head like cotton. In fact being soft was as integral to Sally Jean as her family name or their home on the Battery. It was the adjective most likely to be spoken, in conjunction with some feature of hers or another, when castaway beaux remembered their days in Sally Jean's favor, or when admiring friends sat with her at her dressing table. Sally Jean knew how people thought of her; she knew how the boys brushed their fingers against the skin on her shoulders as if she were made of clouds and spun sugar, things that would melt away if you touched them with your mouth. She knew how the girls admired her, just to the brink of envy, but not beyond. They couldn't really envy her after all, not in a jealous way, because she was so kind, so generous, so pliable—so soft. Sally Jean knew all of this and yet she held all their compliments at arm's length, at the length of one pretty, soft, white arm, because she knew that being soft, just like being young and beautiful, was part of her arsenal. A weapon that she could call upon later, when life really began.

Sally Jean sat alone. Her small hand rested proprietarily on the pink-papered hatbox that occupied the seat beside her, making clear to the boarding passengers that she had no interest in company. Ordinarily Sally Jean would have generously made conversation with any sort of seatmate. But this trip was different. It wasn't that she was afraid of being accosted by an unsavory character with hooch on his breath and bad intentions up his sleeve. And it wasn't because she had hoped to lie down for a bit during her journey; she was as awake and as happy as she'd ever been. She needed to sit alone because she herself was undergoing a transformation.

Sally Jean felt a certain anxiety that if she didn't change along with the world, along with the air that was being ripped through with aeroplanes, along with the oceans that were being swum by women covered with grease, along with the country itself that was getting smaller and faster and full of cars, she would be left behind like a moldy tombstone in St. Phillips cemetery. When she was a girl, she used to walk through the cool quiet graveyards, reading the epitaphs until tears would spill down her soft cheeks. Her face would be wet, but she wouldn't feel sad, just full and proud, as if she understood something. But in the last few years, things had changed. Women could vote now, for goodness' sake, not that she was twenty-one or had any intention of doing so, but the fact remained that she could do so many things. She was tired of sweet tea, tired of grits, tired of religion, and tired of the past. Maybe if the Confederacy had won its ancient war she could have stayed in Charleston, but it hadn't, and she was up to her ears with the melancholy of it all. The same languorous, long-rooted world in which she had grown up now seemed hopelessly at the periphery of life.

There were external manifestations of Sally Jean's transformation as well. With each stop of the train, she compared herself to the new passengers and made adjustments to her attire accordingly. Only a couple of hours into the journey she had realized that her hat, just purchased last week at Berlin's, was not going to make it to New York atop her head. A clever-looking girl with sleek red hair had boarded in Baltimore, and Sally Jean had immediately felt the frothy thing burning against her scalp. As quickly as she could, she had removed it and pushed it unceremoniously into the hatbox. Soon after, she had unbuttoned the top two buttons of her blouse, and at the next stop, casually removed her white gloves and stuffed them into the hatbox as well. About her hobble skirt and thick cotton stockings, she couldn't do a thing. She needed a short dress and, if she could somehow manage it, silk stockings.

Silk stockings seemed absolutely necessary, the more she thought about it. She couldn't hardly exist without them! Her legs began to itch under the girlish, old-fashioned cotton, and she wished that despite the hour the stores would be open when she arrived. How could she afford them, though? Half a thought flashed into her mind: Brett. Brett would surely understand and take her to Saks Fifth Avenue.

And then the second half of the thought joined the first with a clap, startling her like thunder: Brett. Tall, handsome Brett with his neatly cut uniform and steel gray eyes. Brett whose neck smelled like limes and in whose arms she had danced, night after night, during all the summer dances, two years in a row. Faithful Brett, who had written her nearly daily all through the war. Sweet Brett, who had known her when she was just a girl and had waited for her, who had let her grow up while he fought his wars and earned his money. Dearest Brett, as she had called him when she wrote her perfumed letters back, filling pink pages with vague ideas about love and life that she meant more as musings than as professions. Brett, whose lips had kissed hers on the veranda of her parent's house late one June evening.

When the first shots of the Civil War were fired on Fort Sumter, the good people of Charlestown had sat on their porches and verandas, juleps in hand, and watched as the battle began. And then, some sixty years later, Sally Jean had sat in the very same place and watched with perhaps a similar interested detachment as a young man from Asheville declared that they would spend the rest of their lives together. Whatever she had said that night was true when she said it, but it had felt unreal, as if what she said could go nowhere in that heavy, unmoving air. But now, in the brightly-lit train car, with the city buildings growing sharply outside her window, the whole thing seemed horribly lucid. She was traveling to New York because she was engaged to marry Brett Blakely.

And before Sally Jean could reconcile that solid fact with the new self that was tentatively blossoming inside her mind, she was at Grand Central Station. She had arrived. She made her way through the crowd, hatbox in one hand, suitcase in the other, and though she held her head up proudly, she felt like everyone was snickering.

Sally Jean bristled and walked as fast as her long tight skirt would allow. And then again she remembered Brett. She stopped, looked around, scanning the bustling figures for a tall gray-eyed soldier. He was nowhere to be seen. Her indignation was tempered with hope. Maybe this was going to be easier than she had thought. As impossible as it was for her to understand how a gentleman would be willing to throw her over, it sure would simplify matters. She did hate scenes.

She heard thunderous footsteps and turned just in time to see a hulking young man in an ill-fitting green suit and a feathered hat running up behind her.

"Sally Jean!" the young man bellowed.

"Why, who on earth—Brett!"

The whites of her eyes grew at the sight of him, and it was only with conscientious effort that she softened them into a look befitting the occasion.

"Darling!" he said as he pulled her close to his sweaty cheek.

"Oh, honey," she said as she pushed him away. "Not here!" This with a smile and a look toward the oblivious crowd around them. "Oh! Let me just look at that extraordinary suit you have on. Somehow I thought you'd be in a uniform forever."

He spun for her, tipped his feathered hat and picked up her bag and her hatbox, and they began to walk toward the exit.

"Pretty sharp, huh? And you wouldn't believe the deal I got."

She hummed noncommittally. No deal could have been too good; the suit was dreadful. Thick, green, out of fashion, and it concealed quite effectively his fine figure. Sally Jean felt a flash of outrage at this costume, as if he had wooed her under false pretenses, in disguise. She had kissed a soldier and awoke to find herself with a man who wore a feathered hat and a clumsy old suit.

His face was flushed with excitement, the creases around his eyes and at his mouth white in contrast. He leaned in close and she could see tiny droplets of sweat clinging to his upper lip.

"You must be exhausted, darling."

And suddenly she was. Sally Jean feigned sleep as they rode to the hotel in Brett's creaky old Model T and didn't look out the window once; she wanted to leave it fresh for when the city was hers alone. Brett had arranged for separate but connecting rooms, and it wasn't until she was in her single bed with the door to the other room safely bolted, that she allowed herself to open her eyes fully. This wasn't going to do. She wasn't going to be the same girl who sat passively on that veranda. She wanted to feel things, to be things. She wanted to be a modern woman, and getting married at eighteen to a man in a feathered hat wasn't part of her agenda. Having confirmed this with herself, she closed her eyes and fell into a deep sleep.

The polite knocking at the bolted door awoke her from a deep dark sleep.

She called through the door, "Just a minute, honey. I seem to have accidentally locked this silly thing."

"Take your time. I'm going to go down and have a cup of coffee. I'll come back in twenty minutes and take you to dinner and a show. I know this really fantastic place."

He parked carefully along a curb, hemming and hawing the car into position while Sally Jean regarded him with barely concealed irritation. He seemed a little nervous, and she worried that he was taking her to a party to which they hadn't been invited.

"This is it," he said as they stopped in front of an unremarkable brownstone marked 333 with bronze numbers. "You do know these people, don't you, honey?" "Well, not exactly, but you'll see. I came here with a fellow from the office."

Oh, poor Brett, he clearly doesn't belong in the North, she thought, her pretty jaw clenching. They entered the unlocked door and instead of a parlor were greeted with a darkened staircase. She didn't want to go down; it smelled like spoiled milk and wet wood. At Brett's insistence, Sally Jean followed him down the rickety staircase and nearly ran smack into a gigantic man with wide-legged trousers and a matchstick between his lips. The giant didn't say a word, just looked at them.

"I think we're in the wrong—"

"Texas sent me," Brett said to the giant. And to Sally Jean's surprise, the giant took one heavy step to the side and indicated the door behind him with a nod. As he did, Sally Jean thought she saw the flash of a gun beneath his dinner jacket. She was about to dash back up the rickety steps when Brett opened the door and she saw into the room beyond.

It was like looking into the peephole of a sugared Easter egg and seeing the miraculous jeweled world inside. A splendid dining room, all red velvet and chandeliers, spread out before her, filled with the most elegant people Sally Jean had ever seen. And there was a stage at the front where a tuxedoed band was playing. She couldn't have dreamed that such an opulent place could be hidden in the bowels of the world like this, behind such a door, beneath such a staircase.

They sat at a table right near the front. Brett ordered a very fine dinner for them and they were able to drink real cocktails. It wasn't moonshine or some stuff from someone's bathtub, but real liquor from real bottles. It tasted like freedom to Sally Jean. And the show! There was a comedian who made Brett laugh like Peony, her horse at home—her horse in South Carolina—and a juggler who juggled martini shakers and finished his act by pouring a drink for a bald-headed gentleman at the table next to theirs.

After that trick Brett looked over at her with a gentle, proud smile, and she felt a small part of her heart melting under his glance. She smiled at him sweetly and felt a sort of sleepy nostalgia for him. Brett was a good man, honest and true, patient and kind. The lights dimmed; a new act was coming on. Maybe she wouldn't be able to stay frozen after all; maybe she'd just soften and melt back into being his girl, being his wife. She wasn't even sad about it, just felt a kind of sweet remembrance as if she was being led into a dance that had been going on for years and years. Maybe she was going to lose the battle for secession all over again.

And then the woman came on stage: tall, all in blue, with black bobbed hair. She beckoned with one lean arm and then there was a whole crowd of them, leggy girls in sapphire-blue costumes with bands of diamonds strung round their heads like glittering crowns of thorns. Sally Jean sat straight up in her chair, forgetting for the first time that day what she looked like and what others must be thinking of her. Brett squeezed her hand, but she pulled away. There was a miracle taking place on stage. The music was deep and suggestive, full of sliding trombones and a timpani beat from a tightly pulled drum. And the dancers—they moved like mermaids, like horses at the Derby, like angels. They were made of lightning, flashing across the stage with their legs high in the air. The past seemed to dissolve around them as they set forth some sort of dancing manifesto, a vision of the future described in kicks and spins. When the act finished, Sally Jean clapped as loudly as anyone in the theater.

Brett turned to her.

"That wasn't too much for you, was it, Sally Jean?"

His face reflected concern and, to her, an artificial sense of propriety. As if she hadn't seen women's legs every time she took a bath! She smiled at him in the same way she might smile at an old woman talking about the exorbitant fee for overdue library books. And then the next act began.

The women had changed their costumes, adding long gold skirts and Egyptian-inspired headdresses. Their eyes were rimmed extravagantly in kohl. Sally Jean drank her cocktail in one swift swallow without taking her eyes off the stage. The music was silky, Middle-Eastern, and the girls, the women, the dancing horses, were even silkier. Sally Jean's eyes flicked across the stage, looking for the woman with the black-bobbed hair—there she was, at the far left of the line. And though the black-bobbed woman wasn't in the center for this number, Sally Jean was sure that everyone was watching her alone. Everyone and everything was drawn to the woman, and Sally Jean felt that any second, the stage itself would tilt toward her and all the dancers would slide uncontrollably to the left, pulled by her immense gravity of being.

Unlike the others, the woman in the black bob didn't smile; her face was incredibly still, fixed in an odd expression Sally Jean couldn't name, and her eyes, which peered out into the crowd, seemed not to be looking at the enraptured audience but somewhere else, into the future or into the past, as if she could see angels and phantoms. This woman, this creature, this future-dancer, this is who Sally Jean wanted to become.

Two more acts followed, and then the lights went up and the air seemed to return to the room. On the ride home, Sally Jean kissed

Brett twice out of pure exuberance. And then it was night and then it was day again. Sally Jean put off visiting Brett's aunt and, after getting a new short dress and a pair of silk stockings with seams along the back, claimed she was too worn out to shop for her wedding dress. But when eight o'clock came, her energy miraculously returned and Brett found himself driving to Forty-fifth Street once again.

The show was just the same as the night before: the comedians; the singers; the sketch about the man from New Jersey who found a cow in his closet; the lanky woman who swung a long string of pearls around her neck while singing the national anthem; the martini juggler (this time Brett was given the martini and Sally Jean joyously ate the olives from a tiny plastic sword); and then the real show, the dancers.

Just as the night before, the air thinned and the moment froze as the sapphire girls took their places. Sally Jean was fixated on the black-bobbed dancer, staring at her as if she were a ring in the window of Van Cleef & Arpels. And when the show was over, Sally Jean felt the same sense of rejoining time. There was another act afterward and Sally Jean relaxed back into her seat. She smiled at Brett.

"You've been really terrific to me, you know that Brett? It's like we're sitting here side by side and I feel like I'm with one of my best friends in the entire world."

"Best friends? I should hope we're—"

"Absolutely. Really the best," she cut him off. She didn't want to talk about who they were to each other or who they had been. Her world was splitting in two. Her future had two paths and she could only take one. "And I just want you to know how grateful I am for you taking me here."

"Why sure, Sally Jean, why sure. After all, you *are* going to be—"

"Look!" Sally Jean whispered insistently. "Look at the table next to us."

Brett saw an urbane bald-headed gentleman and recognized him from the night before. He watched as the man pulled out a chair for a young woman. It took Brett a moment to recognize her as one of the dancing girls.

"It's *her*," Sally Jean intoned breathlessly. "Let's watch."

Dutifully Brett watched as the dancer, now dressed in a low-waisted burgundy cocktail dress and a matching cloche, sat with the older man.

"Do you think that's her husband?" Sally Jean whispered into Brett's neck.

The older man and the black-bobbed woman talked quietly together. The woman leaned on one tanned arm, and Sally Jean could see lean, hard muscles flex beneath her skin. The man said something. The woman glanced toward the back of the theater, nodded to the man, and removed her necklace. It seemed to be made of pearls, black pearls alternating with white pearls, and Sally Jean had never seen anything like it. Handing them over to the bald man, she strode back, past the tables, toward the door where they had entered.

"Guess he wanted his stones back," Brett whispered loudly. "She's probably his mistress and his wife just showed or—"

"I wouldn't mind another cocktail," interjected Sally Jean with a kiss.

Brett suppressed his surprise, and without comment began to flag for a waiter. After a minute he gave up and went to the bar himself. There was a line, and he was gone some time. Left alone, Sally Jean fixed the elderly man under her soft-eyed scrutiny. Soon after, the woman returned and, sitting beside the man, retrieved her pearl necklace and allowed him to assist with the clasp. She conferred again with the man, her face almost hidden behind the swing of her black hair, and seemed to indicate that something satisfactory had taken place. As she drank her cocktail—what looked to Sally Jean to be a gin and tonic—another man approached the table.

The older man stood and shook the younger man's hand. He slapped him convivially on the back and gestured to the seat on the other side of the woman. A waiter came by Sally Jean's table and, without a thought, she ordered a gin and tonic. She watched as both men talked to the woman with the black-bobbed hair. The younger man was wearing a sharply cut suit and a peppermint green shirt, and she imagined for a moment that he was the man she was destined to marry. He and the black-bobbed woman laughed, and Sally Jean felt a pang of jealousy, of desire, fresher than anything she had felt with Brett since she was fifteen years old.

Soon Brett returned to the table.

"I got you an old-fashioned, darling."

"Well, aren't you sweet, but somehow I ended up with this."

She held up her almost empty drink. Brett looked at the lime in her glass like it was a rare goldfish.

"I didn't know you drank gin."

"Me neither. You know they used to think the juniper in gin drove women crazy. Isn't that funny?"

"I think I heard something about that," he said grimly.

The hours passed and the crowd only seemed to grow. Sally Jean watched as different people stopped by the table next to theirs and paid homage, sitting with the group for a while, exchanging kisses, and then departing for another table like a jolly school of fish swimming wherever crumbs of gaiety and laughter were offered. She watched how the younger man stared at the black-haired woman. *He's in love with her,* she decided. Sally Jean sighed. *Nobody loves me like that. Nobody.*

Brett touched Sally Jean's arm tenderly but couldn't get her attention. He was beginning to grow restless; early the next morning he had to be back at the office where he worked as a copywriter. But Sally Jean gave no indication of readiness to depart and Brett didn't want to displease her. He began to work over some ideas for the ladies' shaver campaign. *Sell the sizzle, not the steak,* he reminded himself. *What on earth sizzles about ladies' leg hair?* After what Brett counted to be her fourth gin and tonic, Sally Jean announced that she wanted to meet the black-bobbed dancer.

"I've just got to talk to her! Look what fun they're having."

"Aren't we having . . . a good time? This here is fun, isn't it, Sally Jean?"

"Yes," she said, weighing the question. "But it looks like they're having some kind of important fun. Do you know what I mean?"

He had no idea what she meant. In fact, as he thought back over the last two days, he felt there were quite a few moments during which he had had no idea what she meant. And she was drinking so much. She must just be nervous about the wedding. Feeling a surge of love for her, he reached over to pat her hand reassuringly, and found it missing.

He spotted her standing at the adjacent table, the short skirt of her dress riding up past her knees. Brett blushed. But before he could jump to her rescue, she was seated at the table, clinking glasses with the dark-haired dancer. Brett sat back down and sipped at his drink contemplatively.

"Well, aren't you just a gem for saying so," said the black-haired woman in her breathy voice, shaking Sally Jean's hand like a man.

"I think you were just, I don't know how to say it, like an angel out there. Like an angel and also sort of like my horse, Peony—"

"Peony!" The whole table laughed.

"That's her name. It's a flower."

"Isn't she a gem," said the woman, turning to the older, bald-headed man.

"A diamond," he concurred.

"A diamond in the rough," said the younger man, looking at her with a flash in his appraising eyes. He winked at Sally Jean and the black-haired woman laughed.

"Ardita," said the black-bobbed woman looking directly at Sally Jean.

"Come again?" asked Sally Jean politely.

"Ardita O'Reilly, that's me."

"Oh, I'm so pleased to make your acquaintance! Sally Jean Baker, that's me."

Again the table laughed, but their laughs were friendly and warm.

"She's the real McCoy, isn't she? A gen-u-ine innocent."

"I know! Let's keep her! Why don't we just adopt Miss Sally Jean Baker here, and keep her all for ourselves?" This was Ardita, breathless, delighted. "How about it, Mr. Whiskers? What do you say?"

"Is that you?" Sally Jean asked the elderly man sincerely, "Are you Mr. . . . Whiskers?"

The table roared.

"That's what they call me," he told her confidentially, "on account of my excessive hairiness!"

"But you don't have—"

And then they all laughed, including Sally Jean.

"I'm the proprietor, the owner of this particular establishment," said Mr. Whiskers. "Ardita is my greatest find, my lovely ingénue. And the rudely silent gentleman to your right is Tom Valentine."

Tom Valentine gave her a generous smile and, with an exaggerated flourish that didn't deny the genuine chivalry of his actions, half stood and planted a kiss on Sally Jean's hand. Ardita clapped with delight.

"And I am Brett Blakely."

The table turned and Brett stood there, looking like a Boy Scout who got run through the wrong wash cycle.

"Sally Jean's fiancé."

Awkwardly Brett pulled up a chair and introductions were made. Mr. Whiskers ordered another round of drinks. The men started to talk of the Great War and Sally Jean had a moment to look at Ardita. What she saw made her lose an ice cube down the front of her dress. Ardita had one blue eye and one green eye. It wasn't the kind of thing you couldn't see from the audience, but up close it was undeniable. Sally Jean stared into those eyes and the rest of the room disappeared. She wanted to swim in them; get drunk in them; vanish into their blues and greens. Ardita smiled and Sally Jean smiled back; an infant hypnotized by the most beautiful mobile.

"Hi," said Sally Jean.

"Hi," said Ardita. And her eyes flickered with that same strange look Sally Jean had seen on stage. Was it passion? Anger? Resignation? All Sally Jean knew is that she wanted her own eyes to be blue and green and hard and full of secrets.

The next half-hour passed as in a dream. The band picked up their instruments and decided to play for their own enjoyment. The music was wild and fantastic. The air was thick with smoke.

One song ended, and before the next began, Sally Jean heard Brett talking confidentially to Mr. Whiskers.

"All I can figure is she's getting something out of her system. After all, once we're married—"

Sally Jean interrupted, "Sorry, honey. But I'm not getting something out of my system at all. In fact I do believe I just got something into my system."

Brett took in a breath. Since when did Sally Jean talk like that? Since when was she so bold, so hard?

"Sally Jean, darling, you've had too much to drink."

"I know, isn't it grand?"

Brett stood up and pulled Sally Jean by her elbow. "Not so much, Sally Jean. Not so grand as you think." And then with the uncomfortable smile of a parent whose child has just thrown a tantrum in a public park: "Good night, everyone. It was a pleasure to meet you. I'm sorry about all of this. She's just not used to drinking, that's all."

"Don't be ridiculous." Ardita stood up. "She's an absolute gem, Brett."

"I've got to say just one more thing," said Sally Jean. "This"—she gestured to the room at large—"all of this. This is what I want. I want to be on stage."

And then Brett tugged Sally Jean by her elbow one last time and pulled her out the door, up the reeking staircase, and into his car outside. The ride home was dreadful. Brett sulked and Sally Jean was forced to wait. As many drinks as she had had, her mind was still calculating. A scene was inevitable, sooner was probably better than later, and she knew enough about alcohol to realize its potential as a social lubricant for all occasions. Breaking off one's engagement wasn't an ordinary social situation, but she knew that it would ease the wretched words out of her mouth and then blur the whole episode, like a watercolor left in the rain, so that neither of them would remember it too clearly in the morning.

Morning brought a horrible knocking at her door and a puffy-eyed ex-soldier who called her some unprintable names and then tearily professed his eternal devotion. These two strategies were employed by Brett in alternation, growing to a rapid-fire rhythm, like a marching-band drummer beating two sides of his thundering drum as he marched down a hopeless street right into a brick wall. Sally Jean comforted Brett as best she could and returned the engagement ring in a moment when she thought he was too tired to heave it out the window. He pocketed it, kissed Sally Jean on her soft blond head, and, in a final torrent of swears and endearments, disappeared out her door.

Sally Jean spent the morning in bed and soon fell back asleep. When she awoke, instead of feeling blue, she felt clean and well rested. She looked out the window of her hotel room, truly seeing the city for the first time. The light was sharp, and everything seemed terribly alive. She dressed and went for a walk around Manhattan and felt the energy of the other pedestrians enter her blood like a strong cocktail. People were everywhere, moving, going places, doing things. And those were just the people she saw; she knew now that there were people below the earth, terrific parties full of glittering people and magical music.

She kept walking through the streets, enjoying the fresh summer air. She made her turns at random, attracted by a tree whose leaves were just starting to turn or a barbershop with a spiraling pole, but she adopted the pace of the crowd around her, hustling as if she had somewhere to go. She walked until her lungs ached and the soles of her feet were flat and hot. When she finally stopped to rest, she looked up and saw a row of familiar brownstones. It couldn't be. And yet, crossing the street and reading the brass 333, she knew that it was. She thought for a moment, and any passerby would have taken her for a lost young woman trying to get her bearings—which she was, in a way. *What else can I do?* she thought, and opened the door and went down the stairs.

Soon autumn came in earnest, and though Sally Jean knew the leaves were dying, were dead as they fell to the sidewalk, they seemed to her, in their vibrant reds and yellows, more alive than ever. She had been at Mr. Whiskers's for five weeks now and had been performing in the revue for nearly a week. Mr. Whiskers had been impressed with how quickly she picked up the routines. For the month before she had been allowed to perform, Sally Jean had watched from a stool backstage, her soft, white arms moving in sync with Ardita's rangy limbs, memorizing her every move. During rehearsals, Sally Jean had worked herself exceedingly hard, pushing against fatigue and biting back tears when she missed a step. And when the girls were sent home, Sally Jean begged Ardita to teach her more, to tell her what she was doing wrong. She wanted to be Ardita's pupil, her slave, and when Ardita praised Sally Jean, she felt like a millionaire.

When Sally Jean graduated to the stage, she experienced the thrill of applause for the first time in her life. Although she was sure that Ardita had earned most of it, she was nevertheless grateful to bask in its warmth. Life was good. She got along well with the other dancers and had even allowed Bernard the martini juggler to take her out for a dinner at a fine restaurant where the meal cost more than a week's salary. She rarely thought of Brett. When she did think of him, he was a storybook character in her mind, a soldier who had been in the war and then mysteriously faded away. At some point she realized that she had always assumed he would die in the war and that she was vaguely disappointed that he didn't, as if by surviving he had shown his intrinsic weakness.

Sally Jean's parents were very sorry to hear that the engagement had been broken off. Somehow they had gotten the impression from Sally Jean's letters that it was Brett who had thrown her over and so were more than willing to send money until a reconciliation could be made. This money kept Sally Jean in a small apartment on Bank Street and her legs in silk. The letters to her parents also served a second purpose of reminding Sally Jean of who she used to be. Sally Jean realized that this aspect of her character, this old sweet nonthreatening Sally Jean, was terribly useful. So even while she nourished the new Sally Jean—the silken-legged, cosmopolitan flapper—she kept her old character in play. It was this character who chatted sweetly with Ardita whenever she got the chance. It was this character who asked for Ardita's advice on new dresses and begged Ardita to teach her how to smoke cigarettes. It was this character who amused Ardita with her exuberant innocence, holding tight to her hat as Ardita sped them along Broadway in her lime green Opel Reinette. It was this character who gasped with admiration when, after asking Ardita why she didn't have a driver, Ardita replied that no one could drive fast enough to suit her taste.

And it was this character, this aspect of Sally Jean, who rapped softly on Ardita's dressing room after the show one Friday night. Ardita called for her to come in, and though when Sally Jean opened the door she found her only vaguely dressed, wearing a tangerine-colored kimono that appeared to have lost its belt and ashing a cigarette into an empty glass of champagne, Ardita was not the least embarrassed.

"Sally Jean! At last!"

Sally Jean nodded enthusiastically and clutched her pocketbook to her stomach modestly.

"Well, come on in. Be a sport and help me with this champagne, won't you? It's the real McCoy."

Sally Jean nodded again and, consciously tipping her head down so that her big brown eyes were at their most sincere, asked if Ardita wanted to join her for a little supper later. Ardita laughed and Sally Jean laughed too, as if the invitation was a bon mot.

"Can't, but do hang on and have a drink? I'll be back in a sec."

With this she threw her lanky body off the settee and swished out of the room. Sally Jean was left alone. Slowly she took in the small dressing room, her soft eyes flashing like a camera. On Ardita's dressing table, she found a small basket filled with jewelry. She rooted among the baubles until she found the necklace with the black and white pearls. She held it up to her neck and admired herself in the mirror. She arched an eyebrow and laughed softly.

"These?" she replied to the mirror. "Oh they're nothing, doll. Just something I throw around my neck when I haven't got anything better to do."

She dropped the necklace back into the jewelry basket and examined the items tucked into the dressing table mirror. There was a snapshot of Ardita with Mr. Whiskers that must have been taken some time ago. In the picture Mr. Whiskers looked the same, but Ardita was young—she couldn't have been more than fourteen years old. The young Ardita wore that same strange expression that Sally Jean couldn't place. There was an ink drawing of Ardita and the girls in their sapphire costumes; a map that appeared to be an old drawing of New York with odd markings made in red pen, surely some inherited document; and tucked into the mirror frame, a brittle old rose gone black with time. The rose had a small card attached with ribbon and Sally Jean opened it with one finger. "You say when and I'm yours. Tom." She read it over twice and crossed the room.

She opened a teak armoire and found Ardita's shoes. Dozens of them, lying in wait for Ardita, black and silver and red, with buckles and heels and silky bows. She pulled out a worn silver slipper and touched it gently, fingering the satin. She put her hand inside, feeling down to where Ardita's toes had strained against the fabric, stretching out the satin so that the shape of her ghostly foot remained. After a moment she carefully replaced the shoe next to its mate, and closed the door. She opened another, smaller closet and had to catch her breath. She leaned in. This closet was filled with weapons—knives mostly; they looked like they might be artifacts from Africa or China or somewhere far off. Some were made of metal, most of wood. She reached out slowly and touched the tip of a wooden knife, pressing her finger hard against its point. She took a deep swig of champagne. How terribly exotic! Leave it to Ardita to have a thrilling hobby like collecting knives. She wished she had thought of it herself. She closed the door and drained her champagne.

She drifted back across the room to the dressing table. She opened a jar of cream and spread some on her cheek. She picked up Ardita's bottle of perfume, noted its label, and absently spritzed it on her neck and on her wrists. It smelled exhilarating, musky, just like Ardita. And then, as if intoxicated by the perfume, she quickly reached up to the rose, deftly untied the ribbon, and slipped the card from Tom Valentine into her purse. At that moment the door opened and Ardita returned.

Sally Jean looked into the mirror and fluffed at her hair innocently.

Then to Ardita's reflection, "Do you think I should bob my hair?" she asked quickly.

"Why?" Ardita smiled and stretched languidly on the settee.

Ardita had returned wearing what appeared to be men's black pajamas and diamond earrings. Sally Jean tugged at her cocktail dress.

"I don't know. I feel like a change I guess."

"You shouldn't, you know. You should stay innocent Sally Jean Baker for as long as you possibly can."

"Why?" asked Sally Jean, sounding to her annoyance like a whining child. "You're not innocent."

Ardita laughed. Sally Jean was feeling more and more frustrated. She pulled at her hair in the mirror, approximating what it would look like short. Then the door nearly pounded down, and before Ardita could respond, a troupe of glamorous madmen poured in, bearing more liquor, a bottle of champagne, and a basket of oranges. These were some of Ardita's friends; Sally Jean had met some of them in passing and they all seemed to be displaced nobility, counts and archdukes, or polo players or heiresses from Chicago.

"Oranges all around!" bellowed a tall bespectacled gentleman with hair the color of the fruit he bore and a curious galaxy of freckles sprawled across his face.

He began to toss oranges to all the various guests; some caught them and some let theirs fall to the floor. A voluptuous woman with unnaturally blond hair picked up three oranges and began to juggle them. She was better than Bernard, thought Sally Jean. Sable coats and silk wraps were tossed to the floor, thrown over the dressing table, and piled on the settee as the guests prepared themselves for a party. Sally Jean recognized Tom Valentine among the crowd and giggled happily as he knelt before her, kissing her hand. And then another man, whom Sally Jean thought might be one of the counts, knelt beside her as well and took her other hand in his.

"Who, pray tell," he said looking up into her eyes, "is this vision of loveliness?"

Tom introduced them, and the count clutched his spare hand to his chest.

"Maude, be a good girl and kill me now, will you? I can't stand to exist in the presence of such beauty."

Maude, the voluptuous blond juggler, snorted with laughter and flicked her fingers against the count's skull. Before Sally Jean could think of a witty response, the count was on his feet, ripping the foil off a bottle of champagne. She stared at the people around her with amazement. This was it; this was the center of things! Then Sally Jean felt Ardita's warm, strong arm around her shoulders.

"Sally Jean, doll, you'd better go."

Her heart sank to her feet and hardened into stone.

"Why? I . . . I don't want to."

"This crowd. They're a little odd, that's all. I just wonder if you'll have a good time."

Someone put on a record and the room filled with jazz.

"I'll be fine," insisted Sally Jean coldly, and danced away from Ardita toward the count.

The champagne cork popped, exploding like a bomb, and Sally Jean squealed. The count laughed and pulled her into his arms.

"How gorgeous you look when you scream," he murmured into her ear. "You should be in the pictures."

Flattered to no end, she blushed sweetly, but then Tom took arm and danced her away. The party grew like a well-kindled fire, roaring and roaring and then fading until someone poked it with a funny remark or a new bottle of booze and the sparks relit and it roared again. Glasses filled and bottles emptied. Ice cubes made music that echoed in the tinkling laughter of the women and the soft flirting of the men.

At one point Sally Jean found herself seated on the floor next to a brunette who looked like Theda Bara. She asked her about Tom. He was so well off and yet he never seemed to work. He had mentioned that he was often in the South and in Canada, too. Was he, could he be a rum runner?

The brunette howled.

"A rum runner? No, I'm afraid the old boy hasn't the sea legs for that. Mr. Tom Valentine is just your plain old run-of-the-mill millionaire bootlegger."

And the next thing Sally Jean knew, she was dancing with Tom again. The whole crowd danced and they drank and the night came heavily upon them. The conversations looped and turned; Sally Jean understood phrases and then lost the strand as the words bent and twisted together like a woven sea grass basket. She stopped trying to follow the lengths and just admired the pattern as it twisted on and on into the night. At one point, just before the sun came up, Sally Jean awoke to find herself curled on the settee, a bottle still clutched in her hand. When she looked around, she couldn't find Ardita. The count was gone too.

"She's gone out," explained Tom. And Sally Jean took his hand in hers.

+ + +

The trees blossomed with their dead orange leaves and slowly released them, letting them fall like pennies from an old man's hand, until the branches were bare and Central Park was full of skeletons. Sally Jean enjoyed the coming of winter, appreciated the pink the cold pinched into her cheeks, and anticipated eagerly the fireplaces near which she would sit with her new friends, Ardita's friends, and drink hot drinks and sing cheerful songs.

Her confidence as a dancer had grown and she no longer asked Ardita for her help or watched her out of the corner of her eye as she had when she first performed on stage. Offstage, she still watched Ardita, though, more than ever. Each night after the performance, Ardita would go directly back to her dressing room. Then she would stay there and entertain her friends; go sit with Mr. Whiskers; or go out on the town, often by herself. No matter the night, Ardita always mysteriously disappeared sometime after one or two o'clock. Sally Jean's theory that Ardita was in love with the count didn't seem to be panning out; after that party, he had never returned to the theater. So Sally Jean decided that Ardita must have a dozen secret lovers and felt irked; how could her idol treat Tom Valentine like that?

And coincidentally, or perhaps not quite so coincidentally, Sally Jean fell in love with Tom Valentine too. He was the perfect man, she had realized. Strong, capable, rich as Creoeses, Tom knew all the best places in the city. And he had such a way about him—it was like he was a soldier all the time. She told him that once, and he had laughed and kissed her on the ear and told her that if anyone was a soldier it was Ardita. Sally Jean had screwed up her pretty face.

"Well, she can't be a soldier, can she? She's a girl."

"You silly Southern Belle," he had said, and she might have been offended except for the way he said it was so admiring.

Sally Jean had never set about courting a man. Where she came from that was a ludicrous idea. But up in New York it was different, and so she went right to work. She hosted an indoor picnic at her apartment on Bank Street and made sure to tell Tom that she'd be much obliged if he stuck around a little afterward. When she finally went to get her hair bobbed, she had Tom come, and held tight to his hand as if she were afraid the barber's scissors were going to slit her throat. And when she performed, she kept her eyes locked on his and kicked her legs as high as they would go.

One night after the show, Sally Jean was gratified to find three separate bouquets waiting for her. Ardita, she counted, had only two that night. Sally Jean took a circuitous path back to her dressing room, carrying around the flowers as if they were a cumbersome baby whose mewling was getting at her nerves. She sat backstage with Bernard a moment, and when he inquired, rolled her eyes at the flowers, as if to suggest her growing popularity was a burden. Back in the dressing room she shared with another of the chorus girls, Sally Jean slowly opened the cards. The first was from an only vaguely familiar admirer, a man called Ivan D'Mengers whom she thought might be one of the counts or at least an archduke. The note asked if she would accompany him to dinner sometime. Sally Jean would have shown off the card to Ardita except she could predict the response. Ardita had lectured her as if she were a schoolgirl about the dangers of counts and men like them. Apparently it was all well and good for Ardita herself to disappear with them into the night, but not poor, sweet, soft Sally Jean.

She ripped open the card on the second bouquet and saw that it was from none other than Tom Valentine. Her heart beat a bit faster and she read this note several times.

*"To Sally Jean.
My silly Southern Belle.
Yours, Tom Valentine."*

She was so interested in this note, in the nuances of meaning just beyond the surface—was the fact that he signed his full name a good sign or a bad one?—that she nearly forgot about the third card. Could it possibly be from Tom too? She tore it open and recoiled at what she read. "My Sally Jean. I'm waiting for you, waiting for you to be mine. Eternally Yours, Brett." Brett! She had forgotten about him almost entirely; did he still live in New York? How completely disgusting! She ripped his card into tiny pieces, and, feeling like her dressing room had been contaminated, hurried into her clothes and left without putting any of the flowers in water.

She raced over to Ardita's dressing room and was about to burst in when she heard low voices through the door. She paused a moment, deciding, and then bent down to fiddle with her shoe strap.

"I have to go, Tom, and I know you don't like it, but it's just the way things are."

"Not tonight, please, Ardita. Just once, please, do what I want!" His voice was loud.

Soon after, Sally Jean heard something crash against a wall inside, something heavy like an ashtray, and she hustled away from the door. Bernard was in the hallway coming toward her, a bunch of small roses in his hand.

"Why, hi, Bernard," said Sally Jean, casual as could be.

"I . . . well, these are for you, Sally Jean." He held the flowers out awkwardly as if they were in some running race together and he was passing her the baton.

"You don't say? I wonder who they're from. There's no card."

She buried her face in them.

"Oh, they're those roses that don't smell," she said, disappointed.

"Actually, I . . . they're from me, Sally Jean."

Before she could reply, she heard Tom Valentine exit Ardita's dressing room and come toward them. She turned.

"Tom, I was just looking for you!" she said, her voice bright and happy. "I'm hungry as a tiger; won't you please take pity on me and escort me to some supper?"

"Sure, Sally Jean," he said, sounding half-hearted, and then, oblivious to the martini juggler's stricken face, added "You have a good evening, Bernard."

And she tucked her arm through his and they exited down the hall, leaving the unhappy juggler in their wake.

Tom was quiet all through supper and Sally Jean was at her wits' end trying to get his attention. She tried to talk about the day's newspaper, but since she had only caught a glimpse over someone's shoulder backstage, she was limited to headlines and the day's weather, which by this point in the night wasn't particularly newsworthy. She moved on to talk of her childhood, a subject that usually amused and comforted Tom, but this too proved futile. She wracked her brain and found it empty as the trees outside.

"I'm not sure about this whole winter arrangement," she tried brightly. "It was fun when it was coming, but now that it's here it's so, I don't know, cold and endless."

Tom nodded and returned to his dinner.

"I don't like seeing my breath rise up in the air like a spirit. I don't like gray skies and I don't like dead trees. I don't like dead things," she said enthusiastically.

"Me neither," he agreed, looking at her full in the face for the first time that evening. "I don't care for them one bit." And then, leaning encouragingly close, "You're wearing Ardita's perfume, aren't you?"

"Oh, does she wear this too? I didn't know," she lied.

And then dessert came and Sally Jean ate it with enthusiasm, trying to keep the momentum going. But Tom was a million miles away, tired and spent, and soon Sally Jean retreated into herself, trying to figure out what was wrong. She lacked something. Clearly she lacked something that Ardita had in spades. What was it? Ardita was beautiful, but so was she, in her different, softer way. Ardita was a terrific dancer, but hadn't Mr. Whiskers told her how well she was doing? And hadn't she received three bouquets—four, if you counted the roses from Bernard—that very night? What was it? Sally Jean licked the whipped cream from the back of her fork. Well, she'd just have to figure it out and beat Ardita at her own game. Sally Jean wiped the corners of her mouth with her napkin and folded it resolutely on her lap.

For the next week the question of Ardita was all Sally Jean could think of. She had taken hold of this thought like a pitbull with a rat, and she wrestled it constantly, unable to relax the jaws of her mind. And then one night during the Egyptian number Sally Jean looked over at Ardita and caught that mystery that had flickered in those blue and green eyes. She understood what Ardita had, what she was. Ardita was sad. Sally Jean's smile grew and she kicked her legs higher. All she had to do was cultivate melancholy.

And so she tried. She walked around the gloomy city, past beggars and one-legged women. She stared up at the gray sky and thought of dead people, kittens with broken necks, and losing her looks. She thought of everything in the world that could possibly depress her. She thought of Brett, but that didn't do any good. She only felt pity and even that was eclipsed by disgust. She thought of her long-dead grandmother, but that didn't work either. She thought of Peony, and that was the closest she came, but mostly what she felt was jealousy that her younger sister might be riding her at that very moment.

Giving up on actual emotion, Sally Jean set about affecting sadness. When Tom asked her what she was doing one evening, she smiled a closed-lip smile and sighed.

"I'll go wherever the wind blows me, I figure."

"Well, a gang of us are heading over to Silveri's for steaks. Want in?"

"No, I don't guess so," she said mournfully.

And when he said, "Suit yourself. You'll be missed," she could have kicked herself.

"I guess I could probably be persuaded," she amended, skipping after him down the hall. "I can't promise I'll be much entertainment, though. I'm feeling awful blue for no particular reason."

And then she forgot all about being blue and ended up dancing on the table while Ardita clapped and laughed her church bell laugh.

Weeks passed and spring began to taunt New York, playing peek-a-boo with crocuses that then were frostbit and warm mornings that turned ugly before a girl could fetch her overcoat. Sally Jean saw a lot of Tom Valentine, more than Ardita saw of him. She felt that just one good night could make him hers forever. When he was in the audience, she could see that he was watching her for most of the show. She kept him in her gaze and counted the number of times his eyes flicked toward Ardita, using the glances as a measure of her battle.

One night, looking out into the crowd, she saw a familiar man. She saw the feathered hat and her heart went right into her slippers: Brett Blakely sitting all alone, staring at her with those cold gray eyes. As soon as the curtain fell, she ran back to Ardita's dressing room and threw herself on the settee waiting for her to return. When Ardita came in, Tom Valentine was right behind her.

"You have to help me!" Sally Jean shrieked. "He's come! That dreaded old fiancé of mine was here tonight and I'm sure he's out there waiting, waiting to—"

"Calm down," said Tom, sitting beside her. "You stick with us, right, Ardita?"

Mr. Whiskers opened the door without knocking and just looked at Ardita. She grabbed her black pajamas and was heading toward the door before he had to say a word.

"Oh, dolls, I've got to run!" she said. "There's someone that I have to . . . deal with."

Tom's nostrils flared, and Sally Jean felt frustrated that he was still stuck on Ardita when clearly she carried on with a number of men.

"Tom'll take care of you, won't you, Tom?"

"If it's not too much to ask, Tom, I'd be so grateful."

"Ask me for the world, Sally Jean. Nothing's too much for you."

He put his fingers under her chin and kissed her on the lips, right there in front of Ardita.

Ardita left and Sally Jean was left alone with Tom. This was good, this was very good, but Sally Jean still couldn't relax. She felt like she had to seal the deal. She wanted Tom to see Ardita with her clandestine lover and have it imprinted in his mind that Sally Jean was the only girl for him.

"Let's go out!" she suggested.

"Aren't you afraid of that old fiancé of yours?" asked Tom.

"Not with your arm around me," she insisted.

And so they went out into the damp and foggy night. They managed to exit the theater without encountering Brett, and Sally Jean led them uptown, hurrying along the street after Ardita's shadow. To explain their pace, Sally Jean claimed she was afraid it would rain and spoil her hair.

"Also I just feeling like moving fast," she said. "Know what I mean?"

"Are you hungry, Sally Jean?"

"Not yet. I just feel like walking."

Ardita crossed the street a few blocks up and Sally Jean followed, keeping Tom in distracted conversation.

"I didn't know you followed baseball, Sally Jean."

"Why sure I do. I think it's terribly fascinating, Babe Ruth and all. Don't you? All those uniforms and rules and men running hither and thither."

Ardita was heading toward Central Park. Sally Jean and Tom followed. The wet grass licked at their ankles and shadows leaked from the dark trees like slicks of gasoline. There was something frightening about this strange island of nature surrounded by stone. The birds that called were haunted and the wind whispered Sally Jean's name in the air. But still she tugged Tom along, determined to end this, once and for all. Somewhere around the boat house, Sally Jean lost sight of Ardita and their pace slowed.

"Why are we here, Miss Sally Jean?" asked Tom. "Are you going to put the moves on me?"

Sally Jean laughed lightly and then changed tack. "I don't know, it's just so beautiful and melancholy here."

"And dark as hell."

Where had she gone? Sally Jean was sure Ardita was around somewhere with her mysterious lover. She didn't want to give up yet. She scanned the horizon. Only darkness, shadows, black like the bottom of a well.

And then the darkness took the form of dark figures. Was this the assignation? Then the figures distilled into the outline of three large men walking directly toward them. Sally Jean's breath turned sharp and Tom pulled her closer.

"You know, let's get lost, Sally Jean. Walk fast."

She did as he told her, but the men kept coming, half-running toward them. Sally Jean and Tom began to run, jumping across paths, heading toward the street. She was running in earnest now, fast as she ever had. A heel broke from her shoe and stuck in a puddle of mud and she continued to run, her eyes peeled open with terror. But there was no escaping. The men hurtled toward them like three loose train cars on a steep grade. Faster and faster they came, thrashing through the underbrush, until Sally Jean and Tom were surrounded. Sally Jean looked up and what she saw terrified her. They weren't men at all; they were monsters.

Their faces were warped and scalded as if they'd been burned in a gas fire; their upper lips pulled back like snarling dogs', and the teeth that filled them were sickening, yellow, sharp as sabers. And their eyes: hollow, yellow and shining, and no pupils—just slivers like a snake's. Inside these eyes was death.

Sally thought she would be sick and then thought she would scream. But she didn't and she couldn't. She just stared. One of the creatures was talking to them. Its voice was like a poison let loose from hell, sharp and searing.

"Looking for us?" it said.

"No, we're just—," Tom began.

"We're not talking to you."

Their soulless eyes were fixed on Sally Jean.

"I'm not . . . I think you're mistaken," she squeaked. "I'm just Sally Jean."

The creatures came closer, as if fascinated by her.

"You can't pretend; we know your smell."

The words disgusted her, and again she thought she was going to be sick.

"It's nice to look at you," one of the creatures said, coming closer still. "I've never seen the Slayer up close. You look so soft. So tender."

"Stay away from her!" shouted Tom, finally finding his voice and stepping in front of Sally Jean protectively.

"Move," one of them said, and the moon went behind a cloud.

"And if I won't?"

In an instant, one of the creatures leaped at Tom, swiping at him with one arm. Sally Jean saw a flash of the monster's claws. Red on Tom's cheek. And then he was on his back. Unconscious.

"You will."

Sally Jean closed her eyes then and, for the first time since she was a little girl, started to pray. She was going to be killed, she was sure of it. What would her parents think?

"What's going on?"

Sally Jean opened her eyes and saw the most wonderful thing in the whole crazy world. Brett Blakely.

"Brett," she cried and ran toward him, throwing herself into his arms.

He looked at her with love in his gray eyes.

"Sally Jean," he said and his voice was so calm and safe. He looked right at the creatures and didn't balk or even shiver. Sally Jean let him hold her tight, pulled him closer. She was astonished by his bravery; maybe she had misjudged him. She looked up into his face for comfort. There he was, good old Brett Blakely from Asheville who drove an old Model T and wore a feathered hat and wanted to marry her. And then his face began to melt.

Right before her eyes he transformed, his features dissolved, wrinkling in on themselves until he had the same scalded skin, the same wolf mouth, and the same horrible snake eyes as the others. She tugged away from him, but his arms were stronger than they had ever been. He laughed at her struggle and, with one hand, tore the top of her dress, exposing her neck.

He addressed the other creatures. "This one was mine. You knew that." And then to Sally Jean, with his fangs at her neck, "Mine eternally."

And then something was upon them, a black cloud knocking them back, bringing them to the still-frozen earth. The rest came in flashes, moments of luminescence separate but strung together like pearls—like black and white pearls. Ardita in black silk with a wooden sword in hand. The white moon breaking from beneath a blue cloud. Ardita atop Brett's prostrate body, outlined by the moon, stabbing him in the chest. Dust. Dust blowing in the wind. The monsters on Ardita, all atop her. A flare of teeth. The wooden sword. A bird calling, calling. Dust in the air, like stars, like a galaxy. The moon like an orange, dust like bubbles in champagne. A monster arm in arm with Ardita like they were dancing, like he was a count. And then more dust, raining over her like ashes from the dead. And nobody left. Just

Ardita's eyes, blue and green like black and white like pearls and bubbles and oranges.

The next thing she knew, she was sitting in Tom's parlor in front of a roaring fire. She didn't know how long she had been sitting there, but she knew that Ardita had been there and now Ardita had gone and Tom was holding ice wrapped in a towel to his head. They were silent for a long time. Sally Jean didn't know where to begin: the monsters, Brett, Ardita. The fire warmed her body, but her mind still felt frozen and her heart felt cold.

"Who is she?" she heard herself ask, on the verge of tears.

Tom looked into the fire and touched the swelling claw marks on his cheek.

"She's Ardita O'Reilly, just like she says. She's a girl. A girl who also . . . I've known her a long time." He lit a cigarette and then threw it into the fire. Sally Jean saw tears thicken his eyes. "She's a girl," he continued, "who was chosen to fight a war."

And Sally Jean listened quietly as he told her about vampires and how they were everywhere, how they thrived in the dark corners of life. He explained how they could be killed and how Ardita had been trained for years by Mr. Whiskers to know how to do it. He told her how someday Ardita would die in the battle against this evil. And yet she kept doing it. She went out, every night, into the dark where monsters waited to kill her. And she did it knowing that she would die.

"I thought she was a flapper," Sally Jean said weakly, unable to express anything bigger. She had known, somehow, that Ardita was something else. She wasn't careless and wild and decadent like the others; she had a purpose. Sally Jean didn't want to be a flapper anymore and she didn't want to be like Ardita either. She began to cry. The tears flowed from her eyes like water from a well-primed pump. Tom moved toward her and put his arm around her, holding her tighter and tighter as the tears continued to come. He kissed her face and she kissed his and they held each other there in a salty sad embrace.

"Do you love her?" she asked through her tears.

He didn't answer.

"Do you love me, Tom?"

"Yes," he said, kissing the tears from her eyes.

"Do you choose me?" she asked. "Do you choose me?" He nodded and her tears slowed into jerking sobs.

"It's going to be okay," he told her, and she saw that he was crying too.

"It's going to be okay, it's going to be okay," she repeated. "We're going to be together, aren't we?"

He nodded and smoothed her hair.

"Forever and ever?"

He nodded again and smiled at her. "Forever and ever."

And his eyes filled again with tears.

"And we can get married and go back to Charleston and Peony can wear a garland of flowers?"

"A bright, beautiful garland of flowers."

He kissed her soft shoulder and she felt different. She had changed and she felt a kind of sadness she had never fathomed: bottomless, hopeless, hollow, and hard. She had Tom. She had won, hadn't she? She smiled unhappily and sat passively and let him kiss at her sweet soft arm.

A GOOD RUN
Greg Rucka

The Slayer Thessily Thessilonikki
The Battle of Marathon

Greece, 490 B.C.E.

She runs.

The ground is hard and dry, littered with stones and the bodies of the fallen, Athenian and Persian alike. She runs barefoot and avoids the bodies, but cannot avoid the stones. They bite at her soles, digging into her skin, and she can barely feel it, but she knows her feet are raw and blistered, and that with each stride she leaves a trail of bloody footprints across the plain. She barely feels anything but a distant and crackling pain from her lungs and a dull hot throbbing from the wound in her side, where the poison entered her body almost four days ago. Her chiton, once white, is now almost black in places, stained with days of dirt and sweat and blood, and linen has torn at her shoulder where a vampire grabbed her while trying to take her throat.

That vampire is dead, as are a hundred others, and she is dying, too, but she keeps running.

She has run nearly three hundred miles in four days, and she is almost finished.

In her right hand she carries her labrys. Perspiration from her hand has soaked the leather-wrapped grip, turning it blacker than her filthy tunic, and fine dust clings to the point of sharpened wood opposite the ax head, the part she uses as a stake when a stake is better than a blade. The handle is scored in several places, where she has used it to block blades or blows or teeth, and the head is chipped. The staking end, however, is still sharp. This is her favorite weapon, the one she has used again and again for almost eighteen years.

But now, and for the first time in her life, the labrys is heavy. The poison riding through her veins makes her hallucinate, and when she hallucinates, she loses her grip. Twice already she's come back to the present from her dreams to find the labrys dropped and retraced her steps to retrieve it. It matters that much to her.

She runs.

Her name is Thessily, sometimes called Thessily of Thessilonikki, though no one she has ever known has ever been as far north as Thessilonikki. It is simply a name, given to the woman who was once a girl who was once a slave and who is now the Slayer.

For a little longer, she thinks. *The Slayer a little longer.*

She is twenty-nine years old, and ready to die.

She is twelve years old, and has been a slave all her life.

Her mother is a dream memory who died before she could talk, and Thessily has been raised in the household of Meltinias of Athens, a fabric merchant. She has been well treated, or at least never abused, because only a fool abuses a slave; they're just too expensive to replace. She has never argued or been difficult, but Meltinias has seen it in her eyes.

Defiance exists in Thessily, and she is biding her time.

Meltinias thinks she is trouble. Smart for a slave, perhaps too smart, and growing dangerously attractive. The girl has hair blacker than the night sky, cold blue eyes that seem to judge everything, and skin that is pale like the skin on the statue of Pallas.

Thessily is exotic, and Meltinias has already pocketed several coins by charging other men for the simple pleasure of looking on her. Now that she is getting to be old enough, he is considering other ways he could make more money off of his prized slave.

In truth, he might have done so already were it not for the unblinking stare Thessily so often turns his way. The look is unnerving. He thinks, perhaps, it is a look from Hades. It is a look that will certainly lead to trouble.

But not anymore, because today Meltinias has sold his exotic, Hades-in-her-eyes slave to Thoas, the high priest of the Eleusinian mysteries. Thoas is the hierophant, and if anyone knows how to deal with Hades, it is he. The hierophant, after all, is the one person in all of Greece who can guarantee safe passage into the afterlife.

Meltinias watches them go, the tall, middle-aged priest and the pale-skinned girl. Thoas was almost desperate to purchase the girl, and Meltinias will live well on the sale for months to come. Meltinias breathes a sigh of relief.

And he catches his breath, because Thessily, now outside the door, has turned and looked back at him, and smiled.

And the smile is from Hades, too.

She is seventeen and Thoas, her Watcher, is at his table in their home, pretending to be at work with his scrolls. It is only an hour before dawn, and Thessily is happy and tired and sore, and when she comes inside, Thoas looks up as if surprised to see her. She knows he isn't; this is his game, and has been since they started.

Every evening she goes out with labrys in hand, to patrol and to slay, and always before dawn she returns, and when she crests the rise above the amphitheater, she can see his silhouette in the doorway of their house, watching for her. Then Thoas ducks back inside, and when she arrives only minutes later, he is always at the table, always pretending that he was not worried.

She loves him for this, because it is how she knows that he loves her.

Thoas looks her over quickly, assuring himself that his Slayer is uninjured. If she were, he would hurry to bind her wounds and ease her pain. But tonight she is not, and so Thoas proceeds as he always does, and asks her the same question he always asks.

"How many?"

"Seven," she tells him. "Including that one who has been haunting the agora, Pindar."

"Seven. Good."

Thessily smiles and sets her labrys by the door, then pours herself a glass of wine from the amphora on the table. "There was something new, a man with orange skin and an eye where his mouth should be."

"Orange skin or red skin?"

"Orange skin. And silver hair, in a braid."

"How long was his braid?"

"As long as my arm."

Thoas nods and scratches new notations on his scroll. "Jur'lurk. They are very dangerous, but always travel alone. You did well."

Thessily finishes her wine and nods and says, "I am to bed."

"Rest well, and the gods watch you as you sleep."

She goes into her room and draws the curtain, then sits on her bed and removes her sandals. Before, in Meltinias's house, she was simply a slave, and not a very good one. Here, living with Thoas, pretending to be his aide, she is the Slayer.

She is damn good at being the Slayer.

She smiles.

She frowns.

It is three nights ago, and she is running through olive groves and down hillsides, trying to protect a man Thoas has told her must not die. The Persians, led by their king, Darius, are coming. They will land their ships at the coast in only three days. Athens has no standing army, and the Persians have never been defeated. It is already assumed that the glory of Athens will fall, that the city will be looted, the men murdered, the women raped, the children taken as slaves. The greatest civilization the world has ever known is only seventy-two hours from total annihilation.

But there is a thin hope, and it lives in the man Thessily follows, a man named Phidippides, who is running to the Spartans with a plea for help. It is 140 miles from Athens to Sparta, through some of the roughest terrain Greece can offer, over rugged hills and through cracked and craggy ravines. Phidippides is a herald, a professional messenger, known for his stamina and his speed, and rumored to have the blessing of Pan. He runs with all his heart, trying to pace himself, yet knowing that time is against him, and Thessily admires him for this, if not for the errand itself.

She understands the wisdom of appealing to the Spartans. They are the greatest warriors in Greece, their whole culture is built around war and honor and service and dying. She knows how fierce they can be in battle, because even though the Slayer is forbidden to kill Men, she has battled the Spartans before.

The Spartans are lycanthropes, werewolves, and though they control their bestial nature, Thessily does not trust them. But because they are werewolves, they can save Athens.

Athens knows only that Sparta is great in the arts of war, not the truth behind that fact. That is why Phidippides runs 140 miles to ask for their help.

Thessily runs because with the Persian soldiers there also travel Persian vampires, and the vampires fear the Spartans.

Thoas has told her that the vampires will do everything they can to stop Phidippides from reaching his goal.

Thoas is correct.

The first assault comes only hours into the run, as Thessily parallels Phidippides's route, staying hidden from the herald's sight, as the terrain turns mercifully flat for a brief while. She leaps across a small creek, starlight reflected on its flowing surface, trying to stay ahead of the herald, and she sees three of them up ahead, using the edge of an olive grove for cover. The vampires aren't even bothering to hide their true faces, and without a pause Thessily frees her labrys from where it is strapped to her back, and she flies into them.

She has done this easily a thousand times before, possibly even more than that. Thoas has never found a record of a Slayer who has lived as long as Thessily, who has survived and fought for so many years without falling for the final time. She has been the Slayer for seventeen years now, she has grown up and is growing old, and though her body is not as fast or as strong as it once was, she is still the Slayer, and there are no mortals alive who can challenge her.

She takes the vampires by surprise, and has felled one of

them with the labrys before they've begun to react. On her follow-through swing, Thessily ducks and spins, bringing the ax up and ideally through another of the vampires, but she is surprised to find she has missed. It is a female, dressed in rags and patches of armor, and the vampire hisses and flips away, and Thessily has enough time to think that perhaps these Persian vampires are a little more dangerous than the ones she is used to when she feels the arrow punch into her side.

It feels like she's been hit with a stone, and it rattles her insides and pushes her breath out in a rush, and she turns to see the archer, the third vampire, perched in the low branches twenty feet away. Without thinking she drops the labrys and takes the stake tucked on her belt, snapping it side-armed, and the point finds the heart, and the vampire's scream turns to dust as fast as his body.

Then the other one, the female, falls on her from behind, and Thessily tries to roll with it, to flip her opponent. She feels a tearing of her skin and muscle and the awful pain of something sharp scraping along bone, and she stifles a scream. The vampire has grabbed the arrow sticking in her side, twisting it and laughing. Through sudden tears, Thessily strikes the vampire in the throat with the knuckles of a fist, forcing the once-a-woman back, and it buys her time.

Thessily is out of stakes. Her labrys is out of reach. With one hand, she holds the arrow against her body. With her other, she snaps the shaft in two, turning the wood in her hand even as the vampire leaps at her throat again. Thessily drops onto her back, bringing the splinter up and letting the vampire's own motion drive the stake home. There is an explosion of dust and the all-too-familiar odor of an old grave, and then the night is quiet again.

Thessily lies on her back, catching her breath. After a second she hears the sound of Phidippides's sandals hitting the soil in a steady rhythm, the shift of the noise as he comes closer, then passes the grove, then continues on his run. There is no pause or break in his stride, and she believes he has noticed nothing, that she is still his secret guardian, and she is grateful.

She tries to sit up and the pain blossoms across her chest, moving around and through it, and she gasps in surprise. In all the years she has been wounded, she's never felt a pain like this. She looks down at the remaining shaft of arrow jutting from her chiton, the spreading oval of blood running down her side, and gritting her teeth, she yanks the arrowhead free. Her head swims, and she sees spots as bright as sunlight. She raises the arrowhead and tries to examine it in the starlight, sees only the metal glistening with her own blood. She sniffs at the tip, and recoils, dropping it.

The odor burns her nostrils as she gets to her feet and retrieves her labrys. The straps on one of her sandals have torn, and she discards the other rather than try to run in only one shoe. She turns and follows after Phidippides, and has only gone three strides when she feels the first distant wash of nausea and giddiness stirring.

And she knows that she has been poisoned.

It is hours later that same night, and she has fought eight more vampires, each time keeping them from Phidippides. The vampires are savage and fast, and she is already tired and hurt, and slowing.

She wins each fight.

She runs.

It is today, and now she runs with Phidippides following, not caring if he spots her, because it is finished and because she is going home.

Behind her lie the remains of the battle, where Athens met its enemy that morning. Six thousand four hundred dead Persian soldiers litter the field, lying together with the bodies of one hundred and ninety-two Athenian men who have given their life for their city.

The sunlight is fierce above, and Thessily trips as she comes off the plain called Marathon. She tumbles through dirt and scrub before she can find her feet once more. She has lost the labrys, and loses precious seconds of her life trying to find it again.

Athens is only ten miles away, now, she can see it in the distance to the south, shimmering with color. Sunlight glints gold off the statue of Pallas Athena, off the tip of the mighty goddesses' spear.

She continues to run. Thoas is there, waiting, and she has to tell him that they won.

She has to tell him that she is ready to die.

She is nineteen, and full of herself, and is fighting a mob of vampires called the Horde, who have taken up residence at Delphi. She attacks with flaming oil and her bone bow, then with her labrys, then with her stakes, and she kills dozens, and still there are more, because they are, after all, a horde.

One gets behind her and puts her in a headlock, yanking her off her feet, and she can feel his breath burning her neck. His breath smells like rotten meat. Another is charging at her from the front, either not caring that she is already pinned, or hoping to capitalize on the moment, and he has a sword in his hand.

Thessily tries to go up, to flip herself out of the headlock and out of the way, so that the one vampire will stab the other. But as she tries to move, she feels the fangs tear at her neck and then the sword punching through her side, and it is the sword that saves her, because after it goes through her, it goes into the vampire behind her, and his teeth leave before he can take her blood.

She screams with rage, and as the vampire with the sword pulls it free, she reaches blindly for his head and snaps his neck, taking the sword from his hands as he dies. She spins with the blade and takes the head of the one who had bitten her, shouting hatred at him as he dissolves.

Thessily staggers out of the caverns beneath the temple, one hand across her belly, trying to keep her insides inside. Dawn is breaking, and she hears the sea and smells the salt, and then the sound of the waves grows louder and louder, and instead of the world growing lighter it grows darker, and she collapses on the road.

She nearly dies. She survives only because someone brings her to the Oracle, and the Oracle knows of the Slayer. The Oracle sends for Thoas and tends to Thessily, and for three days Thessily is unconscious, until finally she awakens, and her Watcher is there, and he looks concerned.

"I'm fine," Thessily says.

Thoas shakes his head.

"Truly, Thoas, I'm fine."

Thoas rubs the crow's feet at his left eye, the way he does when he is trying to find the right words. Thessily smells the camphor and lime on the bandages around her middle, and fights the urge to scratch the wound. In three days it will be healed, and there will not even be a scar. She hears voices singing praises through halls far away.

"You should have died," Thoas says.

Thessily looks at him and blinks, then laughs. It hurts her middle, but she laughs all the same. "When did you learn to joke?"

"It is no joke," Thoas says. "The Oracle tells me that the Horde was to kill you. It had been foretold."

Thessily thinks about this for several seconds. The singing continues, a praise to Apollo.

"Perhaps the Oracle is wrong."

"Perhaps," Thoas says.

The two of them are silent.

"I want to go home," Thessily says.

"I'll get your things," Thoas says.

It is dawn, a day and a half ago, and Thessily is hiding in the shadows of Sparta, listening to Phidippides plead Athens's case. She aches all over, the muscles in her calves and thighs and back drawn taut like sun-baked fishing nets. The wound from the arrow seeps steadily, and occasionally she begins to shiver and cannot stop for a time.

Phidippides is saying, "Men of Lacedaemon, the Athenians beseech you to hasten to their aid, and not allow that state, which is the most ancient in all Greece, to be enslaved by the barbarians. . . ."

She already knows the answer will be no, that the Spartans will not come—or at least, not come yet, though she did not realize this until just hours before, running in the darkness. She wonders why Thoas did not realize this as well.

The Spartans will not march until the full moon, when they are at their most powerful, and of course, that is what their king is telling Phidippides now. Our religion forbids marching sooner, he is saying, it would earn the wrath of our gods. We cannot march until the full moon. If the men of Athens can hold out until then. . . .

Phidippides offers the king formal thanks, bows, and departs, saying only that he doubts Athens has that much time. Thessily admires his diplomatic skill; she has never been good with words, and even though Thoas has spent the last several years trying to teach her manners, Thessily knows she would only make matters worse if she tried to plead the case. Women in Sparta have less standing even than women in Athens, and while she can claim to be the hierophant's aide, that will not grant her respect, only privacy.

She moves from the shadows to the edges of the fortress-city, waiting for Phidippides to emerge, and another bout of shaking strikes her. Her mouth feels full of wet wool, and her vision blurs.

She thinks about her life, and tries not to be angry. She tries not to hate the Oracle at Delphi, who ruined everything.

Sometimes she wishes she had died with the Horde.

Phidippides comes through the city gates, and immediately begins running.

Thessily fights to control her limbs and her thoughts, and follows.

She is twenty-three, four years after the Horde, and she has killed more vampires and more demons than she can possibly remember. She considers asking Thoas what the running total is, but decides against it; the knowledge would be too depressing.

But she is depressed anyway, and Thoas spots this quickly, and asks what is troubling her.

"There is no point," she tells him.

"You are mistaken. You have saved countless lives—"

"But the vampires are legion, Thoas, and they never stop

coming! If I had died at Delphi, would anything be different? Would there truly be fewer vampires in Attica? Would there be anything to mark my passing?"

"If you had fallen, another would have been Chosen—"

"Exactly. I have slain for over ten years! *Ten years,* Thoas, and for what? A list of numbers you record each and every night, and nothing more? And so I will die and another will be Chosen, and another, and another. . . ."

Her voice cracks, and it both surprises and embarrasses her. She did not mean to be so emotional, so angry.

Thoas looks at her with concern and compassion. "Thessily," he says. "There are Slayers in the annals who have been Chosen only to fight for a fraction of the time you've had. You are remarkable, you are blessed, to have battled so well for so long. Your survival is a gift."

She shakes her head, and feels tears rushing up in her eyes, and the frustration is so intense that for a moment she can't speak. Thoas rises from his chair and moves to where she sits on the bench beneath the window. He is old, now, and moves slowly. He puts his arm around her shoulders, and holds her the way every father holds a daughter.

"I just want to be remembered for more than numbers," she says through her tears, and though she is a woman, to her own ears she sounds like a girl. "I want to be remembered because I did something great. Just one great thing."

Thoas says nothing, just holds her and rocks her, and eventually the tears stop.

But the question and the desire remain.

Just one great thing.

+ + +

It is yesterday, and they are returning to Athens from Sparta, running in daylight, and now she is suffering brief hallucinations because of the fatigue and the poison. She lets Phidippides stay ahead of her, afraid of losing sight of him, but no longer worried for his immediate safety.

She sees the Horde and the way they slaughtered families, and she remembers the feeling of the sword slicing through her body.

She sees Meltinias and his thin fingers counting the coins that men have given him to just look at her.

She sees Thoas, at once old like he is now and young like he was then, and she sees herself, and she is old, too, she knows.

She sees ships, seven of them, moving along the coast, galleys with their sails out, Persian soldiers on the decks, and hatches leading below chained shut.

Then she sees the world as it really is, she is still running back to Athens, and it has grown late and the night has fallen. She moves to a side and sprints, skirting Phidippides's position, taking the lead. Again, he seems to not know she is there. Her feet burn.

She sees no vampires, and wonders.

She sees the galleys in her mind, moving along the coast toward Athens. She sees the hatches again. She sees the chains and knows that they are there not to keep what is below in, but to keep what is above out.

She knows what is behind the hatches.

It is almost dawn, and Thessily is searching frantically for Thoas in the near-empty streets of Athens, finding him where the men are donning their armor, preparing to march out to Marathon to meet the Persians. Phidippides has arrived only minutes after her, bearing the bad news, and the decision has been made to fight despite the odds.

Thoas sees her and his eyes go wide and the lines in his face run deeper as he says her name. Breathless, she tries to explain what she knows, but Thoas won't listen, forcing her to sit down, searching frantically for water.

"You've been poisoned!" he says.

She nods, gasping for air, taking the skin of water gratefully, and pouring half its contents down her throat. "It's not important," she manages to say.

"It is—"

"It isn't," she says, and she grabs at his robe and pulls him in close, forcing him to listen. "I can't—my mind is, it wanders, but I know . . . I know *why*, Thoas."

He searches her face, concerned, afraid. She can only imagine how she looks to him, dusty and sweat stained, even paler than normal. She thinks her hair must be matted with dirt and grass and mud.

"I'm not delirious," Thessily manages. "I'm *not*, I *know*. The Persians, Thoas. The galleys."

"They will attack from the water?"

"Yes, but—but—" She shakes her head, desperate. Why can't she make the words come out? Why can't she say it right? *Please understand me,* she is thinking.

"In the ships," she says, the plea in her eyes. "They must be in the ships. It's the only way they can move in the sun."

Thoas's expression smoothes, and he takes her hands in his and nods, telling her to please let go, that she has forgotten how strong she is. She forces her fingers to loosen, and as she does another bout of shaking strikes her, so violently that she is left shivering, curled on her side, with Thoas trying to wrap his cloak around her.

In the streets, the Athenian men are beginning to march down the wide promenade, past the agora, to meet the Persians.

Thessily sees Phidippides, exhausted, joining the back of the line. He is donning his armor as he goes, carrying his spear.

She forces herself to be still again. To Thoas, she says, "I'll need oil."

"How many ships?"

"Seven."

"You're certain?"

"I . . . I saw it in my mind."

Thoas considers this. "I will get oil. And we will pray that you are right."

The sun is blazing and it is still well before noon, and the Athenian men are formed in their lines on the field of Marathon, and the Persian soldiers—the human soldiers—are thundering toward them. Thessily sees the flare of sunlight off metal from the corner of her eye, and she stops for a moment to watch the battle as it is joined. Her shoulders ache, and her side still bleeds. Her labrys is heavy against her back. On ropes slung over each shoulder she carries skins of lamp oil, and the weight of it would not bother her if she hadn't already run over three hundred miles in the last three days.

She knows she doesn't have time to stare, but she does all the same, and a pressure builds against her heart that, at first, she fears is the poison and her death, but isn't. She cannot describe the feeling, but it brings tears to her eyes.

She sees Phidippides, spear low, set against a charge, standing shoulder to shoulder with his fellow citizens, free men, civilized men. Men who have walked of their own free will to a barren plain twenty-six miles north of Athens to fight a battle they believe they are certain to lose. Fighting for their homes and their loved ones and their lives.

She realizes she is watching history.

The sounds of the fighting drift across the plain to her, and then the screams of the dying men. The Persians are desperate in battle and savage, and the Athenians hold their line, and then it breaks, and she understands what she is seeing. One of the Athenian generals—she thinks it is Miltiades, he's the smartest—is trying to flank the Persians. As she watches, the Athenian line breaks into three sections, and the outer two move to the sides, and the Persians are caught by surprise. They cannot go forward without dying. They cannot go to either side without dying.

They can only retreat.

Thessily runs, as fast as she can, for the coast.

If they can only retreat, they will retreat to their ships.

She has to get to them first.

It is noon and the fires on the water are so intense she cannot breathe and has to retreat. The galleys burn slowly, but the vampires inside them burn much faster, and she can hear their screams behind her as she works from ship to ship, the torch in one hand and a skin in the other, dumping oil all over the decks. When she touches the torch to the puddles, the flame races along the cracks in the wood, sucking the air from below.

She leaps from the prow of the sixth galley to the back of the seventh, and douses the nearest hatch with the last of her oil. She drops the torch in the pool, and feels the heat rise around her so suddenly her eyelashes curl.

The hatch ahead of her bursts open, and the vampire who has broken the chains bursts into flames and falls back into the hold. She hears more hissing, and then screams, and she spares a look down as she passes, seeing them crowded together in the shadows, trying to avoid the sun, trying to avoid flames.

For a moment, she almost pities them.

Then she leaps from the last galley to the water, and swims to the shore.

With the last of her strength, she runs.

It is dusk and Thoas is at the gates along with a thousand other Athenians, old men and children and women of all ages, and Thessily tries to keep running, but her legs no longer listen, and in truth, she feels they have earned that right. Her vision is so blurred by tears and sweat and poison that she does not recognize Thoas until he has come out to meet her, calling her name.

She hears tears in his voice.

She falls into his arms, and he cradles her to the ground, her head in his lap.

He kisses her brow and speaks a prayer to Dionysus, to Demeter, and to Kore.

Through lips that are parched and cracked, she whispers to him.

"We won," she says, and though she can barely hear herself speak, a cheer comes from the crowd at the gate. She tries to turn her head to see what has roused them, and Thoas brushes hair from her cheek and shakes his head.

"Phidippides has arrived," he tells her softly. "He brings the same news."

"He can run," Thessily says. It hurts to smile, but she finds one anyway.

"Yes, he surely can."

She shivers, but not so badly as before, and tries again to turn her head. This time, Thoas relents, and she sees that Phidippides is before the crowd, his helmet in his hand. She sees the fatigue take him as he turns toward her, watches as he falters and drops his helmet. He staggers another step, falling to his knees. The crowd behind him surges, then stops.

Phidippides reaches them on his knees, and holds out a hand. Thoas has to take it and put it in Thessily's own. Phidippides' hand is dry, too dry, and there is no heat in it any longer.

"I've seen you before," Phidippides says. His voice is ragged and hoarse. "Running with me at night."

"Yes." The word passes her throat more air than sound.

"What is your name?" he asks.

"Thessily."

He smiles a broken smile, through lips as damaged as her own, and he puts his head on the ground near hers.

"It was a good run," he says.

"Yes," Thessily says, the last of her air slipping away. "It was."

HOUSE OF THE VAMPIRE

Michael Reaves

London, England, 1897

I

The sight of a gentleman ambling down the crowded and ill-lit alleys of the East End after dark was not unique, but it was certainly not common. This neighborhood, containing parts of Whitechapel, Spitalfields, Mile End, and others, was one of the most dangerous and poverty-stricken in all of London, and for someone of obvious means to venture into it on foot, even by day, was remarkable.

Nevertheless, down the narrow avenue the stranger walked, briskly but with apparent nonchalance, all heads turning to mark his passage. The cacophony of raucous voices slowed as he went by, then started up again with increased interest, the multitude of topics now having diminished to just one. Tatterdemalions paused from their endless pursuit of one another across the flagging and through the stinking gutters; shop owners lounged in recessed doorways, blinking amidst malodorous clouds of pipe smoke; and slatterns slowed their strolling to gaze in appraisal or frank admiration. The stranger ignored them all, walking as casually as if he were out for a constitutional in Covent Garden. He swung his ivory-tipped cane in rhythm with his gait, and his top hat was perched at a jaunty angle. He seemed utterly unaware of the area's unwholesomeness.

It was just after nine P.M., the dark of the moon, so not even that celestial body's effulgence could aid in dispersing the shadows. The only things keeping the darkness even slightly at bay were rubbish fires, candles, and the infrequent oil lanterns and naphtha brands. From all about could be heard the wailing of hungry children, the shouts and scuffles of various altercations, and the moaning of the aged and infirm. The winding lane was hardly wide enough to permit the passage of a four-wheeled cab, and it branched off into alleys and cul-de-sacs that were even more restrictive, barely serving to separate the ramshackle buildings. The stench of offal, waste, and things rotten was almost palpable, coiling through the streets like an invisible miasmic serpent. But of all this the gentleman took no apparent heed.

He turned down an alley narrow enough for him to touch the slimy walls of both buildings with his gloved hands. The darkness here was complete and utter; even the faint starlight was blocked by webs of laundry strung between the upper floors. But he did not slow his pace.

The alley, after turning sharply in several directions, opened at length into a small, deserted courtyard. Dark windows and doorways, many boarded over, punctuated the walls. The starlight was unimpeded here, and the crowded buildings loomed overhead at what seemed impossible angles. The court was empty, save for a single figure, dressed in white, standing across from him.

The gentleman moved forward quickly, his cloak flaring. The woman stood with her back to him. His shoes made no sound on the cobblestones. He pulled his gloves off as he approached, revealing long, pale fingers, and reached toward her.

"Elizabeth!" His whisper was husky with longing. "My darling, how wonderful to be with you again!"

At the sound of his voice she turned. Each paused for a moment, then rushed into an embrace. They held each other closely, murmuring mutual endearments, the dreary surroundings and cares of Lower London banished for a brief time. Then they backed slightly apart, still staring lovingly into each other's eyes, and began to stroll slowly about the perimeter of the square, not speaking, content for the moment in each other's presence. At length, as they passed the dark lacuna of a stairway entrance, he turned to her.

"It won't be long now, I promise you," he said. "Once the decree is issued I'll be free, and then you'll bid this disgusting welter of thieves and mendicants good-bye forever."

"Phillip," she murmured, her eyes bright with the promise of good fortune. She drew a breath to speak again—

And the night took her.

One instant she stood before him, young and happy and full of love for him alone . . . and then it was as if the darkness itself reached out hungrily and snatched her away. Paralyzed by shock, Phillip stood staring into the impenetrable gloom. He heard the rustle of something that could have been a cloak, or perhaps even the stir of sinister wings, followed by a brief, sharp cry from Elizabeth . . . then silence.

Silence, save for a rhythmic, measured sound, as of some liquid being drawn by suction . . .

The gentleman gave a shout of mingled horror and rage. He raised his cane and leaped forward into the stygian gloom, only to be met with a single blow of such appalling strength that it sent him sprawling halfway across the court. Dazed, he rolled over and managed to raise himself on one elbow. He stared back at the dark entrance. From it emerged a pale face with eyes red as embers; it seemed to float toward him on a column of darkness. Behind this apparition he could see the stairway entrance. From the shadows an arm, slim and cotton-clad, lay outflung on the cold stones.

The face loomed over Phillip. A line of crimson trickled from one corner of the scowling mouth. The gentleman's final cry was one of utter despair; it rose into the night, blending unheard with all the other screams and shouts of the city.

II

Springheel Jack fled for his life.

He ran in great bounding leaps over the pitched roofs and gables, jumping from tenement to tenement, clearing gaps of fifteen to twenty feet at a time. He hurtled over chimneys and skylights, cloak billowing out behind him like black wings. His speed was such that nothing human could hope to catch him.

Not even the Slayer.

Angelique knew she had no hope of overtaking Jack. That was not the plan. Accordingly she pursued at a somewhat less than breakneck pace, leaping over impediments with practiced ease, the fetid city air pumping in and out of her lungs. Though the life of a slayer was in many ways a difficult one, there were compensations, and chief among them were physical strength and reflexes surpassed by none—none of her fellow humans, at any rate.

She saw Jack put his boot on the edge of a cupola and hurl

himself forward into space to land on a rooftop one floor down and a good twenty-five feet away. Had she taken the time to doubt, she might not have made it. Instead she gave herself up to her training, as the Professor had admonished her so many times. She leaped. Sooty night air fanned her raven tresses . . . then she landed, her legs absorbing the impact with no complaints.

It felt good to be alive.

Jack was still running. He would not be for much longer.

Angelique charged forward and saw the dark figure step out from behind a water tank. He aimed a device at Jack and fired. Before the surprised Jack could react, a net of hemp flowered before him. It enveloped him, brought him crashing to his knees. Angelique heard him roar in rage, a sound no human throat could make.

He surged to his feet. Blue fire erupted from his mouth, incinerating his bonds. But the delay had been enough; before Jack could escape, Angelique leaped onto his back.

Jack roared again and twisted about, slamming himself into a brick wall, with the Slayer between him and the barrier. The impact set off fireworks behind the Slayer's eyes. For a moment her grip slackened. He would have thrown her from him then, but in that moment a thin blade flashed, the point darting toward Jack's chest. Startled, Jack stumbled backward. Angelique wrapped both arms around his neck, gripped his head and twisted with all her strength. The *crack!* his neck made when it snapped was clearly audible.

Springheel Jack collapsed beneath her.

Angelique stood, brushing soot from her skirt and Zouave jacket as the Professor and Gordon approached. "That's that," she said briskly. "We should hear no more about the terrifying Springheel Jack in London, I think."

"Perhaps," the Professor said. "But do not be overly sure,

Angelique. The legend of Springheel Jack has endured for decades. I think it likely more than one Tethyrian demon has contributed to the stories over the years." He picked up his bowler from where it had fallen during the slaying and dusted it off before carefully covering his baldness with it.

The Slayer frowned, but then smiled again as Gordon came to stand beside her, sheathing his sword cane in its camouflaging shaft of wood. "No purpose to worrying about that now," she said. "I trust, Professor, that you noticed the aid Gordon was able to give us a moment ago?"

The Professor scowled, the fingers of one hand tugging at his beard. "It is still not right," he said. "The Slayer walks alone, save for her watcher. The council has made its stance very clear on this, and I agree with them."

Gordon responded before she had a chance to speak. "All well and good for the council to huddle before warm fires and make pronouncements like Parliament, I suppose. But Angelique is the Slayer. It is her life put at risk every night—"

"Which is how it should be!" the Professor interrupted, brandishing an indignant index finger. "Hers and hers alone! This has been the way of it for centuries. Remember: 'She *alone* can stand against the vampires, the forces of darkness—'"

"Enough arguing," Angelique said. In the silence that followed, the tolls of Big Ben could faintly be heard echoing across the distant Thames. "It's three in the morning," she continued. "I think this has been a good night's work. Whether one hand or many did the deed, the important thing is that the deed is done. Another demon lies dead."

The three looked down at the recumbent form. "Professor," Angelique continued, "do you mind tidying up?"

The Professor nodded. "Of course, of course." He turned to the black leather satchel a few feet away and retrieved from it a small phial. Unstoppering it, he sprinkled a bit of sparkling dust over the demon's corpse. *"Facilis descenus,"* he said. There was a rushing sound, a flash of green fire, and when it cleared the body of the Tethyrian demon had vanished.

They found a stairwell and descended to the street. A single gaslight provided scant illumination. "Little luck we'll have finding a cab at this hour," the Professor grumbled, pulling his Inverness closer around him against the chill night air.

Angelique and Gordon looked at each other and smiled. Her heart warmed at the sight of him, clean-shaven and thin in his ragland overcoat, breeches, and boots, all varying tones of gray. Angelique felt her skin tingle as his hand brushed hers. They had known each other for over two months now, and so far everything seemed to be going right. Gordon Mycroft was considered by some—most, in fact—to be a ne'er-do-well with a shady background and equally shady standards. Some thought him a dandy for carrying a cane, not knowing, for the most part, how lucky they were to be spared his skill with the blade it camouflaged. He and Angelique had met on a cold night in the heart of one of London's many cemeteries—he had been there, he'd told her later, seeking inspiration for his poetry—where she had found him fending off the attacks of two newly-risen vampires. She had thought to make short work of the bloodsuckers, but then seven more had erupted out of the darkness. She and Gordon had fought side by side among the timeworn marble slabs, beneath the brooding oaks and willows, and he had been by her side practically ever since.

Her watcher disapproved of her associating with a wastrel poet, of course; from what Angelique had been able to discern, Professor

Peter van Helsing was considered somewhat old-fashioned even by the stuffy and hidebound standards of the council. He had been vehemently opposed to her initial association with young Patch, though even he had had to admit that the ragged urchin's knowledge of the streets and what was happening on them was far more effective than the local constabulary's—or even Scotland Yard's, on occasion. And he had practically become apoplectic when Molly Carrington had entered the picture, despite the ex-novitiate's passionate hatred for the forces of evil. But in the end he had grudgingly accepted the three, though his objections still flared now and then.

And, Angelique reflected as they walked along the narrow deserted street, the Professor was right, in an academic sense. It was unheard of for a slayer to work closely with anyone except her watcher. She was violating rules and traditions that had been accepted without question for centuries. But Angelique Hawthorne cared little about rules, and she knew that even the hoariest of traditions are not immune to change. In the nearly two years since she had been summoned, she had proven to be one of the most successful vampire hunters in the council's memory. So let them grumble, she told herself. It is never prudent to question success.

And, no matter how dangerous or ultimately short-lived her career as a slayer might be, it was still better than the life she came from.

By the time they reached the Professor's manor in Regent's Park, it was after four, and even Angelique was tired. She climbed the stairs, changed into her nightdress, and collapsed gratefully upon the four-postered eiderdown bed.

But, exhausted though she was, sleep danced tantalizingly just out of reach. She was keyed up, anxious. Such restlessness was unusual for her. She had made her peace years before with her calling and the short life expectancy that usually came with it, and she had also learned to snatch sleep when and where she could.

Tonight, however, peace evaded the Slayer. For some reason she found herself growing uncomfortably warm, to the point of perspiration. Impatiently she kicked the bedclothes free, lying exposed to the air in her nightgown. Still the heat plagued her, almost febrile in its intensity. *This is ridiculous,* she thought. *Such a balmy night is unheard of this late in autumn. And yet the breeze does nothing to cool me.*

With a start, she realized that the French doors to the balcony were open. When she had retired, she had made sure they were shut and locked, as she did every night. While it was true that a vampire could not cross a threshold unless invited, other species of demons were not as restricted. Yet now the doors stood thrown wide. The moon was new, only the faintest sliver of a crescent, yet somehow she could see clearly the dead rust-colored leaves stirring on the balcony, could see the lace draperies framing the doors, and the massive dark wood wardrobe against the far wall . . .

And the man who stood cloaked in darkness at the foot of her bed.

Angelique felt her heart frost over. The moment of fear was quickly followed by anger. How *dare* some creature of the night invade her private chambers! She sat up, reaching for the stake which lay on the bedside table—

Or rather she *tried* to. But, to her astonishment, she was unable to move. A paralysis gripped her as if she had been inoculated by some potent drug. Helpless, she lay there and watched as the silhouette moved slowly, even casually, around the bedpost and toward her. Although she could see the rest of the room clearly, his face and form somehow remained in shadow, even when he stood by her side, close enough to for her to touch him . . . and for him to touch her.

He leaned toward her. Angelique could see the twin embers of red that were his eyes and the pale slivers of fangs as he opened his mouth.

Hear me, Slayer. Did she hear the whispered words, touched by the hint of a Slavic accent, or did they echo somehow only within her head? *Do not seek to meddle in matters not of your concern. Some affairs of the night are beyond your station. Keep to your domain, or pay the penalty.*

With a gasp, she sat up. She looked at the balcony. The doors leading to it were closed. There was no one in the room but her.

Angelique's hand shot to the bedside table, seized a hand mirror lying beside the stake. Quickly she inspected her throat.

It was unmarked.

From the far distance, at the very edge of audibility, she thought she heard the howl of a wolf.

The Slayer reached for the heavy duvet, pulled it back up over her. She bundled herself in it, shivering. The night air was very cold.

III

At mid-morning of the following day, Angelique stood in the tiny East End courtyard, along with the Professor, Gordon, Molly, and Patch.

It was Patch who had brought them the news. He had woken them at dawn with his shouts of "Hoy!" much to the annoyance of the Professor's neighbors. Yet even at that early hour they had nearly been too late to inspect the site.

When they arrived, the bodies had already been moved from the court into the avenue. The normal din of costermongers and their customers was subdued now as the man's sheeted corpse was loaded onto the back of a wagon. The woman's body had been turned onto her back, and her eyes were being photographed at close range. Simon Peasbody, a detective from the Yard, was supervising. Professor van Helsing distracted him with questions while Molly and Angelique pulled back the coarse linen and examined the bodies. A quick look was all they were able to obtain before the crowding of curious onlookers forced them away. Even so, they saw enough.

"The marks are there," Molly said. "The fangs of the beast have drained them both." Her thin face, which remained pale no matter how much sun she was exposed to, was even grimmer than usual. Molly Carrington had been an Anglo-Catholic novitiate before having been cast out for defiling the church; she had scooped a hatful of holy water from a baptismal font to fling at a vampire. Now she fought against evil in a more unorthodox, but certainly more effective, way. Her hatred of all things unholy and the undead in particular was a whip constantly driving her.

"The bodies still have blood in them," Angelique said. "They will not rise again in three days."

Molly looked closely at her. "You sound disappointed. Surely you do not wish the curse of the undead upon these poor people."

"No, of course not. Still, those newly risen tend to seek the one that turned them. They might have led us to—"

Angelique paused. For a moment the wan light of the morning sun seemed to pale even more; her vision grew dark around the edges, and instead of Molly's concerned face, she seemed to see another more sinister countenance.

"Angelique! Are you ill? Speak!"

Angelique blinked. Gradually the street around her swam back into focus.

"I'm fine," she told Molly. "A bit of lightheadedness; that's all. Nothing that can't be cured by a plate of kippers and kedgaree."

Molly looked unconvinced, but before she could respond, they were interrupted by the approach of van Helsing and Peasbody. The Professor was shaking his head at the detective and saying heatedly, "Optograms indeed! How can anyone believe such tripe in this modern day?"

Peasbody looked bored. Angelique knew him to be a prissy and officious man who went about constantly swathed in the clinging scent of various pomades. She could smell the one he had used today, a faint paraffin odor. *As stiff as one of Madame Tussauds's waxworks, and about as bright,* she thought.

"Indeed, Professor," Peasbody said. "And how would *you* go about finding the murderer?"

"Fingerprinting. Specifically, the Galton Method. It is the only dependable way to identify a criminal. Even in twins the patterning is different."

Peasbody elaborately stifled a yawn. "I am aware of the process, thank you. But it has not yet been established as being useful in criminal investigation."

"Bah," the Professor said. "Perhaps you should avail yourself of the good offices of that fellow over on Baker Street. What's his name? The one your colleague Lestrade is always popping off for advice."

Peasbody drew himself up haughtily—*like a paraffin penguin,*

Angelique thought, and had to smother her laughter. "Forensic photography," the Yard man said to van Helsing, "is a well-known practice, and, given the importance of this case, I see no reason for the Yard to deviate from procedure. Good morning." And, with a slight nod toward Angelique and the others, he turned away.

"Officious idiot," van Helsing muttered. He frowned massively at Angelique as if she were somehow responsible for Peasbody's dismissal of his suggestion.

"I'm sure Scotland Yard will recognize your genius eventually, Professor," Gordon said. Van Helsing looked suspiciously at him, uncertain if he was being mocked.

"So who's the toff?" Patch inquired, nodding toward the wagon.

"The past tense is more appropriate," the Professor replied. "He *was* Phillip Menzies, Viscount of Kentington."

"That explains why the Yard's involved," Molly said. "Vampires drain these poor souls down here every day, and no one gives a tinker's damn. But let one of their own be attacked, and—"

"Exactly so. This demon must be found, before there is a panic."

They began walking away from the crime scene. Already the normal sounds of the neighborhood were reasserting themselves: the rattle of sewing machines from a nearby sweatshop, an organ grinder's sprightly tune, the noisy horseplay of children. Violent death was nothing new in the East End.

Van Helsing looked at Angelique. "How do you suggest we begin?"

"With some questions," the Slayer replied. "And I think I know where to start asking."

She pushed her way through the crowd, van Helsing and her

friends following. She led them through the crowded, redolent neighborhood, down one twisted lane and up another, until all but the Slayer were completely lost in the warren of cul-de-sacs and blind alleys.

At last they stopped before a side entrance to what appeared to have once been a lower-class lodging house, but which now seemed deserted. "That's a bit more than strange," Gordon mused. "The East End teems with people, yet an entire building stands empty?"

"Not entirely empty," Angelique replied as she kicked the door in.

Within, a long-unused vestibule was barely visible in the dim light. The entrances to still-darker rooms could be seen on either side. The destruction of the door sent lances of morning sunlight down the hall, luminous with dust motes. From within the closest room they heard furtive rustling and uneasy hisses. Angelique, moving forward quickly, caught a glimpse of yellow eyes disappearing into the darkness.

"Professor, illuminate the situation, please," the Slayer said. Van Helsing brought from an inner pocket another of his many inventions: an ingeniously small but powerful electric torch, which bathed the entire chamber in stark, actinic light. The room was empty of furnishings, anything of value having long since been stolen, and even much of the wainscoting torn away for firewood. Dazzled by the glare were four vampires, freshly risen; she could see the rich dark loam of the grave still caked on their clothes and fingers. For an instant the tableau held . . . and then one of the undead ones lunged toward her, howling, fangs bared.

Angelique nimbly sidestepped the bloodsucker's rush; it stumbled forward, off balance, and was abruptly stopped by the wooden tip of Gordon's cane, which speared its unbeating heart. With a sound of muted thunder, it disintegrated. Without looking back the Slayer whipped a stake from a holster concealed by her skirt's pleating and leaped to confront the next fiend. It hurled a flurry of blows and kicks at her, all of which she blocked with the ease of long practice. She saw an opening and struck, lunging into full extension with the stake as a fencer might thrust an epee. Her aim was true, and the second vampire followed the first into dusty oblivion.

Two were gone, and two remained. *No, make that one,* Angelique corrected herself as, out of the corner of her eye, she saw Molly skewer the third gravespawn. The expression on her pale face was grim, but her dark eyes glittered with savage satisfaction as her prey crumbled to nothingness. Then Angelique turned toward the last vampire, which crouched snarling in a corner, held at bay by the cross gripped in the Professor's extended hand. Behind him, Patch took aim with a small but powerful crossbow.

"Stop!" The Slayer's command echoed in the empty chamber. The others looked at her in surprise. Angelique moved to face the vampire.

"You know who I am," she said.

The vampire nodded, its fingers kneading the air as if servilely twisting the brim of a doffed hat. "Aye."

"The one who changed you," Angelique said. "Describe him."

The creature's eyes filled with fear. "I can't. Not the Master. He'll know."

"Tell me," Angelique said, "and we will leave you unmolested."

She heard Molly gasp behind her and knew without looking that Gordon's hand was on her arm, restraining her.

But the vampire shook its head. "He'll know, I tell you. His eyes are everywhere! Even here!"

Angelique saw the thing's gaze shift to a dark corner of the room. The vampire shrieked in terror, then turned and leaped unhesitatingly toward one of the boarded-up windows, crashing through it directly into the glare of the morning sun. It was dust before it had time to hit the ground.

The five comrades stood staring in shock at the open window and the bright shaft of light.

"It knew," Patch said. "Lummie, it *knew* what it were doin'."

Angelique turned and looked at the thing in the corner that had triggered the vampire's suicide. The sunlight made it easy to spot. The others looked as well.

It was a rat. As they watched, it scuttled rapidly along the floorboards and disappeared into a hole in the wall.

Angelique looked at Professor van Helsing. He shook his head in bewilderment.

She looked back at the window. "The Master," she murmured.

IV

"'His eyes are everywhere,'" Gordon quoted. "That's what the vampire said just before it destroyed itself. What could it have meant?"

They were in the laboratory section of what was unofficially known as the Lair, the secret sub-cellar beneath the Professor's manor house that gave egress to London's labyrinthine network of sewers and tunnels. Gordon lounged in a somewhat threadbare Morris chair, Patch and Molly leaned against one of the stone walls, and Angelique paced nervously. The Professor stood near a bookcase, leafing through a handwritten journal. On a nearby lab bench a complicated distillation apparatus circulated liquids of various hues through a glass maze of tubes and coils. A large detailed map of Greater London occupied one wall. The room was dimly lit by flickering gaslight.

"As I thought." Van Helsing's forefinger stabbed an entry in the diary. "It is all here in my brother's account of his dealings with the one called the King of the Undead: Count Dracula of Transylvania."

Angelique stopped pacing. "I've heard of him."

"Of course. If the undead have a potentate, a Prince of Darkness, it would be Dracula. Before his death, centuries ago, he was a national ruler and a potent sorcerer as well. His knowledge of the black arts makes him the most powerful of his kind. His gaze is mesmeric, enthralling. It is said that he can transvect from a man to a wolf, or to a bat, that he can change himself into mist, and"—van Helsing peered at them from over his rimless spectacles—"that he can use, as if they are his own, the eyes and ears of vermin, such as rats."

"But didn't your brother help to slay him in his homeland?" Angelique asked.

The Professor shrugged. "It seems Dracula was not quite as dead as Abraham had hoped. And now he has returned to London. This is a very serious matter. It will take all your skill to prevail against him, Angelique. None of us will be safe until he is destroyed."

Patch sniffed. "Sounds like a tall order, that does."

"He does appear to be well-nigh indestructible," Gordon agreed. "Is there no vulnerability in this creature to exploit?"

"Only one," van Helsing replied. "To gain his dark powers, he had to give up the daylight hours. Instead of simply avoiding the sun like others of his foul breed, he must remain insensible from sunrise to sunset, sleeping in a bed of his native earth."

Silence, save for the quiet bubbling of heated beakers, followed Professor Van Helsing's words. Unbidden in Angelique's mind there arose the memory of her dream: the cloaked silhouette, eyes burning in the shadowed face, the gleam of fangs drawing closer . . .

She shuddered. She was not overly concerned for herself; it was hard to imagine a vampire who could stand against her. But she was worried about her comrades' safety.

A dozen times she had opened her mouth to tell them about the vivid, unsettling nightmare—and its enigmatic warning—that she'd had the previous night. But each time the words seemed to stick in her throat. She wasn't sure why she was so reluctant. The Professor had told her many times that a slayer's dreams could be prescient, warnings of things to come. But she still could not make herself speak of this.

It was Molly who spoke next. "Our course is obvious, then," she said in response to the Professor. "We hunt this Dracula during the day. We find his lair and send him back to hell." She pantomimed thrusting a stake.

"Do not be overly confident," van Helsing said darkly. "Dracula has not survived for centuries by underestimating his enemies; neither should we underestimate him. He may be helpless during the day, but he can bend humans to his will, force them to be his myrmidons. We must be on guard constantly. In fact," he added, "until this evil has been put down, none of us should be alone for even a moment."

Once again uneasy silence reigned in the Lair. Angelique saw Patch, Gordon, and Molly look uncertainly at one another, and read their expressions without difficulty: How were they to know that one of them might not already be under Dracula's thrall?

Though they were anxious to begin the search, Angelique and van Helsing decided it was best to wait until the next day, as it was already less than an hour to sunset.

The Slayer spent the rest of the evening and long into the night training with Gordon in the Lair's makeshift gymnasium area. Van Helsing and the Watchers Council had spared no expense to see that her prowess in the arts of war was as thorough as it was eclectic. Among many other skills, she had been tutored in *Baritsu* and the French art of *La Canne,* as well as fencing, both classic and bayonet.

Gordon participated with gusto in the exercises, adroitly using both his walking stick and the rapier concealed within it to parry her quarterstaff mock attacks. As always, Angelique joyed in the smooth kinetics of her body, her muscles and reflexes working seamlessly at a speed and strength unknown to the strongest of athletes. It had not always been thus.

Before she had been called she had been the third of five children, raised by her mother and uncle; her father had left the country for a new life in the Colonies before she was born. They lived in Shoreditch, renting two rooms for eight shillings a week. At the age of seven she sold matches to help put food on the table, usually no more than a loaf, a penny's worth of hard cheese, and a penny's worth of tea. When she was twelve, her uncle lost his job as a boot-machinist. He supported them for a time in a wide variety of increasingly desperate ways, including making artificial flowers and helping to drive herds of cattle through the narrow city streets to the slaughterhouses, but eventually his savings were exhausted and he was sent to debtor's prison. They never heard from him again, and Angelique had to go to work at a blacking factory to help support the family.

In a way she was lucky, for by being at the factory she escaped the fate of her siblings and mother. The city officials blamed their deaths, as well as the deaths of several other families in the impoverished neighborhood, on a local outbreak of cholera. That gave them the excuse to quarantine the area. But Angelique, like most of the local children, knew more than one way to gain entry to their houses. The removal of some loose bricks disguising a hole in a wall was all it took.

It had not been cholera. Sick people did not smash pieces of furniture to kindling against the walls or stain the floor with spatters of blood. At the time, she didn't know what kind of horror was responsible, but she quickly learned. When she was called, one of her first acts as a slayer was to clean out the nest of vampires who had orphaned her.

Angelique had no illusions about what it meant to be the Chosen One. A short life with a brutal death at its end had been the fate of nearly all of her predecessors. Indeed it could be argued that the ephemeral nature of the calling made the office of the Slayer more effective, because rarely was another activated in the same city—or even the same country—as the last. Thus the power of the Slayer was distributed throughout the world, and, though individuals died quickly, the efficacy of one girl against all the powers of darkness had proven itself surprisingly well over the centuries.

A short life and a brutal death, then. But what of that? Angelique knew that was to be her legacy anyway, like as not. To grow up poor and a woman in the waning years of Victoria's London was to face a life of hardship and humiliation. With little education and no trade skills, most of her friends wound up going "on the game." It was that or starve.

Professor Peter van Helsing and the Watchers Council had taken her away from all that. Now she lived in a fine house in Regent's Park, she wore clothes of fine linen and wool instead of coarse burlap, and she ate food she had hardly known existed in Shoreditch. And her powers as a slayer granted her what even women of noble birth could not have: freedom from the fear of footpads, killers, and others who prey in the dark.

All this, she thought, *plus the comfort of boon companions . . . and true love.* There was no reason to fear death; compared to her old life, Angelique Hawthorne was already in heaven.

When the training period was finished, she sat beside Gordon. "It might behoove you to learn unarmed combat as well," she told him. "Suppose you encounter a sword-eating demon some day?"

"He'll have to eat me along with my blade," Gordon replied, "and then I shall carve my way back to you through his giblets." He pantomimed somewhat graphically to suit the words.

"There's an image to inspire romance," she said, grinning at him.

He grinned back, then looked serious. "This Dracula . . . the Professor seems very concerned by the threat he poses."

She felt a stab of unease, but masked it with a light tone. "You know the Professor. Every danger is a harbinger of universal doom. Hazards of the course. I imagine very few watchers are optimists."

He nodded but did not seem to take much comfort from this. "Still—"

She gently laid a finger across his lips. "Hush. We will find him, and I will slay him. He may be more powerful than the vampires we're used to, but we have faced demons and other abominations both powerful and well-versed in magick." She traced her finger along his jawline, raised his face to hers. "We have so little time together," she murmured. "Let's not waste it in worry over the unknown. The future must wait."

"The Slayer is as wise as she is mighty," he whispered, just before their lips met—

And they were interrupted by Patch's excited shouts. "There's been another one!"

V

The corpse of the latest victim lay half concealed in a patch of trees and tall grass near one of the Crystal Palace's Dinosaur Islands. The swarm of lookie-loos was thick, keeping Angelique and her friends from getting close enough to see anything in detail. By the murmured comments of the crowd, however, it was obvious that the unfortunate was a woman, another member of high society. They hung back on the fringes, next to a statue of a four-footed Iguanodon, half-hidden in thick, eddying ground mist silvered by moonlight.

Professor van Helsing had not accompanied them this time, choosing to remain in the Lair and conduct more research.

"The second member of the upper classes to be claimed in as many days," Molly said as they watched the body being removed.

"True," said Gordon. "Dracula appears to have fairly specific tastes. No doubt he prefers cleaner throats and blood less tainted with gin than he's apt to find in the rookeries."

"Which means," Angelique mused, "he must look enough like his prey that he can move among them and put them at their ease before he strikes."

"According to the Professor, Dracula's intent was to relocate to England permanently," Molly said. "No doubt it still is."

"Didn't the Prof say he was a nob before he got turned?" came from Patch.

"He did indeed—a count, no less. He also said that it isn't enough for Dracula to simply avoid the sun; he must pass the daylight hours asleep, resting in his native soil."

Gordon pressed the knuckle of his index finger to his chin. "He'd be looking for a home near the toffs, then, with room enough to hide some boxes of dirt. Someplace private."

Angelique looked at Patch, who nodded in response. "Me 'n' me boys're on it," he said. "I'll hav't sussed out before dark, or me name's not Archibald Oglevy." He raced off into the night.

Even slayers need some rest, and so Angelique passed the remainder of the night in her bed. But she did not get much quietude.

She anticipated the possible return of her nocturnal visitor—whether he had been a dream or reality she still was not sure—tensely at first, a stake clenched in her hand and a cross and phial of holy water on the table nearby. But gradually, as the hours wore on, she found herself relaxing. This was due partly to exhaustion—the tracking and eventual slaying of the Tethyrian demon posing as Springheel Jack had gone on night and day for over a week—but she had to admit that there was something more: an eagerness, perhaps even a yearning, subtle but unmistakable. At one point she rose and opened the windows, looking out over the sleeping neighborhood. She could faintly hear the exotic cries of various animals in the nearby Zoological Gardens, but nothing else.

Just before dawn she dosed off out of sheer exhaustion. She awoke with a start to the maid summoning her for breakfast.

Patch, hands and face uncharacteristically scrubbed at Cook's insistence, was buttering a scone and grinning a self-satisfied grin. Molly, Gordon, and the Professor had arrived before her. "It appears Patch has come through for us again," Gordon told her.

Angelique listened as Patch described an old mansion in Mayfair, recently sold to an anonymous buyer who would only sign the documents after dark. He spoke with a "foreign sort o' way," according to the errand boy who worked for the mortgage company. The place was secluded, spacious, and had a huge wine cellar.

"Excellent," Gordon said. "So, then, a hearty breakfast, a glance through the morning *Times,* and then heigh-ho to kill the vampire before tea." He helped himself to another rasher of bacon. "We'll have this wrapped up in no time."

Van Helsing set his coffee cup down hard enough to spill it. "Again I counsel you, Angelique. This should be the work of the Slayer alone. You cannot risk having your attention divided by—"

"Calm yourself, Professor," Angelique said. "You will upset your digestion again."

The Professor cast a dark look at Gordon, who affected not to notice. When he spoke again, his voice was low and compelling. "Beware Dracula," he said to the Slayer. "He is never where you think he is. He is never who or even *what* you think he is. Do not put too much confidence in the rituals and strictures which bind him. His hypnotic abilities are stronger than anything Mesmer could imagine. He knows of all the forces which empower you. You cannot even begin to imagine those which empower him."

TALES OF THE SLAYER

After breakfast the Slayer outfitted herself, making sure that the hidden holster belt was lined with stakes, that a cross hung about her neck, and that a silver throwing knife was easily accessible from a sheath in one of her kid boots. She also slipped into a pocket a small cruet of holy water. Then the four set out.

Angelique reflected much upon her watcher's words during their journey. She understood his concern, even shared it to a great degree. She felt very responsible for the welfare and safety of those who stood beside her against the night. But, as she had told herself many times, they had chosen to live this life. She had not.

The mansion was indeed as secluded as Patch had described it. Though it was not dilapidated, it gave the impression of being in disrepair. The mighty oaks and yews surrounding it blotted away the sun, creating a pervading gloom even though the morning was bright.

They moved cautiously, entering the huge house in a manner designed and practiced to minimize attack. Angelique kicked open the door, and Patch and Molly went in behind her, Patch crouched low with cross extended and Molly with her crossbow ready to fire. From behind them Gordon shined a torch, quickly and expertly illuminating the shadowy corners and nooks. Once they were satisfied no threat was in evidence, they moved on. In this way they gradually investigated every room of the manse's upper and ground floors.

They found no vampires. Nor did they find any boxes or containers of soil, which Professor van Helsing had said would be a sure sign of the vampire lord. At last the only place left to investigate was the cellar.

They slowly descended stone steps into the darkness, Gordon's torch barely serving to show them their way. The shadows seemed almost alive, crepitant and hungry, pressing in from all sides with malign force. Though Angelique was thoroughly familiar with crypts, sepulchres, and other underground domains of the dead, still she found this cellar as unnerving as any mausoleum. It seemed to whisper to her, the darkness did, in a cold thin voice she could not quite understand, no matter how she strained her ears. A glance at the white and set faces of her friends told her without question that they felt it too. There was no doubt that evil, ancient and unspeakable, had walked the mossy stone floors of this place.

They found huge and empty wine casks, furniture piled in corners, and other domestic detritus, but no caskets of earth. At last Angelique reluctantly declared the mansion empty of the undead.

Patch was disappointed that his lead had yielded no results. There were indeed other places to investigate, but only this one had fulfilled all the criteria. Angelique headed back for the stairs, motioning the others to follow. "Let's be about it, then," she said. "We can surely get one more place checked out before—"

They all heard the sound at the same time: the unmistakable creaking of long-unused hinges. They froze, then slid into formation with practiced ease. Gordon moved the light, letting its beam slide over the seeping walls, past a stack of wooden buckets, to come finally to rest on a thick, iron-hasped door that they had somehow missed previously.

The door was slowly opening.

Quicksilver-fast, Angelique plucked a cross from its sheath, twirling it momentarily around her fingers before letting it settle securely in her grip. To her right, Molly raised her crossbow; to her left, Gordon partially unsheathed his sword cane; crouched in front of her, Patch loaded a slingshot with a holy wafer.

The door creaked open further. An aperture appeared, revealing utter blackness.

Something leaped out of the darkness toward them.

Molly fired. The wooden shaft struck the wall just above the cat's head. The coal-black feline changed course with a yowl, fleeing into the dark cellar depths.

Angelique, Patch, and Gordon relaxed, looking at each other somewhat shamefacedly. "Bloody hell," Patch gasped. "Thought for sure it was Dracula at first."

"How do we know it wasn't?" Molly asked.

The vampire hunters looked at each other in sudden apprehension.

"He can change himself into a bat or a wolf," Molly said. "Are other animals in his repertoire as well?"

"The familiars of witches have been known to take the semblance of black cats," Gordon pointed out.

Angelique turned toward the stairs. "Outside, quickly, while we form another plan."

She felt somewhat better when they were out of the house. The sun rode through a high mist, its blaze obscured to the point where the disc was visible. But still it was sunlight, which meant they were safe for the moment from the undead.

"We must turn to our second choice for Dracula's lodgings, Patch," the Slayer said.

The lad looked chagrined, but before he could reply, they all reacted to a sudden sound, a sort of whistling crack, from beyond the trees. Looking up, the Slayer saw a small egg-shaped object hurtling overhead. It arced and then started to fall. *"Look out!"* she shouted, shoving Gordon to one side. "Take cov—"

Before she could finish the sentence, the object burst and a thick cloud of gas diffused rapidly from it. It settled like a pall over the yard, enveloping them. Angelique heard her friends coughing.

The gas was obviously a soporific of some sort. She saw Gordon and Patch collapse on the sward. She could not see Molly.

A figure loomed before her, indistinct in the mist. She lashed out with one leg, a high snapping kick that would have felled a quarryman. But the haze made it difficult to judge distances, and the strike missed.

She saw he had a gun.

Angelique performed a series of backflips that carried her into a sheltering copse. She heard the gun fire, heard the bullet sear the air nearby. She crouched, trying not to take deep breaths, feeling the numbing effects of the gas seeping into her lungs nonetheless. Her slayer stamina would keep her conscious longer than her friends, but ultimately she too would succumb.

The clouds were beginning to thin. Angelique heard a peal of demented laughter.

Through the diminishing vapor she saw the figure again. There was something familiar about him; she knew she had seen him somewhere before. Obviously he was not a vampire.

"You were warned, Slayer!" The cackling voice echoed about her. "My master is far too smart for you and your pathetic cadre! It was easy for him to anticipate your reasoning and arrange for me to meet you here. You will never find his resting place—he lies with the legends, and his power dwarfs even theirs. Take heed—there will not be another warning!"

The Professor's words echoed in her head: *He may be helpless during the day, but he can bend humans to his will, force them to be his myrmidons.*

A sudden breeze cleared the remaining mist. She could see her enemy clearly now.

It was Detective Peasbody, the Scotland Yard investigator.

Angelique stared in shock. The man was normally meticulously neat and something of a dandy. Yet now his clothes were torn and muddy, his hair matted and the look in his eyes was that of utter madness.

She tried to launch herself forward, to grab him and force him to tell her where Dracula was. But her muscles would not obey her. The narcotic gas had finally had its effect, and the Slayer fell forward into darkness.

VI

Images of fire and ash . . .

Graveyard dust, stirred in a forgotten tomb. . .

Cruciform light strobing. . .

Angelique blinked against the light. After a moment she recognized the chamber she was in: a drawing room in the Professor's house. Van Helsing, Gordon, and Patch were looking down anxiously at her. "What is your name, my child?" the Professor asked.

Angelique blinked again, in puzzlement this time. "Angelique Hawthorne," she replied. "And what is the point of asking me that, pray tell?"

"Good, good," the Professor said in relief, more to the others than to her. "I feared an injury of the brain, but she seems whole. Now—"

She interrupted him, sitting up suddenly. "Molly?" The room

seemed to shudder and shift, and she felt a stab of pain behind her forehead. It cleared quickly, however. "Where's Molly?"

Gordon and Patch glanced at each other. Van Helsing kept his gaze on Angelique. "This we do not know. We must assume that she has been taken by Dracula."

She pushed them aside and rose. "Taken? How?"

"No doubt to insure your noninvolvement in his affairs. It is as I have said before: a slayer is vulnerable through those she loves."

She looked at him, expecting to see rebuke in his eyes, but finding only compassion. "Then we find him," she said. "We find him, kill him, and rescue her."

"There's less than an hour to sundown," Gordon said. "We have no leads, no idea of where to search."

Angelique began to pace furiously. "We can't simply give up! If we don't find her in time, Dracula will—"

She could not finish the sentence, but she could tell from their expressions that there was no need to. Van Helsing had been right, she knew, and now Molly was set to pay the penalty for Angelique's defiance of the council's law.

She realized she was breathing rapidly. She tried to calm herself, seeking her center, willing her racing heart to settle, but with little success.

"Let us not lose our heads," the Professor said. "Even if we do not find him until after dark, the sooner is still the better. Dracula's power waxes during the hours before midnight, and wanes—"

Angelique stopped pacing abruptly and turned to van Helsing. "Wait! There was something that Peasbody said." She frowned in concentration. "'He lies with the legends, and his power dwarfs even theirs.'"

The others watched her, knowing better than to interrupt her concentration. "Back in the East End," she continued slowly, after a moment, "when we spoke with Peasbody, I noticed a curious scent about him. I thought it was pomade, but now I think differently. It was the residue of fumes clinging to his clothes."

"What kind of fumes, then?" Patch asked.

"Paraffin," Angelique replied. "Hot wax."

Madame Marie Tussaud had first brought her fabled wax museum to London in 1835. By 1884 it had settled in Marylebone Road. The spacious, multichambered structure featured many different scenes to tickle the public's fancy, all painstakingly sculpted in pliable wax. But its most popular attraction by far was a room set apart to protect those of nervous temperament, and called for many years simply the Separate Area—a collection of mannequins, death masks, and implements of torture culled mainly from the bloody history of the French Revolution. In 1846 a more appropriate sobriquet was given to it by *Punch* magazine, and it has been known by this name ever since: The Chamber of Horrors.

Angelique moved stealthily through the dark exhibition, one part of her mind marveling at how lifelike the wax effigies were even as she remained alert for possible attacks. She paused before an elaborate Grand Guignol exhibit, with a grinning executioner holding up the just-severed head of a French aristocrat. The images and scenarios within her vision included the aristocratic Dr. Henry Jekyll and his bestial alter ego, Mr. Hyde; the American Lizzie Borden, caught in the act of raising her ax over her terrified mother's head;

and the recently finished reconstruction of Whitechapel showing one of Jack the Ripper's victims lying in a pool of blood.

Peasbody had indeed been right to call them Dracula's peers.

She had not reached the museum until after dark, due to the arrival of a heavy London "pea-souper." Within an hour of the east wind's rising, the evening light had given way to Cimmerian darkness as the air filled with a noxious combination of chimney smoke, marsh gases, and other effluvia. It had quickly become impossible to see more than an arm's length ahead, and her hansom's speed had been greatly reduced.

The museum had closed early due to the fog. Gordon and Patch had wanted to come with her, but Angelique forbade it. She would not take the chance of Dracula acquiring yet another of her friends as hostage.

Now she prowled, silently and cautiously, through the eerie corridors of waxen horrors.

The sound that alerted her could not have been heard by normal human ears, but the Slayer's hearing was attuned for such frequencies. A soft sigh of air above her—she dived forward, rolled, and came up with a stake in her hand.

Nothing. No sound, no movement. Unless . . . Did she hear the faintest echo of an amused chuckle? Or was it only in her mind?

A velvet curtain masked an alcove to one side of her. A few steps put her within reach, and she grabbed the thick material, yanked it back.

And exposed a coffin resting on a small dais.

It was a plain and simple oblong box made of dark wood. No insignia, no description. She had thought the resting place of Count Dracula, Lord of the Undead, would have been more elegant, more impressive. Nevertheless Angelique suddenly felt her throat go dry. The sick taste of fear rose like bile. A sense of dread, undefined but no less powerful for that, enveloped her. She had to force herself to move closer. Stake poised in one hand, she lifted the lid with the other, tilted it slowly back.

Only her training as a slayer prevented her from screaming.

Molly Carrington lay in the coffin's silken embrace. Her hands were folded across her breast, her eyes closed. Her head was tilted slightly to one side, affording a clear view of the wounds in her neck.

Angelique staggered, feeling as though a stake had been plunged through her own heart. Her friend's ashen pallor left no doubt that her blood had been thoroughly drained. Angelique knew that Dracula had done worse than kill her; he had turned her. Her body would rise again, but her soul would be replaced by the animus of a demon. The fiend would use the remnants of Molly's psyche as a template for its own consciousness, but it would not be Molly, any more than one of the wax representations that surrounded them could be mistaken for the real thing. Even so, her soul would echo with the psychic reverberations of her body's possession. Molly had died the death she had feared the most, one that brought with it the most hideous afterlife imaginable. Until the vampire was destroyed, she would never know peace.

And who is responsible? she seemed to hear the Professor's stern voice asking. Dracula had performed the unspeakable deed, but who had put Molly in harm's way in the first place?

She blinked back tears. The only way to make even partial amends was to release her friend from this unholy limbo. She raised the stake.

Plunging it into Molly's heart was harder than plunging it into her own would be. She watched through tears as the corpse in the coffin transformed to dust and dissipated.

Molly. I'm sorry. I'm so sorry....

In her state of utter shock and sorrow, she very nearly did not react in time. He made no sound; it was the movement of air against her cheek that alerted her. Angelique spun about in time to see darkness move against darkness. She saw the pale oval of a face, hideously familiar from her dream, as Dracula came at her with uncanny speed. She barely managed to dodge.

He turned, and now she saw him clearly.

He was younger than she had expected and startlingly handsome, but it was a cold male beauty, with no promise of human feeling in the eyes or the set of the mouth. His face was pallid beneath his black hair, eyes glinting redly, like those of a beast. His attire was formal, a cravat and sash adding a continental touch, and he wore a flowing opera cape that seemed almost to possess a life of its own; it followed his movements more closely than a shadow, rippling restlessly even in the still air.

His gaze caught hers. She felt his eyes searing into her soul.

"Foolish slayer." His voice was almost a whisper, with the faint accent she remembered. "Now you see that I am serious. But now it is too late."

Angelique tried to move, to leap toward him, to bury the stake in the ruffled shirtfront, but she could not. She was as immobile as the statues all about them.

Dracula moved toward her with silken grace. "I have lived a long life and an even longer death. But I have yet to taste the blood of a slayer. I have heard that it is the finest wine the heart can produce."

He made a slight gesture, and Angelique, to her horror, found herself tilting her head back, exposing her neck. She fought her rebellious body, but it was futile. And deep within her she once again felt the urge to give in, the attraction to the dark side that she had experienced in her bedchamber the past two nights.

"Why do you resist?" he asked, honest curiosity in his voice. "For friendship? For loyalty? Human relationships are ephemeral, evanescent. I can offer you a true lifetime . . . one measured not by calendars or clocks, but by cycles."

He stood in front of her now. She noted that his fangs had emerged, though curiously enough, his face had not assumed the monstrous appearance that other vampires did. *The Professor will be interested in knowing this,* a small, detached part of her mind said, knowing that she would not be the one to tell him.

He took her by her shoulders, lowered his face toward her throat. "Your friend was a mere aperitif," he murmured. "She but whetted my thirst. Now—"

Molly. The name echoed in her mind, stirring tides of shame, loss . . . and rage. And with the rage came suddenly the return of her will. Angelique hurled the vampire away from her; he staggered back, stumbling into an exhibit of a torture wheel. She leaped after him, ready to take advantage of his surprise and quickly end the fight. But even as she drove the stake toward his heart he somehow *dissolved,* became insubstantial, a white mist that quickly disappeared.

Angelique stopped, almost unable to credit her senses. She quickly looked about. There was no sign of Dracula.

A cold breeze, as if off a frozen pond, wafted from behind her. She turned . . . and he was there.

With blinding swiftness he struck. It was a backhanded blow, delivered almost languidly, and yet it hurled the Slayer across the room with the force of a catapult. She struck the wall hard enough to break through it, crashing into the adjoining room.

The rich smell of molten wax assaulted her, along with a blast of warm air. She rose, dazed. This chamber was filled with waxworks too, but they were all in various stages of construction. Half-formed statues, human in shape but not in detail, stared eyelessly at her. Shelves lined the walls, filled with jointed wooden arms and legs, busts supporting deathmasks, cans of paint, and all manner of clothing from all eras. In the room's center was a large vat, simmering over a bank of gas jets. Two workers, wearing heavy smocks and gloves, were adding chemicals to the bubbling mixture. They stared at Angelique.

"'Ere, now!" one of them shouted. "What're you about—?"

His eyes widened, as did those of his comrades; then they both turned and bolted for a door in the far wall. Angelique turned in time to see Dracula stalking toward her, eyes blazing with fury.

She reached for another stake, only to find them all gone. She grabbed an ax from a table of medieval weaponry, but as she lifted it she realized it was merely a wooden prop.

Dracula stopped and raised a hand like a conductor demanding music. Angelique felt herself pulled toward him.

She all but flew across the floor in his direction, as though being drawn by an invisible rope. She had barely time enough to snap the head of the fake ax free from the shaft and hold it out before her.

It struck him full in the chest.

Once again, surprise thwarted his spell over her. He looked down at the makeshift stake protruding from his chest. Then he looked up at her and smiled, and she realized that the strike had missed his heart.

By then she was already in motion. She leaped, twisting in midair as she sailed over him, and landed on the catwalk surrounding the wax cauldron. Thick waves of heat roiled from it.

Dracula pulled the stake from his chest and cast it away. Then, with a single graceful leap, he was on the catwalk next to her.

"You pathetic fool," he snarled. "I would have made you immortal."

The hardest part was knowing that she *wanted* it, that a part of her, deep down, would always wonder. And that the desire, that dark desire that had kept her quiet about his nocturnal visit instead of telling the Professor, might have made it easier for Dracula to take Molly from them.

"You could have shared the night with me for eternity."

He stepped forward, one hand thrust out from beneath his cloak, fingers reaching for her throat.

"Forgive me," she said, thrusting one hand into a pocket, groping for what she had put there earlier. "I'm just not ready for that kind of commitment."

Dracula snarled and lunged, and Angelique slashed the air between them with the open cruet of holy water.

The drops struck his hands and face, and even over the bubbling of the molten wax she could hear his undead flesh sizzle. With a cry, he staggered back and fell into the cauldron of wax.

On a sudden impulse she threw the phial in after him.

She was blown off the catwalk by a concussive wave of air as the cauldron erupted. Sprawled on her back, stunned by the blast, Angelique watched in mute shock as a column of wax, writhing sinuously as if possessed of some bizarre life, rose from its center, towering over her. Its plastic surface roiled, and the astonished Slayer saw Dracula's image take form from it, face contorted in pain, fingers clawing the air as if seeking release. Then the column congealed, as if suddenly frozen by some hyperborean wind. It loomed above her, the face and figure rough-hewn as if by some elemental artist, but still recognizable as the vampire count.

Angelique rose to her feet, moved forward, staring at the formation. She had no idea by what alchemy the holy water and the hot wax had combined to produce so effective a prison for Dracula. But that did not matter. A slayer trusted her instincts.

She found a serviceable shaft of wood among the debris, moved to stand in front of Dracula, and raised it like a cricket bat.

"Rest in peace, Molly," she said softly as she swung the shaft. It struck the column squarely. The pillar shattered, fragments of wax raining down around her. From a great distance—or perhaps again just from the depths of her mind—she heard a final scream of anger and defeat.

Then all was silent.

Angelique returned to Molly's coffin, knelt beside it, and wept.

VII

It was dawn when she left the museum. The fog still held London, or at least Marylebone, in its gray grasp. As Angelique walked the streets she might well have been the last live inhabitant of a dead world.

It was certainly how she felt.

Professor van Helsing had been right. She understood now the folly of letting anyone too close to her, of forming any relationships, even platonic ones. Such joys and comforts were not for her. There was room for only one on the path she trod.

She would have to send Patch and Gordon away, she knew.

That would hurt—in Gordon's case, almost as much as driving the stake through Molly's dead heart. But it was the only way. Her conscience could not bear the weight of another loved one's death.

She alone can stand against the vampires, the forces of darkness . . .

She wondered if Dracula were really dead, if she had indeed put the Lord of the Undead to rest for the final time. She realized that it did not matter. If he returned, as he apparently had in the past, she would face him again, or some future slayer would. She could not predict how or why. There was only one certainty in her world now: As long as vampires walked the Earth, a slayer would stand against them.

Alone.

Angelique turned a corner, and suddenly a figure loomed in her path. She stopped short, recognizing it immediately. The red, glowing eyes, the taloned hands, the voluminous cloak . . . they could only mean one thing.

Another Tethyrian demon had taken up the mantle of Springheel Jack.

In that timeless moment, as they faced each other, Angelique knew with bitter certainty that this was to be the sum of her future: A lifetime, most likely very short, of battles and struggles, of victories and defeats, of sacrifice and anonymity. A war against the forces of darkness that would inevitably end in darkness. Without friendship, save for her watcher.

And without love.

The Slayer leaped once more into battle, alone.

ABOMINATION
Laura J. Burns and Melinda Metz

Beauport, Brittany, 1320

"Tonight I kill him," Eliane whispered.

Across the small room, Isabeau began to cry.

"In a moment, dumpling," Eliane called. She used her teeth to tear a strip from the hem of her underskirt. "In just one moment." Eliane used the piece of cloth to tie a stake behind her back.

Isabeau's cries turned to wails. And Eliane's blouse grew wet with milk. She ignored the dampness. She slid the stake free, then replaced the weapon. Drew, then replaced. Finally satisfied, she rushed to the cradle by the hearth and scooped up her daughter. "Oh, my big girl," Eliane whispered, summoning the will to keep her voice calm and soothing. "Soon your toes will be pushing between the slats. You're much bigger than your brother was when he—"

Gervais. Oh, God, Gervais. It seemed like only a few days ago that she held him in her arms just as she held Isabeau now. Her sweet baby boy. Her firstborn, now five years old, with a laugh that sounded like a jaybird's squawk. How many times had she woken to that sound, followed by Gervais pouncing on her, waking her with smacking kisses and demands for porridge with lots of honey?

Gervais is gone, Eliane told herself. I must accept that. Isabeau started rooting around her bosom like a hungry little piglet. Life continues, *Eliane thought. She sat down in the rocking chair Michel had carved and freed one breast for her daughter. It felt wrong that it should, after all that had happened, but life did continue. Eliane began to rock slowly as Isabeau fed, a sensation that was half pain and half pleasure coursing from her breast to low in her stomach.*

Is she taking more than nourishment from me, my innocent sweetling? Eliane wondered. Is she taking in my horror and revulsion at what I must do? Does Isabeau know that before morning breaks I will become a killer, taking revenge on those who stole my son from me?

"It is a curse for what your father and I did," Eliane murmured, gently stroking the down on Isabeau's head. "We knew it was wrong. But Michel and I felt powerless to stop it. And this is our punishment, more horrible than we ever could have imagined. The price of our love was the child Michel and I made together."

"Eliane, pay attention!" Michel shouted as he slashed the sword toward her gut.

Eliane easily twirled away from him, her bare feet slicked with the meadow's early-morning dew. How was she supposed to pay attention on a day like this? It felt as if this were the first day ever created, as if she and Michel were the first humans ever to experience the soft, warm sunshine, the cool grass, the song of the stream in the distance.

"Eliane! This is serious work," Michel scolded.

"Serious work, I know," Eliane answered, stifling a giggle. When Michel tried to sound like one of the strict old priests at the orphanage where she was raised, it always made her feel like laughing. Her watcher was only three years older than she was. And so handsome. No one with lips as soft-looking as Michel's should ever bother to say a harsh word. All the words that came out of that mouth were sweet. It was no use trying to make it otherwise.

Eliane fisted her hands in her skirt and pulled it up above her knees, then whirled around and expertly kicked the sword out of Michel's hand. She swooped it up, but instead of lunging at Michel, she used the blade to slice through the stem of a daisy. "For you." She tossed the flower to Michel.

She'd never been quite so playful with her watcher before. But there was something about the day, the glorious day, maybe simply that after such a long cold winter it was so delicious to feel the sun on her face again. "Isn't spring wonderful?" she cried.

"Concentrate, or I will double the length of your training session for the rest of the week," Michel barked out with his soft, soft lips.

Eliane didn't attempt to hold back her giggles this time. They flew out of her mouth, tickling her throat on the way up.

Exasperated, Michel put his hands on his hips and stared at her. "What, pray tell, is so amusing?"

"Your pretty face doesn't match your sour words," Eliane blurted out. She felt a blush race all the way up to her forehead. Had she actually said that aloud? Sometimes, lying on her pallet at night, she would allow herself to imagine that Michel wasn't her watcher, allow herself to imagine flirting with him the way she'd seen girls flirt with boys in the village. But she'd known she should never attempt to act out her daydreams. She was his slayer. He was her watcher. Love was forbidden for both of them.

"Pretty face," Michel repeated. His green eyes bored into her. Was he angry? Had she pushed him past all limits?

"Yes," Eliane answered, deciding the best thing to do was get back to work immediately. She swung the sword out in a smooth arc in front of her, forcing Michel to jump back. He was not fast enough, and the blade cut through his linen shirt, lightly scratching his chest.

Eliane had a wild desire to put her mouth on the scratch and lick the thread of blood away. The thought had her blushing again. What was wrong with her?

Lightning fast, Michel reached out and freed the sword from her hand. She should have been able to stop him easily, but her hand felt suddenly boneless. Michel dropped the sword onto the grass, grabbed Eliane roughly by the waist, and kissed her.

From the first day we met, this has been wanting to happen, Eliane thought. Then her mind was taken over by a flood of pure sensation: Michel's hands moving slowly up her spine, then tangling in her hair, Michel's tongue brushing against hers; the heat of his body flowing into hers until she couldn't tell where he stopped and she began.

Then the world turned to ice as Michel wrenched himself away from her. "This is wrong," he told her, the words coming out thick and harsh. "We share in a sacred trust. Watchers, slayers must be focused only on the fight against the darkness."

It was what he had told her every day since he brought her here from the orphanage at the age of thirteen. For two years they had trained and studied, but there was no darkness in their little village. Even the Great Hunger had passed them by. Eliane felt blessed here as if no shadow could cross their doorstep. The evil things Michel described did not seem to exist in Beauport. She did not believe she would ever be the Chosen One.

Instead of preparing for the darkness, she would embrace the light.

"It can't be wrong," Eliane said. She took his hand and then sat down in the meadow, pulling him with her. "Not when it feels like this."

"But your destiny—," he protested.

Eliane slid her arms about him. "My destiny is you."

"Our destiny," Michel agreed, his face so close to hers that his lips brushed against her mouth with each word.

Isabeau's mouth slid free of Eliane's breast. Although the baby slept, Eliane continued to rock in the chair that Michel had made. Perhaps if she didn't move from this spot, the day would remain where it was, the sun suspended in the sky.

"Foolishness," Eliane whispered. "Cowardice."

Already the shadows on the stone floor were lengthening. Night was coming. He would be here soon, the monster who had taken Gervais. Her little boy with the jaybird laugh.

My darling boy is dead and cold, she thought. *And that has made me into a monster too. Tonight I will make the town run red with blood. Eliane closed her eyes and pictured the small village of Beauport. She had not been to the village center in years now, but still she could see its semicircle of stone cottages in her mind's eye. Is there anyone left alive there? Have they all been murdered by the demons too?*

Eliane rose slowly and managed to return Isabeau to her cradle without waking her. There was much to do before dark.

Eliane gathered her long, pale hair into a tight knot. Then she began stretching out her body the way Michel had taught her. How long had it been since they trained together? Years. Lovemaking had taken the place of training, and still no evil threatened. The Watchers Council never even sent messengers. She and Michel had grown complacent. Happy. Did Eliane any longer possess the strength and agility she would need this night? She glanced at the cradle, at her sleeping daughter. "I will protect you," Eliane vowed. *"Even if I must die to do it."*

Isabeau was all she had left. Michel was gone. Gervais . . . Gervais was gone too. Eliane would not allow Isabeau to be taken from her as well. A whimper escaped Eliane's lips. She clamped her teeth together hard. This was a time not for tears, but for fury.

Tears streaked down Eliane's face, mingling with the sweat. "What if they find out?" she asked Michel, panting between each word.

He used a damp cloth to bathe her cheeks and forehead. "They won't," he promised. "They won't venture out this far. And we will be very careful."

"But the priest must have registered our marriage. Surely they will become aware—"

A fresh bolt of pain sliced down Eliane's back, cutting short her words. Her stomach tightened until she wanted to scream.

"I see the top of the head," Michel cried. "It's our baby! Our baby's head!"

Eliane choked out a laugh. She'd been so worried about giving birth, especially because she hadn't been able to talk to any women in Beauport about it. She'd kept her pregnancy a secret, not venturing away from home after her condition could no longer be concealed. She and Michel lived in the cottage farthest from the center of the village, and because they had always kept to themselves, unexpected visitors were not a problem.

And it turned out that she hadn't needed any advice from the village matrons. Her body knew what to do with no instruction. Without actually deciding to do it, she began to bear down, pushing the baby along.

Michel grabbed her hand so hard she felt the small bones grind together. "Eliane, wait! Stop!"

Stop? Has he gone mad? Eliane thought. It was well past the time that anything could be stopped. Her muscles tightened, pushing, pushing.

"Eliane, no! The cord. It's wrapped around the baby's neck," Michel explained. "You have to stop pushing or it will choke." Michel pulled his hand free of Eliane's. "I'll get it. I'll fix it. Just stay still."

Eliane dug her fingers into the blanket beneath her. She clenched her jaws until it felt as though her teeth would snap. She curled her toes tightly. And she willed the rest of her body to relax. What was happening? She couldn't see Michel's hands over the slope of her stomach. Had he freed their baby? Did it still live? *It couldn't have died,* she told herself. Not without her knowledge. She and the babe had been connected for too many months; it was almost as if she could hear the child's thoughts, as if they dreamed the same dreams. It would be impossible for it to die without Eliane feeling it to her core. But why wasn't Michel saying anything?

Her body begged to be allowed to push down. It was the only thing that could stop the agony. Eliane tightened her grip on the blanket. One of her fingernails broke free, and she savored the small pain, focusing on it to keep her mind off the horrible urge to push and push and push.

Michel muttered under his breath. Eliane couldn't make out the words. She wanted to ask him what he had said, but she was afraid to loosen the muscles of her jaw. If she did, she might push without meaning to, might squeeze the breath from her child.

"Almost," Michel called. "Almost, Eliane. Yes! Yes! The cord is out of the way. Push! Push now!"

Eliane let her fingers and toes and jaw go slack. All that

tightness rushed into her belly, and she bore down with a strength she hadn't been aware she possessed.

"I have him!" Michel exclaimed. "A boy, Eliane. Our baby boy."

Eliane struggled up onto her elbows. She couldn't wait a moment longer to see their child. Michel lifted the boy by his tiny feet and smacked him on the rear. Silence. There was no comforting wail from the baby. Another smack. Silence.

"Do something," Eliane begged.

Michel lay the baby on Eliane's belly. He used his little finger to clear the baby's throat and tiny nostrils. "He's not breathing."

"He can't be dead. I'd feel it! I know I would!" Eliane cried.

Michel lowered his lips to the baby's tiny mouth. He blew in a puff of air. Another. And the baby let out a glorious shriek. "We have a baby," Michel said, sounding awestruck.

"We have a baby," Eliane repeated. "Our little baby, Gervais." She raised her eyes from the baby to Michel. "This is our family, Michel. This is the most important thing to me now."

"I know, my love," Michel replied.

"More important than being the Slayer," Eliane whispered. "If they tried to come between me and my family, I would go mad." Eliane felt a sort of hysteria growing within her. "What would they do if they knew about him, Michel? Would they—"

Michel silenced her by putting a finger to her lips. "The Watchers Council will never know."

Will Michel ever know what happens here tonight? *Eliane wondered*. Does he know they've killed Gervais, and that I let it happen? I've betrayed not only my own calling, but his calling as a watcher. Will he be able to forgive me?

It's no time to indulge yourself with questions such as those, Eliane admonished herself. She began to perform the pattern of feints, jabs, rolls, and spins that Michel had devised to keep Eliane's slaying skills sharp. There had been a time she'd gone through the routine several times a day. Now caring for the baby and amusing little Gervais—

Eliane stepped on the hem of her skirt and stumbled. She fought back tears as she thought of Gervais. *The demon,* she decided. She would only think of the demon who had taken her boy. There was nothing she could not do to a demon, no pain she could not inflict.

She had been born to be the Slayer. Tonight the demon would discover what that meant.

"What do you think of this funny little creature?" Michel asked Gervais. "Do you think maybe our real baby was switched with a wood sprite?"

"Don't say that to him," Eliane protested. "Isabeau's your little sister," she told Gervais. "Not something out of a fairy story."

"She looks like a troll," Gervais answered, then he gave his caw of a laugh. "Beau the troll!"

Eliane smiled, pushing back the strange feeling that had crowded her all day. She'd slept ill; that was all. She'd had dreams, ghoulish dreams, like nothing she'd ever known before. Still she could feel the dreams, licking at the edge of her thoughts.

But the sun was warm and her children were radiant with life. She breathed in the sweet air and determined to ignore the uneasiness in her gut. Eliane reached out and tickled Gervais under the ribs, his best tickle spot. "Do you think you didn't look the same when you were less than a year old?"

"You always said I was the most beautiful baby in the world,"

Gervais reminded her. "Tell me that story again. About how I almost died when I was getting born."

"You didn't—," Michel began.

He was interrupted by a knock on the door. Eliane's eyes flew to Michel, the old fear of discovery springing up inside her. It had been five years since Gervais was born, and the fear had faded every year. She hadn't received the call to become the Slayer, and both she and Michel had grown more and more convinced she never would. Almost all slayers were called before they reached Eliane's age, never experiencing marriage or motherhood.

"Who is it?" Michel called as he strode to the door.

It must simply be someone from the village who needs our help, Eliane told herself. But people from the village rarely came to them for any reason. She, Michel, and the children lived a solitary life.

"Gaston Roux," came the answer.

Eliane had never heard the name before. But the grim expression on Michel's face made her suspect that her husband had.

"Who is that, Maman?" Gervais asked.

"We'll have to wait and see, won't we?" she answered, struggling to keep her tone light.

Michel swung open the door. Three men stood outside.

"Eliane Ward?" the tallest man asked.

"Eliane de Shaunde," she corrected him, using her married name. All the little hairs on the back of her neck stood up. The nightmare images from her dream invaded her mind once again. This man was her enemy. She could feel it.

"I am Gaston Roux, your new watcher," the man announced. "The Slayer is dead. You have been called."

Heavy silence filled the room. Eliane realized she was not breathing.

"I . . . I am Eliane's Watcher," Michel said. "She has no need of a new one." But his voice sounded high and frightened, and Eliane knew it was useless. They had been found out.

Gaston Roux now turned his cold eyes on her husband. "Michel de Shaunde, my associates will escort you to London, where you will be required to stand trial for your offenses before the Council."

"Offenses?" Eliane exclaimed. "Is it an offense to have a family? To love your wife and children?"

"You know it is!" Roux snapped. "At least you should know. A slayer with children—it is an abomination. Your watcher should have taught you this much."

He gestured to the other two men and they moved forward slowly, positioning themselves on either side of Michel. He clutched baby Isabeau tighter, and a soft moan escaped his lips.

"There is no abomination here," Eliane whispered. "Only happiness."

"The position of Watcher is a sacred one," Roux answered, his eyes on Michel. "The rules of conduct were well known to your watcher."

"My husband," Eliane corrected him.

"What is a watcher?" Gervais asked, his little voice trembling. In Michel's arms, Isabeau began to fuss.

Eliane couldn't tear her attention away from Roux to answer her little boy. Even last evening's nightmares paled in comparison to this. These men wanted to destroy her family! "What if he refuses to go with you?" she demanded.

The two other men stepped closer to Michel, threatening without saying a word.

"He cannot refuse," Roux said.

Michel kissed Isabeau's forehead and gently placed her in her cradle. The baby immediately began to wail. The sounds shredded Eliane's heart. "You're not really going to leave her, leave us?" she asked Michel.

His eyes gave her the answer. They were flat and dull, as if Michel's soul was already absent from his body. "I have no choice," he said. "But I swear I will come back to you." Michel wrapped Gervais in a tight hug. "Papa has to go away for a little while. You be a good boy and take care of Maman and baby Beau."

Gervais's little chin quivered, but he nodded. "I will, Papa."

Michel took a step toward Eliane, then froze. She knew why. He was afraid if he touched her now he would never be able to let her go. It was how she felt as well. Eliane wanted to hurl herself at him, to press her body against his so hard that they would become one, inseparable. But Michel had to go; he had no choice. So she would do nothing to make this harder. She would not give the council members that satisfaction.

"Come back to me soon," Eliane said quietly.

"I will." Michel turned toward the door. Roux's two associates escorted him outside. Eliane stared after them for a long moment, then shut the door behind them.

Her mind reeled. She had closed the door on her entire life. There was no living without Michel. She was not even sure the sun would rise tomorrow over her half-empty bed.

"We must begin training at once," Roux announced. "It is my sad duty to tell you the last two slayers were killed by the same vampire, a demon called Tatoul. He seems to have acquired a taste for slayer blood. Tatoul will soon know your location, and he will come for you, bringing others with him."

Eliane stared at him, shocked. A vampire coming here? Looking for her? She could not fathom such a thing. *He wants me to be terrified,* Eliane thought. *This bitter man has destroyed my family. I will not allow him to frighten me.*

"There has never been a vampire in Beauport. I know of them only through Michel's descriptions," Eliane said. "There is no need for a slayer here. Your council has made an error."

"The council is never wrong," said Roux. He held a stake out to her. "Come. Let us train. You will need all your skill to face Tatoul. He is an old one. His powers have been growing for many years. It is said he can move like the winds of a hurricane, so fast that he is almost invisible to the human eye. Soon he will be here, he and the others. You must believe me. You should feel the call within yourself."

Eliane took this in. She could not deny a certain quickening in her body, almost as if her instincts had been sharpened since yesterday. And there were the dreams, those which haunted her even now. She knew in her heart that he spoke the truth: She had been called.

"I refuse the call," she said simply, trying to ignore the wild rushing that now filled her ears. She almost fancied that she heard evil voices on the wind. But she turned away from Roux, from the stake in his hand.

"That is not your choice to make," Roux replied, his words tipped with steel. "Would you let the people of your village die when you have the power to prevent their slaughter?"

The image of humans being slaughtered like pigs filled Eliane's mind. Poor creatures. Poor helpless creatures. She blinked rapidly, trying to free herself from the gory picture. She had to be strong now, no matter what the price. All that mattered was her family, and her family could not exist without Michel. "When my husband is returned to me, I will take my position as Slayer. Not before."

"I am the Slayer. I will do what I must," Eliane said aloud to reassure herself.

It was almost time. The last rays of the sun were lingering on the horizon.

Eliane heard a rustling in the trees outside the cottage. Not almost time, she realized. Time. She dipped her finger in the small vial of holy water and made a cross on Isabeau's forehead. If the priests were right, the holy water might help keep evil at bay.

"Be strong, my darling," she whispered. "I pray this is enough to protect you."

Eliane checked the stake tied to her back and picked up the crossbow lying beside Isabeau's cradle. A supply of arrows fit neatly into her waistband—arrows Michel had carved to perfection over the years. The sharp wood of the arrows would slide easily into the monster's flesh.

Without hesitation, Eliane moved to the door and opened it. She scanned the small clearing in front of the cottage and the woods that surrounded it. Yes, there was movement in the underbrush. She could see the movement of the demon.

Eliane slid an arrow, wickedly sharp, into the crossbow and raised the bow to her shoulder, aiming at the trembling leaves of the blackberry bushes. She pulled in a deep breath and waited for the demon to show itself.

The rustling grew louder. The leaves shook harder. And a hoof stepped out into the clearing.

The hoof of a doe. She cautiously moved through the blackberry bushes and began to graze on the tender grass at the edge of the clearing. A moment later, her fawn joined her, the hair on its spotted rump looking as downy as Isabeau's wispy locks.

The air left Eliane's lungs in a whoosh. She forced herself to survey the woods again before she lowered the bow. Then she picked up a small rock and tossed it toward the deer. "Run away, Maman. You and your baby aren't safe here."

"Think about the safety of your children, if the fate of those in the village is not enough to soften your heart," Roux said.

He'd been talking for hours as the day turned to night, and all the time a feeling of nausea had been growing in Eliane's stomach. Now it was almost unbearable. "What my children need is their father," Eliane answered, shooting a look at Gervais—still napping, as was Isabeau in her cradle. "You would do best to return to the council yourself. When Michel is brought back to me, I will gladly take on the duty I was trained for." *They will bring me my husband before they let harm come to any of the people here,* she told herself. *I must stay strong.*

There was a knock on the cottage door. Eliane's heart seized up. More trouble come so soon? She straightened her spine, determined not to show Roux even a hint of fear, and swung the door open wide.

A corpse stood outside, bones almost poking through the skin of its face, deep furrows in its brow, and a mouth crammed with fierce, jagged, deadly sharp teeth.

"Tatoul," Roux whispered.

"Vampire," Eliane said, the word spoken involuntarily. She had heard many stories, and even studied sketches, but this was the first time she had ever seen one of the creatures in the flesh. It was so close to her, she could smell the coppery scent of blood on its breath.

Eliane took a step backward, her gorge rising in her throat. She had not been prepared for this, the horror. Michel had never told her of the smell.

"He cannot enter if you do not invite him," Roux reminded her, as if she could ever forget such a basic fact, as if Michel had taught her nothing. His condescending tone roused Eliane. She shook off her feelings of fear and disgust. Before she dealt with the vampire, she must deal with this odious man, Roux. He was merely a watcher. She was the Slayer. She held all the power, and she must not forget that.

The watcher tossed her a stake. She let it clatter at her feet.

The vampire raised an eyebrow. "Clumsy for a Slayer," he commented, showing even more teeth as he smiled. "I came tonight hoping for some amusement, but—"

"I'd have caught it if I wanted to," she answered. "Caught it and killed you where you stand."

"Easy to say. Much harder to do," Tatoul answered.

"Not if I chose to," Eliane answered, pleased that her voice came out firm and strong. "And if things go as I hope they will, I will soon choose to." She shot a glance at Roux. He stared back at her, his eyes as hard as rocks. "But until then, you and your kind are free to do as you will, without fear of the Slayer."

Tatoul hissed in a breath. "Even if what I will is to sink my teeth into your pretty white throat, taste your sweet slayer blood?" he asked, his hunger-filled eyes sliding to the point just above her collarbone where Eliane could feel her pulse beating.

"Have you lost your mind?" Roux began, running toward her.

Eliane shot out a hand and caught him by the throat. In one swift move, she pinned him against the wall next to the door. Now he and the vampire stood side by side, one in the cottage, one outside. Her twin enemies. She held Roux still as she addressed the vampire.

"There are some limits to my generosity," Eliane answered. "Me and mine—my son, my daughter—are untouchable." *Surely Roux will order my husband home now,* she thought.

"I don't make bargains," Tatoul told her, sliding his tongue across his cruel incisors.

"And I don't ask for favors from your kind," Eliane replied. "I occasionally give warnings, if I'm in the mood."

The vampire inclined his head. "I'll spread the word, pretty Slayer. And here is a warning for you. You choose not to fight. Do not imagine that we will do the same."

Eliane started awake.

It was dark in the cottage; the only light came from the last dying embers of her cooking fire. Her hand flew immediately to Isabeau, and she breathed a sigh of relief at feeling the babe's chest rise and fall in sleep.

She had been dreaming of slaughter. The demon stalked through the village, tearing apart the innocents there. This time he did not even play with them the way a hunter toys with its prey. This time he tore them limb from limb, eating their flesh as they watched with dying eyes.

Was I really dreaming? Eliane thought. *Or am I seeing through the demon's vision?*

It was not likely that she had fallen asleep. She knew he came for her tonight, and as the Slayer she did not need sleep the way others did. No, this was not a natural sleep. It was a spell, a trance he forced on her.

She had seen evil deeds before this, although never quite so vividly. Indeed every night since the vampires came she had dreamed of the village. She had witnessed the horrors committed there, the men and women tortured. The vampires did not kill the villagers right away, preferring to draw out the agony.

But this time, Eliane was spared no detail. This latest vision was so powerful she could actually feel a lump of flesh sliding down her throat. Worse, the sensation was enjoyable.

Eliane knew why the demon was sharing each sensation with her. The vampires wanted her. The innocent villagers were simply bait, there to lure the Slayer from her home.

She stood. She would wait no longer. She would go to him, and bring death with her.

The Slayer would take the bait.

The scream came from only inches away.

Just on the other side of the door, Eliane thought, pressing her hand against the wood. *Someone is being attacked right outside.*

Isabeau answered with a wail of her own. Gervais had given up on screaming. He just sat in the corner now, rocking to and fro and watching Eliane with big, terrified eyes. *Michel's eyes,* Eliane thought, smoothing the fair hair back from her little boy's forehead.

"Try to be brave, my love," she murmured, leaning in to kiss him. "Soon Papa will be back, and then the monsters will all go away."

"You foolish wench," snapped Gaston Roux. "The demons have just slaughtered a man on your very doorstep. The undead frolic among the cottages of your town. Your children are on an island surrounded by blood and gore, and yet you tell them stories of salvation?"

"Be silent!" Eliane growled. "I've told you I'll not listen. You've taken my husband, and until he's returned, I will not hear a word you say."

The words were strong, and her voice did not waver. But Eliane knew she could not hold out much longer. She had thought refusing the call would be a simple matter of standing up to the Watchers Council. She hadn't realized that the call came from within her. Her very blood sang with the desire to be out in the night, stalking her prey, destroying the undead who roamed Beauport, stopping the slaughter of the innocents. During the sunlight hours, all was calm. But come sundown, the unsettled feeling in her stomach returned, and her senses were heightened almost beyond bearing.

The vampires had taken the village. Though her cottage was almost a mile from the center of Beauport, Eliane could hear the screams on the air, could smell the stench of death. It was impossible, she knew, and yet the noises and the odors plagued her. Her pulse seemed to pound against her skin, pushing for release. Sleep brought her no solace, for with sleep came the dreams—dreams of the hunt, the freedom and power of tracking her nemesis. In these dreams, all her heightened senses were put to use—to smell the beasts, to hear their undead footfalls, to sense with her body the nearness of the demons.

The call was so irresistible that when she woke, it was all she could do not to fling open the cottage door and throw herself into slaying just to satisfy the needs of her body. And to avenge each and every one of the innocents the evil ones had taken.

But then she would look at Gervais, her darling boy, and see in him her husband. She could not abandon Michel. She would not give up on their love, even though it cost the life of every person in

Beauport. She looked at Gaston Roux. How could he be allowing all this slaughter to happen?

"Do you know why the demons haunt this town?" Roux asked. "It is because they know you are weak."

"I am not weak," Eliane said, though she felt faint with the need to hunt. "I will not weaken."

"You fight your own destiny," Roux pressed. He moved toward her as if he could sense that her slayer's instincts were battling with her reason.

"Michel is my destiny," Eliane gasped. "And our children—"

"Maman! Maman!" Gervais's shrieks filled the room. "Maman, there's blood!" He sobbed uncontrollably.

Eliane rushed to her boy and pulled him into her arms, turning his face to her chest to spare him the sight. There was indeed blood. Running under the doorway and pooling at a low point in the dirt floor. And the puddle was growing. So much blood.

Eliane felt sick. She raised her eyes to meet those of Gaston Roux. "Where is it coming from?" she whispered.

"The vampires cannot come inside your dwelling," Roux said. "But they can invade in other ways. They are teasing you, showing you just how horrific their power is when they are unchecked by a slayer."

Eliane frowned. "I do not need a lesson. You are not my watcher, and I am not the Slayer."

"You deny your sacred duty. You are no better than those soulless wretches out there. We are all doomed." For the first time, Roux sounded frightened. "This is but your first taste of true evil. I tell you, Eliane, there is much worse than what you have seen. Tatoul, the leader, has walked the earth for centuries. Your heart would stop if you knew all that he has done in those years."

There was a moan from outside. Eliane's breath caught in her throat. Whoever had been attacked out there, just inches from where she stood, was still alive. Was this the blood of that poor unfortunate? Maybe she could still help him. She rushed to the door and pulled it open, ignoring Roux's yell of protest.

With the door came the body. A young woman's body, held fast to the door by means of a knitting needle stabbed through her stomach and into the wood. She was nearly naked, and had clearly been tortured. The telltale wounds of a vampire's teeth marked her neck, her wrists, even her leg. Her head lolled about as if her neck could no longer support it, yet still she lived.

Eliane retched, but now Gaston Roux grew eerily calm.

"This is your work," he said. "Are you proud?"

Eliane peered into the darkness outside the door. Who was he talking to?

"This maid was your neighbor, a lass from your own village. A lass whom it was your duty to protect."

Eliane stared at him. He was talking to her. He was blaming *her* for this atrocity.

"How dare you?" she cried. "I have not done this! I am no monster! It is your fault the village is unprotected. You had only to bring Michel back to me—"

"Silence, selfish wretch!" he thundered. "You were born to be a protector of the people, a force of light, one who sacrifices her own needs for the benefit of others. Yet you, mindful only of *your* wants, have left the people vulnerable. You've brought the undead here like vultures to a funeral. Here they are free to wreak their evil. Here they feast and grow strong—"

"And don't think we don't appreciate it," a smooth voice broke in.

Eliane whirled back to the doorway. Outside stood the vampire, the first one she had seen, Tatoul. He looked stronger now, his pale skin firm and his lips red from drinking blood.

"We've been frolicking in your little hamlet for two weeks now," the vampire said. "It's rare that we have such a prolonged period of feeding."

Kill him, a voice inside Eliane urged. *Take the needle from the girl's belly and stake him through his unbeating heart.* Eliane held tighter to Gervais, fighting the urge. She must think of Michel. She must put her family first.

"But I must confess we are getting bored," Tatoul went on. "We want the Slayer to come out and play with us. How many more corpses do you need to see before your anger gets the better of you?"

"I will not give in," Eliane whispered.

"Then you are killing these people yourself," Roux told her, his voice shaking with fury. "The undead horde will move on to the next village and the next. All those people will be murdered just like the people of Beauport, and their deaths will be on your head."

"He's right, you know," the vampire remarked.

The need to hunt was almost unbearable. "I will not give in," Eliane repeated.

"As you wish." Tatoul reached out and lifted the arm of the girl on the door. He raised her limp wrist to his mouth and slowly bit down, his yellow eyes never leaving Eliane's. The girl moaned again, too weak to do anything more.

Eliane was struck dumb with horror. But Gaston Roux was not.

"I will kill you myself, you damned creature!" he yelled. Before Eliane could move, Roux leapt through the doorway, leaving the protection of the cottage. He did just what Eliane had thought of: grabbed the wooden needle from the girl's stomach and pulled it out.

For Eliane, it was as if time itself slowed, but the actions of the others sped up. All at once, she heard the girl's scream of pain as her body fell to the ground, the wound gushing blood like a fountain. She saw Roux lift the wooden needle, heard his roar of anger. She saw the vampire's smile. Saw his hand move with the speed of lightning, catching Roux's arm and snapping it in half. She saw the vampire spin the watcher, pulling him close, bending to his throat.

She saw Roux's eyes meet hers, filled with terror and a silent plea for help.

Then the vampire bit down. Blood ran everywhere—down the Watcher's neck, over his white shirt, down the vampire's chin as he drank hungrily.

Gervais squirmed mightily, trying to escape the horror. But the Slayer within Eliane did not even register the movements. Forgetting her son, forgetting all other concerns, the Slayer leaped forward, through the door. She hurled herself at the vampire, heedless of the child who still clung to her neck.

They were outside now, no longer protected by the dwelling. The vampire roared with pleasure and dropped Roux to the ground.

"You join the fray!" Tatoul cried, dancing away from Eliane's assault. "You have become the Slayer!"

The words hit her like cold water running down her back. "No," she gasped, reining in the Slayer instincts. "No, not without Michel."

She stared about her as if seeing through new eyes. She stood outside, unprotected. Gaston Roux lay at her feet; his lifeless eyes would no longer watch. Her little boy screamed in her ear, terrified beyond all reasoning. From inside, baby Isabeau's cries matched her brother's. And the vampire stood not two feet away.

"No?" he repeated. "Not even killing your watcher will make you accept your call?"

"No," Eliane whispered.

Tatoul studied her. "I think you have lost your way, Slayer," he murmured. "But no matter. Once you tried to bargain with me. I told you I make no bargains."

He seemed not to move. Yet suddenly Gervais was gone from her arms. The weight of her darling boy, the heat of his skin—gone. The vampire stood ten feet away now, though Eliane had not seen any motion. *It is said he can move like the winds of a hurricane, so fast that he is almost invisible to the human eye,* Eliane heard Roux's voice whisper in her memory.

"You and yours are not untouchable," Tatoul said.

In his arms he held Gervais—her child, her baby. He still screamed. He still looked at her with his father's eyes.

The vampire bit him. The monster's deadly sharp teeth sank into the babe's soft neck. Her child's lifeblood spilled out, feeding this unholy hunger. From inside, Isabeau's wails grew louder.

It is an abomination, something whispered inside Eliane. *A slayer cannot have children, a slayer and a watcher cannot know love.*

They were being punished.

Eliane flew at the vampire, but he was gone. Again she had not seen him move, but now he stood behind her. He smiled, fangs dripping the blood of her son.

"You have let me grow strong," he mocked her. "And you yourself are weak and untrained."

She ran at him again; again, he eluded her. Eliane let out a sob. Gaston Roux had been right: She had not truly understood evil until this moment. She had not seen the villagers killed, had not had to watch them die. Not like this.

"Your child's blood is sweet," Tatoul murmured. He stood now near the edge of the clearing around her cottage. Gervais lay limp in his arms. Isabeau's screams were fading. Eliane's head swam. She watched helplessly as the vampire leaned again to her son's throat, sipped again of his life.

The vampire moaned ecstatically.

Eliane moaned in response. She wanted to shake off this dream of horror, but could not. She seemed rooted to the ground now.

"Intoxicating, the death of a child," Tatoul said. "His final moment of life." His yellow eyes held Eliane's own as he drank the last of her son's blood.

Then he turned and melted into the darkness, Gervais along with him.

Eliane collapsed to the ground as if only the vampire's will had been holding her up. The Watcher's body lay in a pool of blood. The village girl's twisted corpse lay across the doorstep. Inside, Isabeau cried softly. Gervais was gone.

"My baby," Eliane gasped, unable to breathe through the pain that filled her soul. "My darling child."

Suddenly she heard him behind her, only a few steps away. "I will come back for the other one," he whispered.

By the time Eliane turned, he was gone again.

"Farewell, my beauty, my sweet one," Eliane whispered. Isabeau played with the rattle Michel had carved and watched with wide, innocent eyes as Eliane tucked cloves of garlic into the cradle. Finally she lifted the cross off her own neck and placed it over her daughter's head.

ABOMINATION

"I have let innocent people die." She leaned forward and kissed Isabeau's forehead. "But maybe God will have mercy on you if I pay for my sins," she murmured. "I go to face the demon."

"There is no need," said a voice behind her. "The demon has come to you. Tonight we will take your second child."

Eliane straightened, still looking down at Isabeau. Her senses were sharp, almost painfully so. She could smell the demon at the doorstep, and she could smell the others who had come with him. They were outside, at least fifty of them, surrounding the cottage.

They wanted the baby. Their hunger was so intense that Eliane could almost taste it. He still wove his spell, sharing everything with her.

"More than the baby," the vampire said. "We also want you. Blood of the Slayer is the strongest blood there is, I hear. When I have drunk you dry, I will dance in the air, I will survive even in the sunlight, and I will be unstoppable. The babe is simply a whet to my appetite. You are my true desire."

"I am not prey," Eliane told him. "I am the hunter."

"You are no hunter," he spat. "You are weak, a miserable slave to your emotions. So you have ever been."

"No longer. Now I understand true evil. Now I know that I have the blood of innocents on my head. I have learned the error of my ways," Eliane said. "I am the Slayer. Tonight I will kill you . . ."

She turned to face the demon. His pale hair fell across his tiny forehead, and he watched her with his father's eyes.

". . . Gervais."

"I do not believe you," said her son. He smiled a cherub's smile. "You put your family first. I heard you say it over and over to the Watcher."

Eliane looked over his shoulder. Behind him stood the vampire who had killed him, Tatoul. Before her mind had recognized the creature, her body took action. Moving quickly, fluidly, she reached behind her back and removed the stake from its sheath of cloth. A jerk of her wrist, and the sharpened wood streaked across the room, embedding itself in the monster's chest. Once more, his yellow eyes met hers.

"Slayer . . ." Tatoul whispered. Then he exploded into a fine, ashlike dust.

"Do you see?" Eliane asked Gervais. "My first kill. Now I am truly the Slayer."

The little boy laughed. It sounded like the harsh caw of a crow, no longer like a jaybird. His tiny features transformed, thick ridges marring his perfect forehead, Michel's beautiful green eyes turning to the yellow eyes of the undead.

"Did you think he was still the leader?" Gervais mocked her. "Why should I care if he's gone? He was a thorn in my side."

He stepped forward, and Eliane hesitated. She had thought seeing her boy's living corpse would be difficult, but in truth, seeing this transformation was even harder. How could it be possible that this was the child she'd held in her arms?

"Has there ever been a vampire sprung from a slayer before?" he asked. "I don't think so. I take after you—my blood is strong."

"It was you today," Eliane said, "weaving a trance about me. The dreams had always been just dreams before, but today I saw clearly. I saw the atrocities. It was you. That's why the dream was different."

"I share your blood, Mother," the vampire said. "I see your heart. You and I dreamed together when I was still in the womb. Don't you remember?"

Eliane did remember the connection she had felt to Gervais, even before he was born. But she also remembered the dream of today—the monster tearing peasants apart, no longer as a hunter but now as a senseless butcher. No longer drinking blood, but now also eating flesh.

The creature that wore Gervais's face smiled as if he could hear her thoughts. His full baby lips were deep red, his cruel fangs as sharp as the stake hidden in Isabeau's cradle.

"Yes, I have eaten them all," the vampire said. "I grow tired of Beauport. I will move to a larger village now, and then on to the cities. There is no one to stop me. But first I will take the rest of your blood."

He stepped forward, his small feet teetering on the very brink of the doorway. He could come no further.

Eliane reached for the baby's cradle.

"I will keep the family together, Mother," the vampire said. "Your blood will join mine. And Isabeau's blood. And when I find my father, I will take him as well. You two created me. You shall share in my crimes."

"Our love created you, and it was wrong," Eliane whispered. "It is my duty to correct that mistake." She closed her fingers around Isabeau's rattle and pulled the toy from the baby's hand.

"Mother—," Gervais began.

"Stop," she said, moving toward him. "I will give myself to you if you spare the babe."

The vampire smiled, revealing his fangs. He held out his chubby little arms. "Then come and hug me, Maman."

Eliane had reached the doorway. She stepped across the threshold and knelt to hug her son. His baby arms went around her neck, his mouth seeking her vein. As his fangs pierced her flesh, Eliane felt again the sense of seeing through his eyes, of feeling his sensations. Triumph, she felt, and insatiable hunger. Her blood filled his mouth, coursed through his body like a drug.

He is an abomination, Eliane thought. *A vampire sprung from the Slayer* . . .

His gaze fell on the baby's cradle, and the hunger increased. Eliane saw what he saw, felt his desire for Isabeau.

As darkness crowded her vision, Eliane yanked the ball off the top of the rattle, leaving only the sharpened wooden handle. Michel had whittled it to a deadly point. It was so with most of his carvings; he had wanted Eliane to be always prepared.

She plunged the stake into her son's back and through his heart.

"Your father and I love you, Gervais," she whispered into his soft hair.

The blood within her grew hot, too hot. She felt what Gervais felt: fire running through his body, white-hot like the fires of hell, burning him from the inside out. So hot . . .

As Gervais turned to dust, Eliane felt the heat within her own body. The heat which consumed her as it took her firstborn child. Flames filled her vision, and she realized that they came from herself.

Eliane fell forward on the ground, watching the fire spread from her body. "I have paid for our mistakes," she whispered.

Then all was fire.

London

The cold stone hallways echoed with footsteps for the first time in the month Michel had been here. He leapt off the straw pallet he slept on and hurried to the thick iron door of his cell.

The watchers didn't consider this a dungeon. They called it a retreat, a place for him to meditate on his transgressions until he was ready to ask forgiveness. But all he could think of was Eliane's smiling lips, the way her breathing matched with his as they lay on their bed. The way baby Isabeau's soft skin smelled, the sound of Gervais's impish laugh.

Would they let him out now? He already knew the answer: No. Eliane was the Slayer. He had never doubted that she was truly called. He'd seen the strange new light in her eyes on the morning that Gaston Roux came. And as the Slayer, she had a duty that transcended her duty to him or even to the children.

Had Eliane understood that duty? He wasn't sure that he had made it clear to her. Those years when they were so happy together, had he let his own duties as a watcher slip? He feared it was so. He feared that Eliane would put him first, put their love before her calling. But surely if there were vampires, she would fight them. Surely if the villagers were in danger, she would know that her first duty was to protect them.

Michel tried to swallow his fear. He had not taught Eliane the importance of her post. He had let her believe that love was the greatest calling of all.

They had made a terrible mistake.

The door swung open. A woman stood outside. Michel stared at her, then slowly sank to his knees.

"But what became of her?" the Elder asked impatiently. The Watchers Council was depending on him to bring back a satisfactory answer. He did not like to rely on the occult, but in the present situation it seemed the only option. The council hadn't received any news of the Slayer or her watcher, and at such times they turned to people such as this medium for help. It was an errand little to his liking.

"I cannot see clearly," replied the medium. "It seems there was a great fire. The villagers are all dead, and there was a tremendous amount of blood, but no bodies. They all must have burned, dead and undead alike." She shivered—it was indeed cold in the tiny hut where she lived—but she did not open her eyes or break her trance.

The Elder ground his teeth, staring at the medium as if he could force the woman to see all that had happened in that faraway place. "How did the fire start?" he demanded. "Where did it start?"

"At the Slayer's cottage," the medium said.

"And Gaston Roux?"

The medium was silent for a moment, her eyes moving under closed eyelids. "He was not there. I cannot see him." She gasped. "There is an intense heat. It scalds me from within." She opened her eyes and stood. "I will not seek there again," she announced.

"But my council has no records," the Elder protested. "We watchers must find out what happened. We do not know how it's possible that the one life was spared among so many—"

"Eliane the Vampire Slayer is dead," the medium snapped. "Another is called. That is all you need to know, and I will not seek there again."

Michel wept on his knees before the woman.

"You are free to leave here now," she said. "The Watchers Council has found you a position in Ireland."

"My wife?" he asked, though he already knew the answer.

"There is a new slayer," the woman said. "The village of Beauport has been burned to the ground."

Eliane was dead, then. Michel hung his head and sobbed. "I should have been there to die with her," he cried. "Her transgressions and mine were the same. Why should I be spared rather than Eliane?"

"Because you are needed here," the woman said gently. She held out a small bundle. "She was found in a circle of destruction. The land was burned for a mile around, but her cradle was untouched. The Watchers Council says it is a sign of forgiveness."

She placed baby Isabeau in his arms. Michel gazed down at his daughter's face, looked into her big blue eyes. "She has her mother's eyes," he whispered.

"It's no small thing, to be the child of a slayer," the woman said reverently. "And your wife killed a village full of vampires, from what we can tell. This little girl will have a blessed future."

The medium left Michel alone with is baby daughter, his entire family. "You will have a blessed future," he promised Isabeau. "I will devote my life to that."

Isabeau smiled up at her father, as if she understood his words. Then she opened her lips and spoke a word of her own, her first word:

"Demon."

DIE BLUTGRÄFIN
Yvonne Navarro

Hungary, 1609

"What evil is it they do, my *vigyázni*?"

Standing beside Kurt Rendor in the frigid darkness, fifteen-year-old Ildikó Gellért saw him start when she said *vigyázni*—*guard*. It was the closest the newly called Slayer could come to the word *Watcher* in their native Hungarian, and also her first true acknowledgment of his post in her life. She knew he would take it as a huge step for their relationship, a hint that the fierce and headstrong Ildikó might finally accept Rendor's experience, if not his authority.

Rendor hunched inside his woolen cape, and Ildikó knew he was feeling the bite of the wind in every joint of his seventy-year-old body. While she and her Watcher hid in the tree shadows at the forest's edge, the moonlight was still strong enough to break through the wintery cloud cover and the swirling snow; more often than not, there was plenty of light with which to see the figures in the clearing a hundred feet away. They bent and straightened, bent and straightened, fighting with something on the frozen ground.

"They bury the evidence," Rendor said finally. He kept his voice low, knowing the treacherous wind could switch directions at any moment and carry his words to the ears of those they spied upon.

Ildikó strained to see in the darkness. "They murder?" she whispered.

When she would have started forward, Rendor stopped her with a hand on her shoulder. "Wait," he instructed. "You will do a greater good if you hear me out and plan your moves with care."

She paused and said nothing for a few moments as the figures, dressed in much sturdier clothes than she and Rendor, finished their task then hurried down a path at the other end of the small clearing. While the Carpathian Mountains rose cold and majestic behind them, Ildikó knew the path across the clearing would ultimately wind back through the foothills to Castle Csejthe. "Whose bodies did they hide?" she asked quietly. "Those who have fallen prey to vampires?"

Rendor shook his head, then steered her into the forest and back toward the village. Wolves howled somewhere on the mountainside, their cries multiplying and echoing mournfully. "Not to vampires," he told her as they picked their way through the snow. "Serving girls—the latest victims of *die Blutgrafin*."

The Bloody Countess?

Ildikó looked at him sharply. "Countess Bathory did this?"

"These are the rumors, yes." The wind had risen, driving the snow in vicious circles in the air and slapping it against their faces, making them both huddle deeper into their garments. "She—" His murmured sentence ended suddenly, the words choking off in surprise as something leaped on him from the heavy darkness of the surrounding trees.

Rendor went down. *Wolf*. Ildikó thought and surged forward, intending to grab the hide of the snarling form. Then her hands gripped flesh—*cold* flesh—and she realized it was a vampire. Desperate and cold, starving enough to try an attack even when outnumbered. Oftentimes the wintry mountainside would do her work for her, the vicious weather numbing a vampire until the creature could barely function and found itself too far from shelter come dawn. This one had clearly felt that the last of its strength was better pitted against two foes than the frigid hand of nature.

She hauled the beast backward then realized Rendor had come with it—the dreadful thing had managed to clamp its teeth into one of her Watcher's shoulders. Even as the creature grunted with short-lived satisfaction, she could hear the elderly man fighting not to cry out, knew he was afraid the noise would draw more unwanted attention in the night. He pounded on the vampire's head to no avail, the snow making his blows slide harmlessly aside.

But Ildikó's strike would not be so easily ignored. She let go of the bloodsucker's wrist and buried her left hand in its matted hair instead; her right slid under its chin and she hooked her thumb and middle finger on each side of its jaw, digging in viciously until its jaw was forced open and the hold on Rendor released. The thing's mouth gaped, but its hiss of anger died abruptly as Ildikó pushed it backward and off balance—right onto the jutting limb of a dead tree.

Ildikó ignored the dust as it died and rushed to her fallen Watcher. "Are you all right? How badly are you hurt?" she asked urgently.

"I'll survive." Rendor was gasping with pain as she helped him upright. "We must get home quickly and cover the blood smell lest it draw another attack. I fear I would not be able to fight such an encounter."

"Of course." She ducked under his arm and used her shoulder to carry a good part of his weight. "Lean on me."

He did so, and they had taken only a few short steps when the question she was already dreading came. "Ildikó, did you not sense the night beast before it attacked? Not at all?"

The Slayer was silent for a moment, but the truth had to be admitted. "No."

Rendor said nothing more about it, but Ildikó knew it weighed heavily on his mind. She had trained and tried to learn the ways of a Slayer, and in most things she felt she didn't do badly. This, however, was her biggest shortfall—her inability to perceive a creature of the dark when it was near—and it was something for which her Watcher could provide neither mentoring nor training. This lack of intuitive skill had occasionally hindered her in the past, but tonight it had nearly cost the life of her Watcher. Ildikó swallowed, feeling ashamed and small, as though she had let down the one person she most hoped not only to protect, but impress.

She decided to turn the subject back to the countess, the castle, and the burial they had seen—anything to take their minds off this nearly fatal failure.

"The countess," she said. "You said she takes young serving girls?"

"Yes." Rendor's breathing was labored. "I will tell you more when we get inside, after we have cleaned my wound, supped, and rested a bit."

Like it or not, Ildikó was left to her own thoughts, as it took them another twenty minutes to get through the trees and make it to where they lived, in Rendor's small house at the outermost edge of the village. Set apart from the others, Rendor had once been a successful farmer; now grown old, he had sold off all but the small piece of land upon which his home was built. He was a man who loved solitude, and it had pained him to see the space that ensured that dwindle; still, while the surrounding earth had been turned and tilled by its new owners, his privacy was not yet threatened. No one saw him and the young Ildikó take refuge inside against the brutal, late Hungarian night.

After Rendor washed and wrapped the puncture marks in his shoulder, he then set to preparing a simple meal, something hot to chase away the cold. He set water to boil in the iron pot above the fireplace, scooped out a bit to make tea, then added a handful of root vegetables, herbs, and a chunk of dried mutton. While he worked at that, Ildikó braved the outside wind to fetch more fuel for the fire, then she spread their outerwear to dry.

"Tell me of the countess," she said when the meager soup was ready and ladled into trenchers in front of them. Its pleasant aroma mingled with the stronger scent from the still-steaming tea. "And of these rumors."

She had slain many vampires since her calling a half year previous, and often her Watcher, despite his great age, had helped her with these endeavors, tossing her a well-timed weapon, even setting a blow or stake himself a time or two. Oddly, tonight's excursion appeared to have taken more out of him than a dozen of the others combined. This seemed to go beyond the injury he had sustained, as though what he was about to reveal were a weight nearly too great for him to carry. *If such is the case, is it not better that he should share this burden with me?* she wondered.

Now Rendor leaned forward on his chair and gripped his mug tightly, warming his hands on the rough stoneware. "The Countess Erzsébet—Elizabeth—Bathory came to us as the young bride of Ferencz Nádasdy. She has been in Castle Csejthe for nearly twenty years, and while the count himself ran about the countryside battling the Turks, his wife had free rein in his absence. It is said that she . . . grew bored with the everyday tasks of raising her family and running the royal household."

"Bored?"

Rendor nodded tiredly. "She was a beautiful but obstinate young woman, proclaimed in her youth to be nearly uncontrollable." Ildikó's Watcher glanced at her and smiled faintly before gazing again at the liquid in his cup. "Now she has grown in power and will not tolerate disobedience. No matter what her orders."

Ildikó tilted her head to one side. "And what things does our lovely countess demand?"

Rendor rubbed his forehead and Ildikó was again struck by the way his age seemed to hamper him tonight. This Countess—was she truly so much to be feared? "Some say she drinks the blood of virgins," he said softly.

"*What!*"

He cut off her surprise. "Others claim she only bathes in it, that she is not truly *vampyr*."

"Sweet Lord," Ildikó breathed. "But *why?* A vampire would be bad enough, but if she is not . . . for a human to do such things to her own kind is unspeakable!"

"It is," Rendor agreed. "And while the number of her suspected victims makes her crimes the more monstrous, no one can prove her wrongdoings."

Ildikó gripped the sides of the small plank table between her and Rendor. "How many?"

"Some say . . . several hundred."

It was all she could do not to throw the table aside and shake her Watcher. Splinters from the rough wood dug deep into her palms as she fought to control her temper. "Why have you waited so long to tell me of this?" she demanded. "How many more were you willing to sacrifice, and for what?"

"I am not *willing* to sacrifice anyone," Rendor shot back. "Least of all *you*, Ildikó." He paused for a moment, then inhaled deeply. "To be truthful, for some time I have sought to prepare you for exactly this—to face *die Blutgrafin*. But I do not feel that you are ready. Tonight was evidence of that."

Ildikó inhaled, willing herself to calm down even as her face flushed with embarrassment. "I am sorry you are disappointed in me. But though that one skill may be lacking, it is only a small thing—I can do much else. Why do you not acknowledge that, Rendor? I am strong, capable—"

"Because you cannot simply go rushing into Castle Csejthe," her Watcher said sharply. "It is a huge place, filled with people, darkness, and more importantly, the *unknown*. You seem apt to dismiss it, but that 'small thing' could be the very sense that saves your life! Ildikó, this is far beyond the blood beasts you have battled in the forest, or even the nest of *vampyr* you discovered in the cave at Skole. If the countess is to be your next adversary, your past foes will seem like insects by comparison, easily crushed and hardly consequential. This is no mere human with whom you must deal, nor is it a feral beast of blood with little to consider beyond its hunger. The countess is no doubt the worst of both the light and dark worlds, a human with a soul who walks in the day, but who possesses the black heart of a devil."

Ildikó lowered her gaze. "It is hard to believe such a person exists," she said in a quiet voice. "To slaughter so and be without conscience—perhaps she is in league with a vampire, or under the spell of a demon. Because to be so evil and still function beneath the eye of God in the sunlight . . ." She shook her head, then her chin lifted. "Be that as it may, she is still just a woman. I will—"

"You will what?" Rendor interrupted. "You forget that this 'woman' carries the benefits of royal blood and family. She conducts herself with impunity from within a closely guarded castle. She has relatives and servants and soldiers, likely hundreds more than you or I have seen, who inhabit that abominable fortress she claims as her home." Her Watcher brought his tea down on the tabletop so hard that the now-cooled liquid splashed out of his mug and made a sloppy wet circle on the wood. Rendor pointed at it. "She is like this cup," he told her. "The ruler of a small country surrounded by servants and a constant entourage. If you think you can simply announce yourself and request an audience, you are sorely mistaken." He ran one hand across his forehead. "No, we should wait until your skills are more fully developed, until you can feel the night beast that might surprise you from the shadows. Six months is far too soon for you to face an adversary such as this."

"We cannot wait any longer, Rendor. Perhaps we have even waited too long already. You *know* that—every week that passes marks the death of more innocents. If the countess is a night beast, it is my duty to destroy her, the very reason I exist as a Slayer; if she is a monster in woman form, then her crimes must be exposed to the king in the courts of Hungary so that he can punish her as he sees fit." Frustration made her hands ball into fists. "But *how?*"

Rendor pressed his lips together. "Those we saw tonight were no doubt several of her personal serving maids," he said. His mouth twisted downward. "Tonight they buried perhaps another half dozen unfortunate victims. I have heard that there are many more of these sad, hidden graves."

"What is she doing to them?" Ildikó asked suddenly. "You never said."

For a long while Ildikó thought he wasn't going to answer. "It is rumored that at first the countess only beat her charges," he finally replied. He pulled the collar of his coarse shirt closer about his neck, as if just to speak the words chilled him more than the November night. "Her temper ran high and quick, and quite often. As the years of her reign increased, the villagers whispered of torture and depraved acts of the flesh, and the pastors talked of young girls who perished from 'strange maladies' while under the attentions of the countess. But upon her husband's death in 1604, *die Blutgrafin* began to overshadow even her own evil. Now she believes she can retain her youth and beauty for the remainder of her life by draining and bathing in, and perhaps drinking, the blood of young virgins."

Ildikó's eyes widened. "Then she *is* a vampire!"

But Rendor shook his head. "That is not confirmed. Her servants—the ones who survive—are relentlessly loyal."

Ildikó stood and began to pace the tiny, one-room house. At one end was Rendor's small bed, at the other her pallet on the floor, and she covered the distance in only a few strides. "Then I will have to get into the castle," she decided. "The countess is always sending ladies-in-waiting to secure new servants. I've paid little mind to such matters in the past, but I will make it a point to be among the next group selected to serve."

Her repeated pacing took her past the table, and Rendor reached for her with surprising swiftness. His fingers locked around her wrist and his touch was dry and papery, stronger than she'd expected. "Listen well, Ildikó. You must use great care in this matter, perhaps even reconsider. I cannot be of assistance to you should you gain entrance to Castle Csejthe—I have had no time to prepare, no time to find and make ties with those within who might come to your aid should you need it. Hear me well when I say again that I do not believe you are ready for such a battle as this. I know not if this evil woman has turned to true vampire, but in the eyes of those of royal blood, my influence is as that of a gnat on the hide of a great beast—not even noticed. Once the doors close behind you, there is nothing I can do, and no one to whom I can turn if you need help."

Her first impulse was to shrug away his concerns, but Ildikó made herself stop and think about his words. Perhaps it was because she was finally gaining a measure of maturity, or an appreciation for Rendor's wisdom, that she realized what he said was true, frighteningly so. All her life she had been an outcast among her peers because of her lack of interest in or skills with the feminine arts. Asking her to turn a tapestry thread or prepare a boar for roasting was the same as demanding she construct a stone dwelling of her own—she had as little knowledge of the first two as she did of the last.

Three years ago she'd been a wild runaway from her parents' gypsy camp and Kurt Rendor had saved her life, taking her in and giving her shelter on just such a night as this. When her calling as Ildikó the Vampire Slayer had come six months ago, her life had changed again, even more drastically than before. Under the guise that she was the granddaughter of Kurt Rendor's deceased cousin, she'd gone from a nomadic child to the charge of a respected village elder; from there she'd ultimately been told that the safety of those within her small world, literally whether or not many would see the next dawn, rested on her young shoulders.

She'd never had much in this world, but what she did have

she'd gotten these last three years. Inside the castle she would be more isolated than she had ever been, cut off not only from the outside world but also from her savior, the only person in the world who likely cared if she lived or died.

Still, in her heart Ildikó knew she had no choice. Because if she did not stop *die Blutgrafin* . . .

How many more unsuspecting girls would perish?

"From now on you will accompany me to the market each morning," her Watcher told her when they rose at the next dawn. "It is well known that the countess sends her ladies-in-waiting not only to supervise the purchases of the housekeeping staff, but also to peruse the maidens for suitable additions to her entourage."

"Shopping? With . . . money?" Ildikó looked at Rendor doubtfully. Surely he hadn't forgotten how poorly she had fared with his repeated attempts to teach her reading, writing, and addition. "My numbers aren't very good."

"Yes, shopping with money." He tapped the small money bag hanging on his belt, but his expression softened. "Don't worry—I'll be there to do that part. You just take care of positioning yourself properly when the time comes. And you must remember—absolutely no behavior unbecoming a maiden. This means no arguing with the other girls, or being disagreeable with anyone." He sounded frustrated already. "I do so wish we had more time to ready you—the spring would be better."

Ildikó scowled and shook her head in answer to his hint. She disliked the learning part as much as he, but she knew it was necessary—the countess's women were unlikely to choose her if she seemed unladylike or ill-tempered. She would not voice her doubts to her Watcher, but it might already be overly hopeful for her and Rendor to believe this plan would gain her access; unfortunately, it was the only plan either had been able to devise.

"And you must clean up a bit." Rendor's semi-irritated tone pulled her thoughts back to the present. "Bathe yourself, and keep your face and hands clean at all times. Pay particular attention to the fingernails. And you must wash the dirt from your garments regularly."

Bathing? Washing? Wastes of valuable time, but again Ildikó kept her silence, recalling the differences between her and the other girls of the village. Some of those contrasts could not be changed—her hair, for instance. The battle to destroy the nest of night beasts at Skole had been intense and brutal, her injuries extensive. It had taken Ildikó several weeks to recover, sequestered in their small home while the cuts mended and the bruises faded. The scars were easy to hide once she was well again, but Rendor had been forced to cut her hair to a boyish length, even with her chin, to eliminate the ragged chunks that had been torn out by the vanquished vampires. Once long and luxurious thanks to her gypsy heritage, her short, shiny locks would now be much more fitting on a man. Ildikó actually preferred her hair cut this way—it was easier to care for, and appearances weren't something with which she was often concerned.

Rendor pushed the frame of his bed aside with one knee, then reached into the space between it and the wall. When he straightened, he held a small, well-filled money bag that Ildikó had never seen before. "Today at market we will purchase another dress for you," her Watcher announced. "This way you will always have a clean garment to wear."

Ildikó frowned. "Surely the money would be better spent on food," she said.

Rendor lifted one eyebrow. "Sacrifices must sometimes be made in order to achieve a goal," he told her. "If we are to have a chance of getting you inside Csejthe Castle, you must be properly attired."

Ildikó pressed her lips together, then nodded. "You're right, of course."

"Come on then," he said. "It's time for us to start the process of turning you into one of the countess's serving girls."

The day was no less cold for the sun that was shining down on the village, the breezes swirling down the mountainsides no less sharp. Huddled into capes and scarves, shivering despite the deceptive brightness, people hurried about their business and spent as little time as possible in the bitter outside air. Ildikó could not have put into words how much she despised these simple, everyday tasks, nor could she have said specifically why. Perhaps she was more suited to the life she had fled, that of a wanderer with her family's gypsy camp along the borders of Hungary and Romania. Wild and free—at least to the extent that a woman was allowed to be such—she and her family had traveled with a dozen other families and lived out of their wagon.

But no, that life had not fit well with Ildikó. She had wanted something more, something . . . illusive and unnameable. Never would she have imagined the contentment she had found in Rendor's simple household, the evenings of sitting before the fire, sometimes talking and sometimes not. The lessons he tried to impress upon her were frustrating but not so much that she had ever considered abandoning the effort, and when he had told her one beautiful spring morning that she was the newly called

Vampire Slayer, Ildikó had finally understood in her soul what the word *destiny* meant. She was fated to find Rendor and this small village and, perhaps, fated to face the dreaded Countess Elizabeth Bathory.

"This would suit your niece well, would it not?"

Their first stop was in a small fabric shop, and the owner, an older woman of nearly fifty years, held up a dress invitingly. Ildikó cringed when she saw the feminine cut—a gathered bodice above a high-cut waist—but at least the material seemed sturdy, and the dyed dark blue skirt would hide stains. She didn't have the buxom build that adorned the frames of most of the other girls in the village, and if nothing else, the style of this dress might conceal that shortcoming.

"Hold it against yourself," Rendor instructed. Ildikó did so, feeling self-conscious as her Watcher and the shop woman eyed her up and down. "Yes," he said. "I believe it will. How much?"

The woman named a price that made Ildikó wince, but Rendor countered with a lower offer. The two haggled for a while and finally agreed on an amount that Ildikó still believed was robbery. Be that as it may, her Watcher paid it and waited as the shop woman bundled up the dress and tied it with a bit of string.

Outside the bright sunshine had disappeared, blocked by a building cloud cover. They fought the biting wind and turned gratefully into a slightly larger shop in the village square. Ildikó wasn't sure what they were after, since they had plenty of root vegetables at home, as well as bread and cheese. Then she realized that Rendor wanted more than simple foodstuffs—he wanted to expose her to the other villagers and find out what was going on in the area. She hung back and listened to him chat with others from the village, waiting as they shopped and browsed and talked about things she basically considered worthless. What did it matter in her world if Magdolna was now betrothed to József, or if Alisz and Hajnal had just reached their fifteenth years and their seamstressing skills were remarkable?

Her impatience was running high when she felt Rendor grip her arm and pull her to his side as he spoke with an elder named Barna from the village. The well-dressed man was nearly as ancient as her Watcher, although clearly not as well preserved—his teeth were crooked and blackened, his skin creased with the ravages of age below a crown devoid of all but a wisp or two of gray hair.

"Oh, yes," Barna was saying. He turned to Ildikó and gave her a smile that made her shudder inside. "My two youngest daughters were in the market square and caught the attention of the countess's ladies-in-waiting the last time they visited the village." He nodded vigorously. "They've been at the castle for nearly two months now, so busy with their new duties they've not had time to even send us word. But we've been well paid for their services."

Two months without word—does not Barna think that strange? Has he not noticed the aura of fear that must surround talk of the countess and her entourage? Ildikó barely stopped herself from frowning; obviously his concern was more for the sums tunneled into his money bag by the royal family. God help this man's children, but she had a terrible feeling that they might have been among the nameless girls buried in the various graves outside the castle walls.

Barna leaned in close to Rendor and lowered his voice, as if what he was about to say were some great secret. "It is said in the village that they will return the day after tomorrow," he said confidentially. "If your goal is to have your niece selected for service, you would do well to clean the girl up a bit and have her at the seamstress shop at midday two days hence." Barna's gaze flicked around. "Should she be chosen, they will pay you—" He finished the sentence with a whisper in Rendor's ear.

Rendor nodded, and Ildikó was gratified to see that his expression didn't change—the coins meant little to him. "We'll consider it," he said, then added, "thank you for the information."

Barna beamed, the self-purveyor of valuable advice; no doubt now he believed that Rendor owed him a favor. "My pleasure."

Finally the other man was gone and her Watcher turned to her. "Two days," he said. "It isn't much time to prepare you."

"Prepare me?" Ildiko asked. "In what way?"

"There are more things you must know," Rendor said. "Mannerisms more befitting a young lady. The absence of these may well cause you to be passed over." Ildikó had no idea what he was talking about, so she said nothing, choosing instead to follow him around the shop as he made a few purchases—a small feminine-looking satchel, a delicate comb, a pair of light-colored stockings that Ildikó thought looked incredibly uncomfortable. She wasn't so daft that she didn't realize these items were for her, but was she really going to have to don those ridiculous leggings and carry that comb in a purse? *How can a Slayer be expected to fight if she is bound in such clothing?*

"Come along," her Watcher said. He held up the dress and the items he'd just purchased. "We have the tools and we have the time. Now we must prepare the package."

Rubbing her arms beneath her cape, Ildikó stood with perhaps fifteen other girls outside the small shop owned by the most talented of the village's seamstresses. Despite her popularity, the woman's store was small, as was apparent by the need for them to wait for the countess's ladies outside when inside a warm fire burned on the hearth and the customers and a few employees enjoyed tea and mulled wine. There was an undercurrent to the crowd—nervousness, discomfort, *fear*—and Ildikó heard more than a few girls whisper to each other of the countess's rumored cruelties, how their families had ignored their pleas to stay home in favor of the possible compensation. *How sad,* Ildikó thought, *to have so little control over your own lives and fate that others, even your relatives, could decide, based only on their own greed, whether you might live or die.*

None of the others spoke to her, none stood by her side. The last two days had felt like the longest of her short life, Rendor's repeated lessons in proper speaking, attire, and demeanor difficult for her to comprehend. Had her Watcher's efforts succeeded? She felt no different than before, and she certainly looked the same as always save for the too-girlish dress and the stockings covering her legs, useless but for the added warmth they provided. Perhaps she would grow to find them comfortable when—*if*—she were taken into Castle Csejthe. Yes, she'd been told the right things to say and the way in which to speak, but she had no experience of such things in day-to-day living, in the real world of sewing and housekeeping and accounts. Rendor, who awaited the outcome with many of the other adults in the nearby shops, could teach her only so much—the rest of her learning would have to come from the surrounding girls, whether or not they wanted to associate with her.

Ildikó sidestepped a bit nearer to the closest three young women, pretending to study the hem of her dress. They didn't say much, murmuring now and then about the cold and their parents, talking of sewing and using terms of which Ildikó had no knowledge. She might not do well with reading and numbers, but she quickly picked up on their mannerisms and speech patterns, the way they carefully pronounced each syllable rather than running everything together like the common peasants. Fearful or not, Ildikó knew each of these girls hoped that they would be an exception to the rumors, that they possessed some special skill that might catch the attention of a royal servant and guarantee them a better, and *safe,* place within the Bathory household. *Everyone,* the Slayer thought ruefully, *holds fast to the belief that the bad things within the world would always happen to someone else.*

"Why do you crowd us?" a voice beside her suddenly demanded. Ildikó glanced sideways and saw Marika, a pretty, blond-haired woman of sixteen summers. Her brown gaze was full of derision. "Surely you don't believe that you will be brought into the countess's service?" She laughed, and a few of the girls around her joined in while the rest simply stood and looked on miserably, stomping their feet for warmth as they waited for the royal entourage. "Perhaps you haven't recently seen your reflection in the washbowl," Marika continued. "'Tis well known that the countess prefers her serving ladies to look like *ladies.* The mannish style of your hair will hardly draw her eye. Whatever were you thinking to trim it in such a fashion?"

Ildikó started to retort, then Rendor's warning about being disagreeable made her bite back the words. There seemed to be no one around to notice, but who knew? "It just . . . seemed like a good idea when it was done," she finally muttered. The other girls giggled among themselves, and Ildikó felt her cheeks redden and her ire rise. She might have taken the conversation a step further had not three carriages bearing the countess's coat of arms rattled to a stop in front of the shop. Steam plumed from the mouths and noses of the great black horses. Their hides were covered in ornately embroidered saddle blankets, and carved headpieces were strapped to their skulls. Marika forgot Ildikó as they all stood a bit straighter and reflexively smoothed their hair into place beneath their hoods. It was a contradictory situation—being pressed to service Elizabeth Bathory might not be the goal for many, but they still didn't want to face the shame of being passed over and having to return to their families.

Waiting with the crowd of young women, Ildikó was happy to be out of Marika's attentions, since it gave her a chance to surreptitiously study the carriage and the two women who exited it. She and Rendor had heard about them, Jó Ilona and Kateline, and the rumors weren't good—it was said they were responsible for not only recruiting serving maids but also sometimes personally disposing of them when they . . . were no longer needed. Perhaps it had been them performing the late-night burial Ildikó and her Watcher had witnessed that night outside the castle.

Now, despite the bitter temperature, Ildikó and her companions tried to curtsey appropriately then stand tall during their inspection.

There was little remarkable about the countess's two main ladies, other than the obviously better quality and warmth of their garments. Jó Ilona was the older one, with a face road-mapped by time and the elements, her iron gray hair escaping her cap in frizzy tufts around a face that Ildikó immediately pegged as not to be trusted. Kateline wasn't quite so old, but she was still past the bloom of youth; she reminded Ildikó of the gypsy camp followers she'd seen in her own childhood, women who did whatever they were told so long as they were given food and shelter in return. Of course, those women had not done such things as the unspeakable deeds committed by these two.

Jó Ilona began plucking girls from the bunch huddled together and directing them toward Kateline. One here, another there, and how many would be chosen? Five? Six? Surely no more than that, and Ildikó realized that the maximum number would be reached long before the two ladies made it to her position near the end of the group. Many of the girls were trying to slip toward the back without being noticed, their fear of the countess turning to slyness—where was the shame in saying they had not been chosen because the queue had filled before they were seen? Counting on that, Ildikó pushed her way quickly toward the front of the waiting girls, ignoring the mumbled, unladylike curses sometimes directed at her when she bodily moved a girl from her path. In only a few moments she was at the front, and only three girls had been selected so far; this was the best position she could get, and now she had only to somehow sell herself to Jó Ilona.

The old woman paused and studied the girl standing beside Ildikó, then frowned and moved on. Ildikó's sensitive hearing picked up the young maiden's nearly inaudible sigh of relief, then the Slayer stood straighter as Jó Ilona stopped in front of her. For a few seconds, she was at a loss; Render had passed along the rumors that Countess Bathory preferred well-endowed blondes. What on earth could she, slender and dark-haired, do to catch the eye of the woman's recruiter?

Her gaze met and locked with that of Jó Ilona's, and more than anything, Ildikó wanted to scowl at the evil she saw in those watery brown eyes. Instead she forced herself to smile boldly, then drop into a deep curtsey. Her bow wasn't perfect, but the winter cape and the skirt of her dress hid where her feet would have made the move too awkward.

"Stand up, girl," the old woman rasped. Ildikó obeyed and

found Jó Ilona standing only inches away and peering at her. "Open your mouth."

Again, Ildikó obeyed, thinking crankily that she was being inspected as would the local mare before breeding. Jó Ilona's next words drove that impression even deeper. "Good teeth," said the countess's lady, then she reached forward and dug her thin fingers into the flesh of Ildikó's shoulders and upper arms. "Strong, too. Healthy. You'll serve us well for chores and such—go to the carriage with the others."

Rendor's plan had worked! Ildikó curtseyed again then did as she'd been instructed, struggling to mask a triumphant smile. Hustled to one side by Kateline, she waited with the three others chosen so far as Jó Ilona walked the remainder of the line and pulled out two more of the young women, including Marika. Mixed as it was with the dread of their families' displeasure, the relief on the faces of those left behind was still obvious.

It felt like forever before they were moved into the carriage. Though cold, it was at least out of the brutal touch of the wind. Crowded together inside, they could at least build up a bit of warmth as they began the long and bumpy ride through the foothills. Although they knew one another, most of the girls were quiet as they contemplated what might await them at Csejthe Castle. Unfortunately, Marika seemed inclined to do little but snipe at Ildikó.

"How interesting that the countess's ladies should select you," the young woman said to the Slayer. With nothing to occupy their attention but dire thoughts of their future, the other girls seemed grateful for Marika and her words, eager for something else upon which to focus. "But then I suppose that even the countess needs workers in the kitchen, or perhaps women to clean her chamber pots."

There were a few nervous giggles from the others, but Ildikó wasn't deluded by Marika's insults. She had found herself in terror-filled situations too many times not to recognize when someone was hiding behind bravado, masking their apprehension by lashing out at whomever was closest. Poor Rendor had suffered her harsh tongue many a time over the last half year. "Yes," was all she said. "Perhaps she does."

Marika said nothing, but one of the others, a young and pretty girl whose name Ildikó didn't recall, leaned forward. Her eyes were wide, and even in the cold, a line of nervous perspiration rimmed her upper lip. "Why is it you do not seem afraid?" she demanded. "Have you not heard the stories? Do you not know what fate probably awaits us?"

Ildikó tried to think of something to respond, but before she could the words of another girl cut her off. "My mother says you're a witch," she announced. She sent a hard stare at Ildikó, then glanced meaningfully at the other girls. "Perhaps *that's* why she isn't afraid—she thinks to ally herself with those at the castle."

Now the rest of them were staring at her in horror, literally trying to push away from her in the tiny carriage. "Don't be absurd," Ildikó snapped. "I'm no such thing."

Marika sat up straighter, deciding to again join the conversation. "Then why else would you be chosen with the rest of us?" she demanded. She gestured at her golden hair and well-fed frame, then arched an eyebrow at Ildikó's more lithe build. "You must have . . . cast a spell upon the countess's ladies to make them see you as they see us."

"You heard her," Ildikó shot back. She could feel herself getting irritated despite her resolve to remain patient and understanding. "She believes I am strong and healthy enough for chores. 'Tis nothing more than that."

"So you say," muttered one of the others.

The carriage hit a particularly nasty bump and the banter stopped as they all tried to find handholds. The roughness of the ride increased, and Ildikó was grateful for it; she was tired of defending herself against these gossipy, narrow-minded young women. How foolish that they would condemn her out of hand when in the not-so-distant future it was to Ildikó whom they might have to turn for help. Sometimes Ildikó thought that the wiles and whims of men and women ensured their own fates.

She was split from the others almost from the moment they were taken into the great hall of the castle. Ildikó watched with a feeling of foreboding as the others were ushered up the stone stairwell and into the shadowed recesses of the upper floors. Would she see them again? Would she be able to save them? Only time would provide the answer, and meanwhile the air inside the castle carried the heavy aura of fear. The servants went about their tasks quietly, sweeping, dusting, and working ceaselessly to add to or repair the heavy tapestries hung to block the dampness and drafts from the stone walls. Laughter was seldom heard here; when a few muted chuckles did escape, the sound was quickly muted, overridden by the fear of drawing unwanted attention.

As Jó Ilona and Kateline disappeared with the others, Ildikó was turned over to the housekeeper in charge of the countess's larder, a florid-faced woman named Judit who, even at this early hour, had obviously already been tasting of the castle ale. The Slayer was given an apron, then instructed to perform a multitude of mundane but physically demanding tasks—no wonder Jó Ilona had felt her muscles. The hours passed quickly, with Ildikó keeping her eyes and ears attuned to everything, learning who was who and what went where as she carted supplies back and forth and learned of necessity how to turn a knife on cooking meat and vegetables; apparently the midday meal was the big event of Csejthe Castle, and everything must be perfect. One of her first unspoken lessons was that it was best under any circumstances *not* to draw attention to oneself around the countess or her main ladies-in-waiting; the second was to never, *ever* question the whereabouts of a serving girl who suddenly no longer reported for her duties.

No matter how she tried, Ildikó was never allowed in the great hall during the meal that first day. Judit kept a hawk's-eye watch on her during that time, perhaps suspicious of all the questions Ildikó had been asking. She could hear the revelry and laughter, and they certainly went through enough food—a small army would have been well supplied for a week on what was wasted and thrown to the rather well-fed dogs and beggars. Ildikó herself enjoyed a small meal of ground meat, goat's cheese, and bread, forgoing the offered ale in favor of fresh water. By the time she did manage to slip back into the main hall, the countess had already retired to her chambers, and other servants moved around and picked up the leavings, using rush brooms to sweep the expansive floor clear of food droppings.

Ildikó was given a pallet to the side of one of the kitchen fireplaces and instructed to keep an eye on the fire during the night and make sure it didn't go out. She didn't mind; becoming a Slayer had given her an entirely new perspective on the night, and she'd never needed much sleep. Besides, there were other things she wanted to do during the dark hours here, and tending the fire would give her the excuse to be up and about when others might have expected her to bed down like a normal person.

Csejthe Castle had a . . . *smell* about it. Unpleasant and heavy, Ildikó's nose recognized the combined scents of blood and death and decay, and no amount of cooking smoke or airing could hide it. Even in its latest hours, the castle was never quiet—animal sounds filtered in from the courtyard, unintelligible voices were carried down on the tiny drafts and wind currents that worked themselves through the cracks in the heavy stonework. There were always servants and soldiers about, far too many for Ildikó to attempt exploring the darker recesses of the huge castle, the winding passageways and corridors that led to areas far larger than she could imagine.

Still, Ildikó would not give up.

Over the course of her first week, she had seen the girls with whom she had been brought here only intermittently, but those few glimpses had been enough to give her comfort that they hadn't—yet—been harmed. By the time the Sabbath had come and gone, however, fully half of them had mysteriously gone absent; no one said anything, and her inquiries were met only with dismayed glances and whispered reminders that some things were better left alone. As he had warned might happen, Ildikó had heard nothing from her Watcher, and it was obvious the worst had already befallen her peers. Ildikó could no longer bide her time and wait for opportunity—if she was to prevent the other three, and countless others, from perishing, then she must make her own way and not wait for happenstance.

A little past midnight, Ildikó slipped from her pallet in the kitchen, her path taking her within inches of another fitfully sleeping servant—it seemed no one in this castle slumbered well. Tied in the folds of the cumbersome skirts was the satchel Rendor had bought her, its only content the wooden stake that had served

Ildikó well during her short time as the Vampire Slayer. She had no idea where to go, not even an inkling as to which direction marked the way to the countess's living quarters. What she did have, however, was that same Slayer-developed sense of hearing; as she moved farther away from the kitchen than she'd ever gone, she began picking up the cries of a person—female, and agonized—somewhere in this desolate structure. It was toward these muted sounds that Ildikó moved, scurrying from one shadowed corner to the next like a rat avoiding the household cat.

Up a flight of stone steps, down a nerve-wrenchingly narrow hallway, then she found another flight of stairs leading upward. The cries were clearer now, and while the average man might miss them, the faint words, over and over, of *"Mercy, I beg you!"* pierced Ildikó's heart and fed her determination. Closer then, and she took another turn, viewing the hall that stretched long and dark beyond it with dismay. There was no place to hide here, no doorway or alcove in which to slip should someone enter it from the other end. Still, the shrieks of pain were closer now, undeniable; if she wished to find and help whomever was being tormented, it seemed this would be the only avenue.

Ildikó sucked in a breath, then hastened forward.

She didn't quite make it.

"Stop right there, wench."

She would have dashed forward rather than obey had not another figure stepped into view and blocked the hallway at its farthest end. Chewing her lip, she turned back and found one of the countess's soldiers, a private guard by the looks of his dress, striding toward her; when she glanced over her shoulder, she saw that the other figure wore the same garments—she was trapped.

"Identify yourself," said the first guard. His voice was completely devoid of warmth, his eyes dark and unreadable. "I've not seen you in these rooms before."

Ildikó's brain worked to concoct a suitable story, something plausible but that would still conceal her true identity. "My name is . . . Marika," she said. "I've been summoned to assist the countess with her wardrobe in her chambers."

The other guard was close to her now, *too* close, and Ildikó stepped back a little, wanting to feel the comforting presence of the stone wall behind her. The second man was taller than the first and thin, with deep-set eyes and hair that hadn't seen wash water in at least a season. There was a smell about both of them that Ildikó didn't like, different from the one that permeated the castle's rooms, but it was hard to place it beneath the stench of their unwashed clothes and skin.

"Marika?" the first soldier repeated. He met the gaze of his fellow guard over Ildikó's head. "What do you think the chances are that this"—he gave Ildikó an unpleasant-looking leer—"this skinny half-girl would have the same name as the busty young thing who services the countess as we speak?"

Ildikó flinched inwardly as the dual impact of the man's words sank in. Yes, they'd already guessed she wasn't who she claimed; worse, the real Marika was suffering under the countess's less-than-desirable ministrations right now. *I have to get in there and see if I can save that girl.*

"So," said the smaller of the two men, "the wench is *lying*."

"True," agreed the other. His gaze raked her. "Besides, I really don't think she's the countess's type, do you?"

"Let's see." His oversize hand snagged one of her arms, fingers digging tightly into the skin. Ildikó tried to pull away from the uncomfortably cold and painful grip, but he only held on more tightly, then he shook his head and gave a nasty laugh. "With that short, dark hair and flat chest? Not likely."

His companion nodded. "You know, if we take her to the captain of the guard, he'll likely throw her in chains in the dungeon, leave her there until she starves and dies."

"It would be a terrible waste," the other agreed. "Of a good *meal*."

The empty eyes, that too-cool touch . . . Ildikó jerked out of the guard's grasp just as his gaze flickered yellow and his facial features melted into a portrait of evil. She didn't have to look to know the other soldier was a vampire, too—were there others just like them where the hallway turned right at the far end? Here, God help her, was a prime example of the consequences of her inability to sense a vampire's presence—this creature had actually placed its filthy hand upon her and she *still* hadn't realized it was a bloodsucker.

She felt the larger vampire's spittle on her neck as he hissed in anticipation; it was cold and smelled of things pulled from a wet grave. Ildikó twisted away and brought her elbow up hard into the creature's nose as her right hand dug into her skirt and found the bag Rendor had given her, felt the comforting grip of the wood through the fabric. With his nose smashed, the guard's cry of pain was thankfully muffled, and she let instinct guide her—in less than a second, the stake, still encased within the fabric satchel, found its mark in the center of the first soldier's chest. Vampire dust exploded in front of her, and had she possessed the time, Ildikó would have been thankful for the absence of battle armor; as it was, she could only gasp as the other guard lunged at her and got a choke hold around her neck.

Her head immediately began to pound and black and gold

sparkles flitted across her vision as her air was cut off. Growling, the beast crowded against her, forcing her back against the wall and giving her no room to get the stake up and into position. It took everything she had to snake one arm up on each side of his and clasp her hands, then angle them sideways until his grasp on her neck broke. She had one blessed moment of full air, but instead of backing away, he pushed her even harder, throwing his full weight against her slighter frame. Her precious breath went out of her lungs as she was slammed against the stonework and her arms flailed outward.

Fast as a snake, the vampire tried to bite her; just as quickly, Ildikó squirmed in one direction, then another. "No," she said through ground teeth. "I will *not* be your evening meal, you vile thing!" The beast pressed against her again and this time she let it; for a second, he hesitated, then she felt his entire body stiffen. The last thing he saw before he erupted into dust from the stake she'd driven into him from the back was her bright, victorious smile.

But Ildikó was anything but clear of danger. Caught up in the battle, she'd overlooked the noise they'd made—her furious statement, the grunts and growls of her two attackers. New excited voices drifted toward her, coming from just around that turn in the hallway—at least a half dozen men, probably more of the countess's guards come to check on their brethren. Her battle here was lost, and she had no choice this night but to retreat.

God would have to help Marika. Ildikó had lost her chance.

The screams of the night before weighed on Ildikó's mind, more so because she knew the young woman who had suffered so. Death was never good, but had her memory held the cries of a faceless stranger she would not have been as down in the heart, as . . . *connected* to the atrocities being committed somewhere within this heavily guarded stone fortress. She had saved many people from the village in her short time as a Slayer, but always the darkness had kept their faces from her, and hers from them. She had left her own family behind of choice, and while she respected Rendor and followed his guidance—more so of late—this was the first time Ildikó had seen or heard evil visited upon someone she knew personally, a girl with whom she'd shared conversation. It mattered not that their words had been far from cordial; the impact was far deeper because it had struck down a face she knew, a voice she had heard, a name Ildikó had uttered from her lips.

The morning dragged, with Ildikó's chores seeming meaningless and her mind spinning in all directions but unable to come up with any plan but to try the same entry tonight. The notion was fraught with potential trouble. The least of these was that the captain of the guard had doubtlessly noticed his missing men and his suspicions would be raised, resulting in an increased guard. Worse, what if the captain is himself a vampire, his men more of the same? If that were true, how convenient that such an army guarded Countess Elizabeth Bathory!

But there seemed to be no other option for Ildikó. If anything, even more servants wandered the area than in the previous days, even more soldiers and merchants. Each able-bodied man and woman who joined the castle's population this day decreased her chances of getting to the countess's chambers this eventide, and Ildikó became more frustrated as the hour wore late. If she did not figure out something soon—

"You there, girl. Come forward."

Ildikó almost missed the command, so absorbed was she in

her own speculations. The old crone of a housekeeper, however, had no intention of letting it slip by; she reached out an aged hand and pinched Ildikó hard on the soft flesh on the inside of her upper arm. It stung enough so that the Slayer's head whipped around, and she nearly dropped into a fighting stance, then at the last second she remembered where she was and her need to keep her identity a secret. The housekeeper gestured angrily at her to heed someone behind Ildikó's shoulder and hissed something at her, the words too heavy with ale to be intelligible.

Ildikó turned and found herself face-to-face with the lesser of the countess's ladies-in-waiting, Kateline. The woman's face was, as always, drawn and tired, her dark eyes rimmed with shadows that testified to many sleepless nights. "You look of sound mind and health," she said. "We have need of your assistance with matters elsewhere."

Ildikó curtseyed, snatched up her cape and satchel from their spot by the fireplace, and obediently fell into step behind Kateline. The older woman led her through the main hall and into the courtyard. Outside the shadows were lengthening and the cold was increasing, quickly bleeding away what scant heat the ground had managed to pull from the winter sun. The little village down the mountain always had a pall over it during the harsh winter months, but the houses this close to the castle, literally within its gloomy shadow, bore an atmosphere that was oppressive and unabashedly fearful in the evening. People rushed about as if their very lives depended on it, and if what she had encountered last night was any indication, finding shelter and safety before darkness fully descended really *did* mark the boundary between life and death . . . or undeath.

Ildikó's senses sharpened as Kateline guided her to a doorway that led out of the courtyard proper. Their footsteps crunched in the snow, and voices filtered through the sparse trees; not too much farther waited three more people—Jó Ilona and two more serving girls, their faces pale and terrified as they awaited the bidding of their mistresses. On the ground at their feet lay their task: the burial of two elongated shapes bundled in heavy fabric, clearly the bodies of two who had been considerably less fortunate. Ildikó barely hid her anger as she grasped the shovel handed her. *Is Marika one of these poor dead souls?*

Angry she might be, but common sense still ruled. Yes, she wanted to avenge these two and the others who had fallen victim to the countess. To do so, her objective was to find her way to the cause of their death, the bigger target back inside the castle. Out here she would hold her comments and tongue, and trust in her instincts to guide her actions.

Thanks to Ildikó's superior strength, the onerous chore went quickly, enough so that Kateline and Jó Ilona took note. Their work completed, the girls were herded inside and sent back to their normal duties, but Jó Ilona gestured for Ildikó to hang back as the others left. Standing before the crone, Ildikó felt . . . *soiled* beneath her gaze. Odd that Jó Ilona's eyes now seemed more than old, rheumy but far too knowing, tainted by the darkness of what had passed before them. When the old woman folded cool, dry fingers around her wrist, Ildikó had to search for a new strength within herself to keep from yanking away.

"You are assigned to help with cooking duties, yes?"

"Yes, mistress," Ildikó answered.

Jó Ilona nodded, the movement more a confirmation to herself than anything the young Slayer needed to interpret. The woman's eyes shifted left and right, as though she were making sure no one else was within hearing range. "A girl, strong such as you, and with aspirations to a better station in the household, could go far in the castle," she told Ildikó in a raspy whisper. "If she could hold her tongue about certain matters."

There was no mistaking that here, finally, was an avenue that might take her within striking distance of the countess herself. But caution was still called for; wary of appearing overeager, Ildikó made a show of giving Jó Ilona's words careful consideration. "You mean I am not to repeat to others what is seen or heard during the performance of my duties?"

"Exactly." The countess's lady peered at her and her fingers dug into the Slayer's flesh more firmly. "Are you capable of silence, girl? Be wise in your answer, for there will be no chance for turnabout."

Ildikó nodded solemnly. "I am most trustworthy."

Jó Ilona released her. "Very well, then. I will show you to your new post at Castle Csejthe."

And Ildikó followed the old crone down the steps into the farthest recesses of the castle, and into the very pits of hell.

There had been times in Ildikó's short span as the Vampire Slayer during which she had been cold and hungry, weary to the bone and injured. Yet even during the worst of those—her battle to destroy the nest of *vampyr* at Skole—never would she have imagined such a place existed as the dungeons maintained by the monstrous Elizabeth Bathory.

The rooms were unexpectedly well lit, but for once Ildikó would have preferred darkness and shadow—anything to help cushion the impact of her surroundings. After leading her down here yesterday morning, Jó Ilona had given Ildikó the barest idea of her assigned duties, then left. The last that Ildikó had heard of the woman was the sound of the heavy wooden bar being dropped into its iron brackets on the other side of the dungeon's main door.

She was trapped down here.

But she wasn't alone.

Ildikó hadn't found them until the crone had left, but at the farther end of the room, chained in place against cold walls weeping with moisture, were four girls. Shivering and moaning, they were delirious with fear and thirst, and while Ildikó murmured words of empty comfort and brought each fresh water, she could neither free them from the stout iron manacles, nor find anything to cover their nearly naked bodies. Sorely mistreated, each girl's flesh was a landscape of wounds, from bruises to cuts to bite marks that bore no resemblance at all to the familiar puncture of a vampire's teeth. A different sort of monster had preyed on these young women, and it was one that sorely needed destroying.

And so Ildikó waited, patiently tending to the girls and biding her time, replenishing the myriad of torches and keeping the single huge fireplace stoked lest the flames go out and they all freeze down here. Her stomach growled with emptiness, and she could only imagine what these pathetic prisoners felt, two of whom had shared the carriage with her only last week. Ildikó hadn't the tendency to hold a grudge, and it pained her greatly to see them imprisoned and in such pain, but while she checked their manacles dozens of times, her Slayer's strength was no match for the iron that encased their wrists and ankles.

There were other things down here, too. Alive and otherwise.

In the realm of the living there were the rats, squeezing in through the cracks and small drains in the stone floors and walls, safely using passageways too narrow for even the castle cats. Insects, too—huge waterbugs and other scuttling things for which Ildikó had no name. Those things, she could deal with—a well-placed stomp of her foot marked the finale for many of the pesky creatures—but it was the—*other* things, items made of wood and leather and iron, that horrified her almost more than anything she had previously encountered.

The rumors had not done this place true justice.

There were tables with stained leather straps, others with thumbscrews, pinchers, rope whips, and chain flails, all dark and nauseatingly heavy with the scent of blood. Had these things been used on the girls chained to the wall? If so, it was little wonder that the imprisoned girls seemed only a hair's length from death. But even though such implements were horrifying, they were dwarfed by the thing in the center of the room, a huge, metal monstrosity that gave Ildikó chills just to gaze upon it. Yet she couldn't *not* study the thing, try to figure out what it did to its victims, what purpose it ultimately served. It seemed to be some kind of . . . *cage,* and God help those caught in its grasp, because if she was understanding what she saw—

"I see you are fascinated by the Iron Maiden."

Ildikó spun, but the honey-coated voice belonged to no one in sight. Her gaze darted from the pools of shadow between each torch on the wall, but still she saw no one. *What manner of beast could hide so?*

Movement then, a blacker silhouette in a valley of darkness by the door—she'd been so focused upon the torture devices that she hadn't heard the stealthy removal of the locking bar, and someone had taken down several of the torches as she'd turned. Before she could speak, more figures moved into the room from the doorway, the heavier, taller figures of the countess's soldiers no doubt accompanying her for safety. As Ildikó waited, Kateline and Jó Ilona stepped forward, the first to cut off her view and access to the figure who could only be Countess Bathory herself. More soldiers hastened to accompany them—how odd that the woman felt the need for such protection from one scrawny serving maid.

But if the countess felt fear, she wasn't the only one. Her mouth dry, Ildikó swallowed and forced her voice to stay calm. She had miscalculated terribly, and Rendor's warnings about how isolated she would be came back in a nasty flood. The Slayer would find no help in this fiendish place, and it was clear that her Watcher, although highly regarded in the village, had been unable to send assistance or even gain entrance to the castle.

Still, there was no time for recriminations. She was where she was—alone—but she would not betray her fear to this monster in a woman's clothing. "I have never seen such a thing."

"It's quite beautiful, isn't it?" came Elizabeth Bathory's answer. The voice floated on the drafts in the dungeon like the ethereal version of a poisonous snake. "I had it made by a clockmaker at Dolna Krupa." If such a thing were possible, Ildikó thought she could actually *hear* the woman smiling. "Such a fine and . . . *efficient* piece of art."

Ildikó grimaced, not sure whether her expression could be seen in the darkness, not really caring. "Art? It seems more a work of cruelty to me."

The countess chuckled but still kept her distance. "Quite overspoken, aren't you? A perilous thing in my service, you know."

The Slayer tensed, but no one moved forward. "My apologies, Your Highness."

The countess waved away her words. "No matter. You are

different from the other maidens," she commented. "More robust, I think. Stronger. My sorceress tells me of your great stamina and health, that you are . . . special." A finger of unease stroked the base of Ildikó's spine. Even for one of Elizabeth Bathory's stature, it was bold indeed to admit to employing a person of the dark arts—of what other things regarding Ildikó did this so-called sorceress have knowledge?

The Slayer tensed again as one of the soldiers moved into the room, but he only set a serving tray on one of the heavy wooden tables, then returned to the shadows; on the tray was a waterskin, bowls of cold goulash, and a few hunks of bread. Even unheated, the smell of the food was enough to rouse the poor girls chained against the wall—no doubt it had been days since they'd had a meal. Still, their senses were too clouded by pain and hunger for them to recognize Ildikó.

"You will tend to these girls," the countess said. "And yourself, also—the cook tends to forget to bring meals to those in the dungeon. I fear this part of the castle makes her uncomfortable." The countess paused, and Ildikó again had that eerie sense of *hearing* the woman's happiness. "I rather enjoy its accommodations. Besides, my Maiden graces this room, and that, of course, makes it my first choice for . . . guests."

Ildikó strained at the darkness, but her heightened eyesight still couldn't make out the number of soldiers on guard with the countess. Nonetheless, she would have to chance it—her opportunities to be in the countess's presence were few and far between. With no idea whether she faced beast or human, her right hand slipped into the folds of her skirt and folded around the stake, then Ildikó risked a small step forward.

There was a flurry of motion in the darkness, of bodies

suddenly moving and shifting. When Countess Bathory spoke again, her voice was farther away and muffled by the knot of people between her and Ildikó. "Don't worry, my pet. A serving girl as different as you should be treated as such, and we'll return to visit later. You shan't be down here alone too long."

A rush of footsteps and murmuring, and before Ildikó could cross the distance of the room, the countess and her passel of servants and soldiers had hastened through the doorway and barred it behind them.

Ildikó balled her fists in frustration, but there was nothing to be done about it—she was still trapped. Knowing it was useless to dwell on it, instead the Slayer retrieved the tray of food and carried it over to the four pathetic prisoners. At first eager, she was ultimately disappointed in the amount of food she could coax each to eat; beaten, sickly, and exhausted, one by one they drank a bit of water and fell asleep after only a few bites of the goulash. Her own stomach was rumbling with emptiness, so Ildikó ate a few bites of the bread and the rest of one bowl of goulash herself, finding it nearly tasteless and greasy, with a bitter edge to each swallow.

Setting the tray aside, she tried to think about what to do next, devise some sort of battle plan for when the Countess returned. But she was tired and it was hard to concentrate—the castle drafts made the torchlight flicker and wave almost hypnotically and she felt sleepy, pleasantly numb—

Suddenly alarmed, Ildikó stood.

And promptly fell face forward onto the filthy floor.

Gasping, with her cheek pressed against the stones, she realized that something had been added to the goulash—no wonder the prisoners, in their weakened states, had fallen asleep so quickly. This was far worse than anything she might have imagined, and suddenly her own mortality and inexperience sank in, her true powerlessness and *frailty* against this woman, the huge royal family, and seemingly endless army of soldiers and servants. She could not succumb to whatever potion or herb had been mixed into the goulash by the countess's sorceress, she *had* to stay awake—

Blackness.

Ildikó felt like she was swimming. In her childhood, her father and the tribe had once camped in a valley along the eastern border of Romania, where there had been a small lake. The water had been cold and not particularly pleasant even in late summer; it had washed over her skin and left chill bumps in its wake, making her want only to get out of its wet grasp in much the same way as she felt now. Oddly enough, she thought suddenly of Rendor, and the way he had rescued her from certain death three years ago, the warmth that had come when as a stranger he had thrown a heavy woven blanket around her shoulders and offered her shelter. If such a thing were possible, she believed to her soul that he would do the same for her now, that he had *been* trying; doubtless his efforts to provide assistance to her over the past week had come to naught. Had not her Watcher warned her countless times that her stubbornness might someday cost her dearly?

"Your skin is such an odd golden color," she heard someone murmur. *"It's as if you've somehow soaked up a measure of the sun—so different from the others."* Something touched her cheek, and Ildikó tried to pull away, then found she couldn't. Her head wouldn't move, her arms and legs were bound and completely immobile. *"It makes you quite beautiful, you know. Very appealing . . . desirable despite your leanness."*

The Slayer dragged her eyes open, then wished she hadn't. The headachy remnants of the sleep potion were nothing compared to the realization of where she was and her upcoming fate.

The countess stood on a raised platform in front of her, excruciatingly beautiful in a fine gown of green silk, her ivory skin and dark eyes accented by the burning torches around the room. Ildikó waited, expecting to see those fine features melt into the twisted visage of a vampire, but the noblewoman only stared at her.

"It is such a struggle to stay young," the countess said dreamily. She held out one hand, and immediately a soldier rushed to help her off the platform. "The very efforts of doing so are in themselves taxing, requiring a never-ending search. I have always known that the best blood comes from pure young girls, but you . . ." Standing below the Slayer now, she reached up and ran a jewelry-covered hand down Ildikó's leg, and the Slayer started as she realized they had completely stripped away her garments. "I'm told you are not as other normal girls, that you possess special abilities. What benefits might I reap from one such as you, so strong and healthy, so *different*? What longevity?"

Ildikó tried to reply and found she couldn't—something cold and painfully hard had been pushed into her mouth and was being held in place by a strap. More bindings were around her head, neck, chest and arms, all the way down her body. She could feel a smooth surface against her spine, rear end, and the backs of her legs—metal?—but she couldn't turn her head to see what was holding her. Such a subtle mistake, the smallest of missed details, but devastating nonetheless . . . while she had thought her uniqueness would help her save the other girls and stop the evil, she had never realized it had served only as her undoing. Those same differences that had served her so well in the fight against the dark side—her strength and stamina, her lean and unfeminine skills—had pulled the countess's attention like a hungry wolf to fresh meat.

"Normally I have serving girls readied for me in numerous ways," the countess said matter-of-factly. Ildikó's eyes widened at her next words. "Heated pinchers or branding generally gets the blood flowing quite richly. But you . . ." Her voice trailed away thoughtfully. "I think it would be best not to blister such lovely skin, don't you?" The woman paced back and forth in front of her, going in and out of Ildikó's line of sight like a puppet in a street show.

"You showed such interest in my precious Iron Maiden earlier that I decided you should experience it firsthand, without all the bothersome distractions that preparation would entail."

The Iron Maiden? Ildikó tried to say something around the metal in her mouth, but it only came out as an unintelligible gargle. Now she wished she hadn't examined the torture device so closely, hadn't seen the hideous metal face on its front and the blood-encrusted spikes that sprouted from the insides of the two doors on the thing's front.

Spikes that would penetrate her body when those very same doors were pushed closed.

Ildikó tried to struggle then, staring down at the countess's dark smile as unseen servants on either side of the Iron Maiden began to slowly close it up. It was a useless effort—she was held fast within the unbreakable iron-spiked grip of the Bloody Countess's beloved torture device. There was no flash retelling in her mind of her own life as the first spikes pierced her skin and sank deep, no sudden divine inspiration about the things she could or should have done to make the world a better place or to banish evil.

There was only the building and excruciating pain, the silent screams of her own agony, and the fading sight of Countess Bathory raising a goblet of collected blood—Ildikó's blood—and toasting her before lifting it to dark red lips.

And even as death enveloped her in its mercifully permanent embrace, Ildikó still wasn't sure if the beautiful, Bloody Countess was truly a vampire . . .

Or if, as a Slayer, she had died for naught.

MORNGLOM DREAMING

Doranna Durgin

Kentucky, 1886

Two entities in need.
 They find each other.
 The primary is demonic in nature, carnal of flesh; it hungers.
The secondary is spectral in nature, ephemeral of flesh; it craves.
Together, they haunt the mountain hollers.

The resounding noise of offended piglets filled the barnyard. Within the barn, Mollie Prater picked out the shouts of her equally outraged younger brother as he struggled to herd the creatures inside without letting the big mean-as-spit sow through the low door.

From the loft above her, Lonnie gave a low laugh, forking down another bunch of last fall's hay for the evening cow feed. "Ferd never gets any better at that."

"Easy for you to say, seein' as you're free of the job now." Mollie scooped a handful of charcoal from one bucket and a handful of hardwood ashes from another, dumping them both in the pig slops and stirring vigorously with the flat wooden paddle she plucked from its spot on the barn partition.

"Count yourself lucky," Lonnie grunted, sending down

another forkful of hay. "You bein' a girl and all—you missed that particular chore."

Mollie said nothing as she stirred the pig slops and worm tonic. No point in it. Girl children had one set of chores, boys another; such was life even if she *had* always been plenty strong enough to handle either. Soon enough she'd have a whole 'nother set of chores—wifely ones. At fifteen, she was well ready to be wed, and after two patient years of courting, Harly Meade was ready to have her. Her daddy reckoned him as a good provider and a faithful man in all ways, and that suited her; a man had to be steady to make his way in these mountains.

She liked, too, that he was tall and straight limbed and had a sweet smile—and that he so often turned it on her, making her feel entirely uncertain of her feet against the ground. In a few more weeks she'd be Mrs. Harly Meade and she'd find out just what there was to being woman of her own homestead, a modest starter cabin in a small scoop on the side of the steep hill.

It was the impending wedding that had her feeling strange these days, she figured. She blamed her excitement for that day she'd woken up with the odd sensation of her own blood tingling through her body, lending her strength a woman didn't expect to have—and for the times since then that she'd tripped over her own movements simply because things came easier than she expected, easier even than her own normal vigorous efforts. She blamed the wedding for her dreams, too—although they didn't seem to be wedding sorts of dreams at all, but mornglom dreams full of darkness and roaring and startling smells.

She'd always had a knack for dreams, but . . . she couldn't recall dreaming in smells before.

Real-life pigsty stink rose to fill her nostrils, dispelling thoughts of early-morning dreams. "Pee-yew," she said in disgust, and decided she'd stirred the charcoal and ashes worm tonic quite well enough. She flipped the latch to the narrow gate blocking the small aisle between the dirt-floored pigpen and repeated, "*Pee-yew.*"

"Can't be no worse than it ever is," Lonnie said with all the airy assurance of someone who hadn't done the pig-worming chore since Mollie had grown tall enough to carry the buckets. He jabbed at the hay, peering down at her through the square entry door in the floor. "You want to worry on something, think about the hay. I hope we've enough to last through the spring cutting."

Mollie might have answered him—if outside, Ferd's triumphant whooping hadn't turned into a shout of protest, a warning that the furious sow had slipped by. If at that same instant right above her, Lonnie hadn't made a surprised and alarmed noise of his own, shouting her name in warning as he fumbled the pitchfork.

She couldn't say if time had slowed, or if it had sped up so fast that events slicked right past her, with her own part in them a thing of startling instinct and speed. She saw clear enough as Lonnie dropped the pitchfork through the loft door right above her, sending it stabbing down at her head just as the old sow charged in with the piglets, and by God didn't that pig have blood in her eye. Slaver flew as she jabbed the air with her sharp tushes, rampaging right through her own squalling babies to squeeze into the aisle with Mollie as her target.

Shouting—pitchfork—squealing—charging—

Mollie snatched the pitchfork out of the air a hair's breadth from her own head and whipped it at the enraged sow.

"Mollie Prater!" Lonnie gasped as the tines jabbed the ground directly before the infuriated pig; the reverberating handle whacked the sow hard on the nose, blocking her path. Stunned, the sow stopped short as Ferd ducked through the pig- and boy-size door cut into the side of the barn, clambering barefoot over the pen slats to the main barn; she gave the world a sullen look and backed up until she reached open space again. Ferd took in the scene with a puzzled look on his rounded boy's face, and Lonnie, crouched over the loft door, seemed to have lost most of his words, for all he could do was say, "Mollie Prater!" once more.

Mollie looked at her hands—her impossibly fast, incredibly coordinated, startlingly strong hands—and said the only thing she could. "'Tain't like I could throw it *at* her. She's still got those babies to suck."

Ethan Bentley stood in the open air of the train caboose platform, watching the twisting rails recede behind the train to be swallowed up by equally twisty hills. He considered it a wonder that the crews had even carved out a place to lay track, with so little room between these unending ridges for anything but deep, narrow gorges and watercourses. No wonder they chose to follow the curve of the hill itself, somewhere between top and bottom—until it reached those places where the hills crammed together and there was nowhere to go but over.

The hills themselves were thickly covered with spring-green trees, poplars and oak and evergreen hemlock—except where the bones of the mountains jutted out, rough granite with mica chips that sparkled in the bright sunshine. A view so different from the streets of New York City, it was a wonder Ethan's eyes could take it in at all.

You have an assignment, the Council had told him—good news and bad. Good, because it meant he would finally fulfill his destiny, taking up the job for which he'd been trained instead of hanging around the dockyards of the city to keep track of the murky creatures who congregated there. Bad, because it meant leaving the city haunts he knew so well and plunging into this deep mountain world of which he knew nothing, and into which he could hardly hope to blend. And *bad*, because it meant a Slayer had died.

Assignment didn't always mean the death of a Slayer; sometimes it meant the death of a Watcher—which was far more preferable. Watchers could be replaced. A Slayer with experience could not. As often as not the new Slayer hadn't been identified or trained before the calling. In this case she lived in an area so remote that Ethan would be hard put to find her at all in the crumpled, winding hollers of Pike County, Kentucky; he'd certainly have no opportunity to study the situation, to introduce himself to the new Slayer, or to ease into an explanation of her calling. There would be no crowds into which he could blend, not Ethan Bentley from New York City. Already he was used to the wary glances, the quick assessment, the challenge of the slightly edged question, "You're not from around here, are you?"

No, these people weren't used to outsiders. The rails and ties unwinding behind him made fresh track, a train route less than a year old and laid in place to haul the precious bituminous coal of southeastern Kentucky. It was 1886, and the world had come to Pike County.

The world, and Ethan Bentley.

Mollie churned milk to butter, sitting on the steps of the cabin and listening to Lonnie talk of coal towns, and how joining up with one seemed the certain sure way for a fellow to put a mark on the world. Why putting a mark on the world had to be important, she didn't know; she'd never wanted or expected anything more from her life than seemed likely to come her way—a good husband in Harly, a family to raise, the chance to look down the holler and take in the beauty of it, green and ripe and full of life. Or in winter, with the frost sparking hard off the trees and the day's sun come to melt it away, bringing enough warmth that most days were just as easy outdoors as in and with only a handful of snows each year.

"I could work my way up to a boss spot," Lonnie was saying, though her daddy just grunted a response, and not any kind of happy-sounding grunt, either. Lonnie must have taken a good hint to change the subject, but she wished, listening, that he hadn't thought to tell about the barn that morning. Or that he hadn't stretched the tale so tall, for surely what she heard wasn't really the way it had happened. She'd been lucky, that's all—not so fast as he described it, nor so calm-headed and deliberate. *Not so oddly—*

Cra-ack!

Mollie looked at the broken butter churn handle in dismay. It had been new-made.

But the jagged ends of the ash wood handle were good and broke. Some hidden flaw in the grain, no doubt. She sighed, set it aside, and examined the gash it had made on her palm, blotting the blood on her apron corner so she could hunt for splinters, ignoring the funny feeling that crept along her spine, the one that said the handle had been perfectly fine, inside and out.

Her mommy came onto the porch, wiping her hands on her own apron after she set down a basket of laundry. "Take these out for hangin'," she told Mollie, and then asked loudly over the broken churn handle, "What's happened here?"

"Must've been crooket inside," Mollie said, picking out a last splinter and scowling at her hand.

"Pour you a little turpentine over that," Lila Prater said, tilting over Mollie's shoulder to have a good look. "Wouldn't want it to come up bad, not with the wedding so close."

Mollie nodded. "Maybe Lonnie'll bind that handle back together long enough to finish this batch."

"I suspect so," Lila said, looking up the long lane leading from the cart road by the creek that ran down the center of the holler. "Here's Adalee, Mollie. She'll keep you company."

Mollie raised her head to discover her best girlfriend coming up the road, heavy with the burden of a sack and the baby within her besides. Mollie waved a hand in greeting and gathered up the laundry basket to meet Adalee by the clothesline. "Aren't you looking fine," she said, admiring Adalee's plumping belly.

"Won't be *me* everyone's looking at come next Saturday," Adalee said, grinning a sly grin. She held the sack out. "I brung you something. For your wedding chest."

Mollie took the sack, untying it to discover a set of pretty white bedsheets, the linen fine woven and the top edge finished with Adalee's lacy tatting. She gasped with delight, and barely stopped herself from pulling the top sheet free so she could see it all at once. "No," she said, "I'll keep it specially clean until the night of the wedding."

"Won't Harly like you on these sheets," Adalee said, conspiracy in her tone. "Him and his fine long legs and good broad shoulders."

"Adalee!" Mollie said, trying for a scandalized tone and hitting only a giggle. "You've been looking at my Harly!"

"I look where I please," Adalee said airily, taking the sack from Mollie to close it up tight again. "There's herbs in there, too, so those sheets'll be pretty-scented when you first use them."

Mollie gave herself a rare moment of anticipation, of herself and Harly in their own little cabin. Harly who loved her, who held her hand as though it were a thing made of china instead of work-calloused toughness. Harly with his shy grin, and who made up for the lack of a certain intuitive spark with his persistent determination. Harly, who knew what he wanted—and that want was Mollie.

Then she turned to the laundry, heaving the first of her father's water-heavy shirts over the fraying line. "Wisht I thought laundry would feel less of a chore in my own household—but I'm looking forward to it anyway."

Adalee grinned; Mollie heard it in her voice as she settled onto an old stump, awkward with the new shape of her body. "It'll get just as old," she said, but then she swapped subjects altogether, becoming more somber. "Mollie, you hear of the christening at the head of Dry Creek Holler?"

Mollie glanced over her shoulder to see the worried wrinkle that drew Adalee's fine brows together. They were much alike, she and Adalee—honey brown hair with summer sunshine streaks and amber brown eyes, both petite of figure and feature. Mollie had better teeth; Adalee had a straighter nose, and they'd both spent much time facing opposite corners in church Bible teachings when they were younger—though the somber Preacher Peavey hadn't ever convinced them that giggling was a sin.

He'd have liked the look on Adalee's face now. "It was for one of the west edge Meades," Adalee said. "You know, that woman what keeps losing her babies before they're born? This time she had herself a live one, a real pretty little girl. Way I heard it, you never saw a man so proud as hers."

"Must've been a right nice christening, then," Mollie observed, twitching the wrinkle out of one of Lila's aprons and moving on to hang Lonnie's britches and frowning her puzzlement at Adalee's somber expression.

"That's what makes it so sad," Adalee said. "So purely awful." She took a deep breath. "This . . . *thing* done come down from the hill, squallin' something fierce, and it stirred them folks up like a pot full of trouble. And it kilt the Meade man, and a Peavey from down near Poor Bottom."

"It *killed* them?" Mollie's hands, full of clothespins and wet cloth, dropped to waist level, and she twisted to look at her friend. "What do you mean, *thing*? Some nasty spring bear, or a wolf?"

"I surely don't. I mean it was a man-beast, a *thing*. I hear its eyes were tore out and weeping vile slime and it still come at them folks like it could see every bit of 'em."

"I never! You're fibbing me!" Mollie turned back to the laundry line with an indignant jut of jaw.

"Cross my heart, I ain't," Adalee said, and the earnest note of her voice made Mollie hesitate as she jammed a second pin down on a kitchen rag. "I'm telling it just like I heard it. It ought to have been the biggest, happiest day of those folks' lives, and it done turned into the worst. They're laying out the bodies even now, and you can go see for yourself if you don't believe me."

"Seein' dead people don't prove a thing," Mollie said, having regained some of her composure.

"It'll prove something when you see what's left of 'em," Adalee said promptly. "It surely will."

Mollie pulled another shirt from the basket and snapped it briskly to straighten the sleeves, pretending to be unaffected by Adalee's words . . . but somewhere along the way, Mollie's head and her heart had turned back to the fading edges of dawn dreams that had been all screams and roaring and fear.

The scent of sorrow on the wind is as sweet as the blood that will follow. Trailing the scent down from the ridge to the crinkle of a holler, the spectral entity soaks up communal grief such as only a funeral brings. He feels the demon's hunger as well, melded as they are—but the demon has learned quickly. From sorrow or joy, from whatever intensity of emotion the humans have emitted to betray themselves, the specter wants more. The demon might feed on his tidbits of flesh, but the specter feeds on that which he failed to allow himself in life.

So the blind demon chases the gathering, knocking over the corpse in its coffin with barely a notice. The demon harries young and old, guided by the specter until that which was once a man has supped his fill on the torment of others.

At that the demon kills swiftly and skillfully, two instead of one after his unusually long pursuit. He unfolds his gruesomely long sixth finger to prepare his feast for eating.

Mollie didn't tell the tale to Harly, and she didn't tell of her uneasy nights. Just nerves, he'd say to that, and most likely be right. As for Adalee . . . "You got to make allowances for a woman with child," he'd said more than once, especially after learning how Adalee had sent her smitten husband walking down the holler after dark, hunting out a neighbor with a bit of sweet pawpaw butter left over from the previous fall.

"Just got to chink the logs," Harly said now, his voice full of pride and pulling Mollie back from her thoughts to the here of things on side of the hill and the new home perched there. *Her* new home. Logs all of the same size neatly dovetailed and debarked, a couple shuttered windows in front to take in the rising sun as it peeked over the top of the opposing ridge. Mollie could well imagine flowers lining the front of the house, some pansies and maybe some hollyhocks at the corners.

"It's beautiful," she said. "It's just purely beautiful. Can't hardly believe you done this all by yourself."

"Not all of it, you know that," Harly said, but he ducked his head at her pleasure and reached out to take her hand. They stood there that way a moment, long enough for Mollie to realize he'd taken the hand she'd cut only the day before, and she felt no pain of it. To remember her astonishment that morning when she'd opened her eyes and discovered not a gash, but healing pink skin. Pink, with a last splinter working its way out.

She'd always been quicker'n most anyone to heal up a cut. But this—

This went beyond *quick*. Way beyond.

Thinking of it, she almost missed the way Harly turned away from both her and the cabin, even while holding to her hand. "What is it?" she asked him.

"I been thinking," he said, and still wouldn't look at her. "So many men're headed toward Black Creek. Spend the week there, come back for the weekend . . . it's a new kind of living, Mollie. They got a company store with special prices for the men, and the kinda goods might elsewise take us years to collect. Things that could make life easier for you, like one of those special clothes washing tubs . . . glass for the windows . . ."

Mollie stood stunned. "Why, Harly," she said, and lost her words. Finally she managed to blurt, "is that what you *want*? To leave this place? To spend your time in the dark underground of those mines?"

Harly's fingers fumbled on her smaller hand; he said nothing.

Mollie felt her throat grow tight. She hadn't thought of him as a man with strong intent, with a drive for other than what he had. She'd thought of him as easily content—maybe *too* easily content, but there were so many worse things a man could be. . . . "Harly, should we have our babies, you'll miss all their growing up. You'll miss *me*—"

His hand tightened hard enough to choke off her words; he turned and looked at her for the first time, his dark hazel eyes earnest. "It's you I'm thinking of, Mollie Prater. What with your own brother talking about heading for the mines an' all . . . I wasn't sure it would suit you to be up here in this small place of ours, watching him bring in fine things for his own."

"Nonsense," Mollie said. "He don't even *have* his own yet, and when he does they're welcome to what he can give him. *This* is what we talked about together. This kind of living, like what was good enough for my folks and yours. Are you changed on that?"

Harly's face was all relief. "No, ma'am, I ain't. I don't care for the idea of being down in those mines, and I don't care for the thought of leavin' you here alone of the week. But it seemed right to offer it to you."

She shook her head. "I reckon to make a marriage right, we ought to live it each in the same place."

He grinned, tugging her onward. "I'm for that," he said. "Just as everyday as it gets, you and me. Say, come around back, I'll show you what I got started of the garden."

Mollie looked at her hand, suddenly just as alarmed as she'd been moments ago. Pink, healing flesh; not even prodding it brought out pain. This sudden healing fit was as far from *everyday* as Harly would ever imagine.

She curled her fingers around her palm and followed Harly out to the garden.

Pikeville wanted Ethan no more than Ethan wanted Pikeville. "Don't swagger," his superiors had warned him. "You won't be on the docks now."

Ethan had never thought to miss the stink of fish and humanity. Or the occasional reek of demon, providing him with such ample training and research grounds—*A Complete Guidebook to the Dock and Pier Demons of Northeastern Harbors,* his pet project while waiting for assignment. "Don't swagger," they'd said all right. "And don't neglect your studies in favor of compiling a guidebook for which only you see the need."

They had never forgiven him for blending so quickly into the city streets upon arrival from London, and a decently upper-class upbringing, he was sure of it. Why else send him . . . *here.* Here, where he'd already had several days of delay simply because the locals didn't know or trust him, professing complete ignorance of the existence of any such person as Miss Mollie Prater.

Meanwhile, his day's explorations revealed that the Pike County courthouse opposite his hotel held the crude records of the births of not one, not two, but seven Mollie Praters of the right age group. Not to mention the *Molly* Prater, and one *Moly* Prater he rather suspected was as much a candidate as the others. Not one of them lived in town; each and every one of them lived in a different holler, as if he could distinguish one of these innumerable wretched hollers from another.

Ethan made a disgruntled noise and stepped into the muddied street, glad that the strong spring sun of the region had dried a walkable path even if he'd packed—and worn—clothes meant for the more severe New York weather. He'd see if the hotel manager could be of any help. The man had become more cordial after several days of prompt payment for the tiny room he'd assigned to Ethan.

Otis was the manager's name, and he greeted Ethan at the desk with something akin to true welcome, his wild old-man's eyebrows twitching in a way that gave Ethan the impulse to flick them off Otis's forehead and stomp them dead. "There's been another one, did you hear?"

As if anyone else in this town would tell him anything, even for the pleasure of spreading gossip. Ethan shook his head. "Another what?" he asked, assuming it would be another in the Hatfield-McCoy feud killings that currently rocked the area. Roseanna Hatfield, modern-day Juliet, lived only a block away from the hotel.

"Set of beast murders, that's what," Otis said with a sense of triumph, seizing on this pristine gossip ground.

Ethan didn't have to fake his surprise. "Murders? Here?"

Otis nodded, leaning over the high counter in a conspiratorial manner. "Worse than murders. Bodies all tore up in strange ways, and it ain't the first time it's happened these past weeks."

"How many times, then? And the bodies . . . may I ask—"

"Four," Otis said, holding up the requisite number of fingers. "First time, just one killin'. After that, it's always been two at a time. And always at a gatherin'—it's been a christening, a funeral, and two weddin's, and didn't that man-beast chase everyone into a palsy before doing the killin'. And them bodies . . . ain't nothing like no one's seen before. There's the marks of the killin', and then afterward . . ." Otis leaned even farther over the counter, and Ethan automatically did the same, then recoiled as casually as possible at the man's breath. "Afterward, the man-beast makes cuts in the poor soul's back, and sucks out the innards!"

Ethan blinked. He remembered to put on a face of startled horror instead of intense thought, but his mind was already racing, filtering through hours of study and memorization. *Raksha demon?*

Except the Raksha was a fastidious diner who killed one victim at a time so as to be able to dine on the freshest possible tidbits. And those tidbits didn't consist of *innards* but of two small identical glands sitting atop the kidneys.

He wished he had all his books with him instead of just a few crucial volumes, so he could check his memory. And he wished, damn it, that he could find Mollie Prater.

He had the feeling his time had just run out.

That *her* time had just run out.

Mollie drew her thickly knitted shawl more tightly around her shoulders, not so much in cold as in sympathy. Below the gathering, thigh deep in cold spring river water, Lallie Beamis and Gerrald Mullins stood shivering, listening to Preacher Peavey and waiting the shock of a full dunking baptism. Mollie shifted toward Harly, who tipped his head down to hear her muttered words. "Believe I would have waited till warmer weather to get so faithful," she said.

Harly was quick about squelching his amusement with a stern whisper. "That ain't respectful, Mollie."

Her father turned around to eye them, so Mollie shut her lips on her reply. If Preacher Peavey caught wind of her disrespect, he'd feature her in a sermon quick enough. Then it would be *her* having to renew her faith with a dunking.

She heard a scuffling in the woods to the side of them where sycamores, willows, and raspberry canes lined the banks of the river in thick cover her gaze couldn't pierce. It came again, and she thought there was a faint grunt as well; she stared at the spot, frowning. Harly gave her a puzzled look, and she kept her voice as low as possible. "Didn't you hear—"

With a sudden bellow, something of gray mottled and flaky skin burst from the underbrush. Gasping, Mollie clutched at Harly; he gave her a little shove. "Run!" he shouted at her, but the creature was already loping manlike toward the small clutch of the Bolling spinster sisters, and Mollie couldn't help a horrified stare as the sisters broke apart and ran screaming for their lives— Myrtle, the oldest of them, darted right for the river and fell in the water at the bank.

Oddly, the beast veered away from her, snarling and hooting and slavering, knocking elderly Mr. Carter on his back but not stopping to hurt him further. Instead it lumbered up the bank at Mollie's own family, scattering them—and veered again, heading at the church where several families had taken shelter.

Mollie just stood there, so flummoxed by its massive man-form, by the odd twisty horns curling down the back of its misshapen head like hair, the odd, matted texture of its skin, the clumpy look of its hands . . . but somehow the thing that just plain turned her stomach was the weepy old scar tissue of its eye sockets above flat nostrils, looking like a man with his nose cut off. She gagged at the sight of it, and suddenly realized that Harly had all but scooped her up and run off with her. His fingers dug painfully into her arm as he tugged to no avail. "Mollie, you got to *run!*"

She crashed into the woods with no particular path to follow and someone's dying scream at their heels. "Harly!" she shouted at his back, knowing that scream could have been her mommy, could have been her little brother. "Harly, we can't leave them—"

He slowed. Stopped, and turned fiercely on her; it didn't escape her how he'd stayed by her side, her and her stupid gaping self rooted to the spot. Now he said, "Mollie Prater, you got a case of the crazies? That thing's worse'n a chicken-eating dog in a henhouse!"

"But—"

Nose to nose they were, all-out yelling at each other like they'd never done before, barely listening to each other anyway.

"But, nothin'! I go back there, it'll be with a gun in my hands!"

Mollie cocked her head, held up a hand. "Harly, wait—"

"A gun in *both* hands—!"

"*Listen!*" she shouted back at him, practically on her tiptoes to put herself on a closer level to his.

They glared at each other in silence, and eventually Harly realized just that. The silence. No screaming, no inhuman hooting and grunting. "It's gone," Mollie whispered.

Harly only shook his head. He let her take his hand and lead him back toward the church, angling through the woods.

They came upon the body without warning. It wore Gert Peavey's pretty flowered dress . . . its radically twisted head had no face to speak of. Two discreet blood trails ran down the exposed back. Mollie went silent and white, and looking at the thing that used to be the preacher's wife, said hoarsely, "I got to find my kin—"

"Mollie!" Harly shouted, yanking her back and throwing himself out in front of her—between her and the beast thing, which crouched silently at the edge of the church clearing, blending right into the trees as it dipped its uncurled sixth and seventh fingers into the back of another limp body, routing around with concentration until the long-clawed fingers came up with a bit of reddish brown organ on them, a tidbit it licked off like a fastidious cat.

It hesitated, sniffed the wind just once, and turned its blind face to them, for an instant—before it charged. Charged hard and true and shaking the ground with its steps, and to Mollie's horror, Harly stepped out to meet it.

It slapped him away like a fly and came for Mollie.

Mollie, feeling absurd and small and terrified, snatched up a dead limb and stepped aside from the charge to whack the creature a good one, a blow that rocked her arm—and stunned the creature long enough for her to dart past and grab Harly as he stumbled to his feet—and this time they found the church path and they ran good and hard and long until Harly couldn't run any longer.

He stopped, bent over with one hand on his knee and the other on his side where the awful inhuman man-beast had hit him, and he stared at her with a look in his eye that Mollie found just as alarming as the creature itself.

Then she followed his gaze, and discovered she still held the dead limb. Not any old dead limb, not of the size a bitty thing like herself ought to have been able to run with. A limb as thick around as her thigh, freshly broke from the tree; she suddenly felt the weight of it.

She'd torn it from the tree. She'd wielded it against the savage man-beast. She'd run with it, kept up with Harly, *surpassed* Harly. She stared at it.

He stared at her.

"—Mollie Prater," said the whisper on the streets. "Trickle Creek Holler." Loud enough for even Ethan to hear, to go to Otis and to hear the old man say it. "Mollie Prater. Whomped that creature with a stick and lived to tell the tale. Saved her man-to-be. An' tomorrow they'll be married."

Tomorrow. He had to get there before the demon. Before more people died. Before they lost a Slayer who didn't even know she'd been called.

Mollie wrapped a damp-palmed grip around her bouquet, only to have her mother gently remove it from her hands and set it aside. "You'll bruise 'em," Lila said, carefully tweaking a flower into place. It was too early in the season for much but tender early blooms, spring beauties with some phlox and bright yellow coltsfoot. "I swear, Mollie, when did you become such a fidget?"

Mollie turned to the wavy image in the speckled mirror, twitching at the blouse of her best dress, a blue-flowered print she'd only worn three times and which now bore slick satin ribbon bows at the cleavage and hem. Her hair was caught up in a ribbon of the same material, and her shoes were new for the occasion. She plucked at the bow by her cleavage and thought of Adalee's sheets fresh-laid on her wedding bed.

Lila slapped lightly at her fingers. "Leave it be. Lord have mercy! Let those menfolk get theirselves ready out there before you pluck yourself apart."

Lonnie and Ferd were out setting up sprays of bright yellow forsythia and pussy willow branches, and her daddy had gone to fetch the visiting preacher. But Mollie, rather than put herself to work outside or in the kitchen, was relegated to the back room where her parents slept, hidden away until the moment of the wedding itself.

"I'd ruther be hanging laundry," she said. "Or hoeing the garden. Or—"

"Harly will be here soon," Lila said, betraying her own emotion as she fussed with Mollie's hair—primping, touching, in the end not changing a thing.

Harly, and the cabin that would be theirs. Harly and the fresh-sheeted bed. Harly, with a baby at his knee . . . Mollie stopped fussing with her dress long enough to envision it, to play it out in her mind's eye like pretty pictures. After today, her whole life would change, and she was ready for it.

Someone gave a discreet knock on the door, and Lila let out her breath in a gust of relief. "About time!" She scooped up the bouquet, pressed it into Mollie's hands, and guided her daughter to the door with a firm hand betwixt Mollie's shoulders. On the porch, they hesitated, looking out at the gathering that filled the front yard and spilled over toward the chickens and the toolshed. Neighbors, friends, family—people she barely knew, besides. People who needed a joyful thing after a hard run of tragedies. Adalee was up near the preacher; she gave Mollie a wave as though only the two of them could see it.

At the edge of it all, a city-looking man sat on a cranky-eared mule, a cap pulled down over his forehead and determination on his face; it gave him a jut-jawed appearance.

She had no idea who he was.

Let him enjoy the wedding if he chose. She forgot his strange presence and found Harly standing up near the preacher with a foolish grin on his face; the grin grew bigger when he saw her looking.

"Go on," her mommy said in an understanding whisper, her nudge subtle against Mollie's back. "Go be growed up, Mollie mine."

Mollie stepped off the porch.

She couldn't say then if time had slowed, or if it had sped up so fast...

With a warbled hooting, the matted-skin beast-man charged from the woods and straight into the middle of the assembly. The stranger's mule reared and dumped him; Harly shouted a command, and two of his cousins lifted rifles they must have had on hand against this very moment.

Mollie found herself over by the toolshed, having dodged easily through the panic of the yard, already eyeing the man-beast's likely course. "Adalee!" she shouted, trying to grab the attention of her awkwardly pregnant friend—but Adalee stood dazed in the middle of it all, one hand on her belly and the other stretched beseechingly in midair, as if it were making up its mind which way she should run.

"This doesn't make sense," someone muttered, and she knew without turning that those clipped syllables belonged to the stranger from the mule. "It's *blind,* bloody *blind,* and it's herding these people like cattle—"

She turned to glare at him. "You know about this man-beast?"

His shoulder was muddied from his fall, but his cap remained in place, its angle more rakish than before. He met her gaze without defiance or apology, although he pretty much owed her one or the other just for being here. "Raksha demon, actually," he said, raising his voice above the sudden bout of screaming.

Mollie flinched against the toolshed, jerking around as Harly yelled, "Shoot it!" somehow knowing it was the wrong thing to do—and watched in horror as the man-beast bounded to Harly's cousins and laid them both out with a single blow of enormous strength. *Dead.* Only a broken neck sat anyone's shoulders at that angle—

"You're the one who can stop this," the man said, coming up closer behind her, his manner as familiar as if he'd known her all

MORNGLOM DREAMING 243

her life and then some. "You're the *only* one." His hand landed on her shoulder, a touch beyond familiar. "You're the Slayer, and you were born to—"

She whirled around, catching him up by the throat with one hand, shoving him hard against the toolshed. His cap hit the ground; his face turned dark red. His struggles were useless. His booted toe hit her shin, and Mollie looked down.

She'd taken him right off his feet.

Despite the differences in their sizes, in their man's and woman's strengths, she'd taken him right off his feet.

She dropped him, aghast, the world swirling around her in a series of screams and hideous hooting and two already dead. "Mornglom dreams," she whispered. Dark predawn dreaming of screams and roaring and startling smells . . .

"It started a few weeks ago," he croaked, relentless, one hand rubbing her finger marks at his throat. "You're stronger, you're quicker, you heal like a bloody miracle—"

"Shut up!" she shouted at him. "You're tetched in the head, you don't belong here—"

"Ethan. And neither," said the crazy man, pointing to the yard, "does *that!*"

The man-beast. The *demon*. It slowed by the scattered chickens; it turned its blind face toward the center of the yard.

"Adalee!" Harly shouted, even as Mollie silently mouthed the same. "Adalee, look out!" He lunged into the yard from his safe spot behind a hemlock, throwing himself between the demon and Adalee. Mollie should have screamed, but it stuck in her throat, making her whole body quiver as the demon struck Harly down and turned back to make the kill. To kill *Harly*.

"*You're the Slayer,*" Ethan croaked beside her, but he needn't have said a word. Mollie had already snatched the scythe from beside the shed and fit it to her hands, quickly realizing that the curve of handle and blade made it an unwieldy weapon. She stepped on the end of the thin metal blade, snapping off the narrowest part of the hook so the remainder was short and wicked and jagged at the end, and then she charged up to the monster from behind and whipped that scythe at the backs of his legs with hours of weed cutting behind her every move. Weed cutting and something else, the speed and strength she shouldn't have and yet did.

Stringy muscle parted with the creak of dry, tearing leather; the demon staggered. It left Harly and whirled on her, its curling-horn hair snapping to stand on end, its extra fingers straight and splayed and reaching for her.

She should have stumbled backward. She should have screamed or fainted or fallen back on her bottom, helpless in fear. She should have died.

She killed it.

Afterward came a complete and sudden silence, as if the whole world stopped itself to take note of her deed. Not a sob, not a cough, not a rustle. Mollie felt the stare of every single person there, people who had gathered for her wedding and found themselves at a slaughter. But she couldn't tear her eyes away from the dead thing at her feet, not for the many long moments of silence. Then, finally, she dropped the scythe on top of it and turned away.

The movement became a signal; someone let out a sob and then everyone started talking at once. Mollie looked down at her own hands, expecting to find gobs of blood and killing gore. They were clean and ready to clasp her bridegroom's. But as she finally raised her head and looked around, finding the members of her family—*safe*—finding Harly and Adalee—*safe*—and seeing that for all the fuss and screaming, no one after Harly's two cousins had died, she saw too the first glimmerings of something that scared her more than even the demon.

They were uncertain of her. They were wary of her. *Harly* was wary of her.

When little Betts Mullins shrieked and pointed her way in fear, Mollie's heart fell away. But from the direction of the toolshed came Ethan's still croaky voice. "What the bloody—" She whirled around, realizing the pointing wasn't for her at all and terrified at the thought of the demon climbing to its feet behind her.

No demon. Instead, a wraithlike hant, all wispy and wavering murk—until, even as Mollie gaped, the thing's facial features jumped into clear, hard definition.

As one, the gathering gasped. Ethan eased up behind Mollie and with leftover harshness whispered, "They know him. Who—?"

Someone else answered, not even knowing the question had been posed. "Asa Peavey! Mean as a skunk even from the grave!"

"Preacher Peavey's grandfather," Mollie added in a murmur, suddenly more trusting of the only body here—stranger or no—who hadn't eyed her so doubtfully. "He passed before I was born, but I hear tell his heart weren't nothing but mean."

Even now, the hant's visage was distorted with anger; it gave a wordless howl of rage that ended, to Molly's ears, in something like a sob. "You've kilt it!" the hant moaned, as much anguish as anger as it looked down upon the mottly heap of dead demon. "I wandered so long before I found it, and you've kilt it!" As it looked up, its features wavered. When they solidified again, its expression had changed—become crafty and determined. "I'll take one of you, then. I'll by-damn take what I need!"

A high, scared-to-thin woman's voice said, *"She* done it! Not us!" and though Molly whirled to see who had betrayed her, she found them *all* looking at her—and her family full of worry, keeping silence. Half convinced.

Ethan stepped up beside Molly—not like Harly, tall and broad shouldered and full of strength, but with a kind of confidence that made her desperately glad for the company. "What," he said with perfect calm, "is it that you need?"

"What I never had," the hant said, as if it were perfectly obvious. "Them things I never felt. All them high feelin's, good and bad. All I got on my own is mad and I'm *wicked* tired of mad."

"Ah," said Ethan, his matter-of-fact tone startling her into taking her gaze from the hant and latching it onto him. He'd resettled his cap, she saw, and he kept a thoughtful look about his fox-narrow features. "Classic situation, really," he said to Mollie, as if they were the only two there with the hant. "An angry ghost who felt little else in life, now doomed to go hunting for what he missed when he was alive. I suggest you all forgive him."

Dumbfounded, Mollie just said, "Do *what?*"

"If he was an angry man, he left a lot of people angry *at* him, feelings they passed down to their children. And if he wasn't still blocking those other emotions, he'd feel them for himself. Forgive him, and he can feel his own feelings instead of hunting down weddings and stealing joy."

"Well, ain't you the smart one," Mollie muttered, confounded by the man all over again.

Ethan gave her a rakish grin, one that vanished as he turned to the gathering. "Forgive him!"

As one, they stared back in stubborn resentment. The hant laughed. Anger-tinged, knowing laughter. "I'll take what I want, be it bodies to use or feelin's to have," he said. "I always had to."

"Ain't that the truth!" Granny Lil shouted at him. "You was a bastid!"

"No!" Mollie said. "When he uses me up, what do you think he'll do? Go away, nice and quiet?"

"He'll come for someone else," Ethan said, quite sensibly. "And another, and another. He'll haunt this community until there's no one left to haunt. But now—look at him now. What a pathetic excuse for a man he is. What a miserable man he must have been! Who among you would choose to live without love? Forgive him, and let him go." But then he made a wry bit of a face, scratching up under his hatband at the ear. Mollie's hand print still stained his throat. "Of course, it won't work unless you mean it."

"Miserable!" the hant said; Mollie would have said he'd sputtered, if he'd only had lips to do it with. "Miserable! I had a good farm!"

"You near starved every winter," Harly's daddy observed.

"I had a family!"

"They hated you," spat Granny Lil.

"I had a long life!"

"And you took it out on every one of us who was alive to bear it," said Uncle Erd, arguably the oldest man in Pike County. "You ain't worth hating, you was so miserable. I forgive you, and you're welcome to it."

The ghost's marbled features wavered into a stricken expression. "You can't do that! I helped this demon kill people!"

Granny Lil said, "Only 'cause you was too miserable to do it your own self." She scratched under her bosom in an unselfconscious gesture and said, "I reckon I don't want to bear the burden of hatin' you anymore."

Harly stepped up beside Mollie; she felt a little leap of hope come in to erase the despair she'd felt at his earlier wary expression.

"I've heared tales of you all my life," he said to Asa Peavey's hant. "I guess they're something to marvel at, that a man so mean as you lived in this world. I thank you for those tales."

It was the final moment to free them all—Mollie's neighbors and kin alike. In a babble of overlapping shouts, they forgave the hant that had been Asa Peavey.

The hant gave a screeching wail and with a final *pop!* that Mollie felt inside her ears, he disappeared.

After a startlingly awkward silence full of people looking at Mollie, the assembled kin and neighbors quietly left, gathering the two dead young men and slipping away with muttered good-byes, as if some silent voice had told them there would be no wedding here today . . . or ever.

Mollie turned to Harly. Tall, broad shouldered, straightforward Harly. Harly who wanted a normal mountain life—and a normal wife. Harly with the wariness back in his face, and sadness in his eyes. He looked at her; he looked at the demon—that which had killed so many and now lay slain by her hand. He knew as well as she that her life had changed forever, and it showed on his face; Mollie felt it deep, in that same place that sent her dreams.

Only the dreams had never hurt so much, never felt so desperate.

Harly opened his mouth to say something; he shook his head instead. And then he turned and walked away.

Mollie turned her hands over, checking them again for some sign of the battle they'd won.

The old gash on her palm wasn't even pink anymore.

"Everything I ever wanted," she said, dazed. "Everything I planned for. My life . . . It's all changed." *Right in this moment.* Or maybe when she'd first felt the tingle of her own blood, or when

Lonnie dropped the pitchfork . . . or when Harly walked away. "It won't never be the same."

Ethan took her strong hands in his, hesitated, and gave a firm shake of his head.

"No, it won't," he said. "You're the Slayer."

She didn't know what it meant. But she knew, somehow, that he was right. And she knew—somehow—he would be there with her through it all.

ABOUT THE AUTHORS

LAURA J. BURNS and MELINDA METZ are obsessed with *Buffy the Vampire Slayer*. In fact, it was the chock-full-of-subtext writing on *Buffy* that inspired them to try their collective hand at television-writing. So far they have written two pilots and spent a season as staff writers on the late, great TV show *Roswell*. In the book world, they created the Roswell High series written by Melinda and edited by Laura. They have relished this opportunity to contribute to the world of *Buffy*.

After obtaining a degree in wildlife illustration and environmental education, DORANNA DURGIN spent a number of years deep in the Appalachian Mountains, where she learned not to get cocky about Things That Go Bump in the Night. When she emerged, it was as a writer who found herself irrevocably tied to the natural world and its creatures (even the ones no one else sees). Doranna hangs around with three Cardigan Welsh Corgis and an amazingly sane Arabian, and drags her saddle wherever she goes. Her online home is at doranna.net.

JANE ESPENSON was on the writing staff of *Buffy the Vampire Slayer* since the third season of the show, and was a show coexecutive producer. She has also written a number of comic books and episodes of other programs, including *Buffy*'s brother-show, *Angel*.

REBECCA RAND KIRSHNER is a bon vivant. Ask anyone.

YVONNE NAVARRO is a Chicago-area novelist who has written a bunch of stuff, including novels, movie and television novelizations, and short stories. Some readers might not be surprised to learn that her first published novel, *AfterAge,* was about the end of world as orchestrated by vampires. In her second novel, *deadrush,* she worked on zombies; both *AfterAge* and *deadrush* were nominated for the Bram Stoker Award. *Final Impact* (which won the 1997 CWIP Award for Excellence in Adult Fiction and the *Rocky Mountain News* "Unreal Worlds" Award for Best Horror Paperback of 1997) and its follow-up, *Red Shadows,* tell the story of some really nifty people struggling to survive when the Earth is nearly destroyed by a celestial disaster. Yvonne wrote the novelizations of both *Species* and *Species II,* as well as *Buffy the Vampire Slayer: The Willow Files,* Vols. I and II, and *Aliens: Music of the Spears.* She also authored *The First Name Reverse Dictionary,* a reference book for writers.

She studies martial arts and loves Arizona (she has been scheming to take over the Phoenix area for years), dogs, champagne, and dark chocolate. Visit her site at www.yvonnenavarro.com, where you can read more of her stuff and see funny photos, plus find out how to get books autographed and keep up to date. Come visit!

MICHAEL REAVES is an Emmy award-winning television writer and a *New York Times* best-selling novelist.

GREG RUCKA is the author of seven novels, including five about bodyguard Atticus Kodiak and his companions. He is the author of several short stories and comic books, and wrote the adventures of Batman in Detective Comics, and the adventures of Tara Chase in Queen & Country. His favorite slayer is Faith.

MEET THE NEWEST CHOSEN ONE IN
KIERSTEN WHITE'S *SLAYER!*

Into every generation a Slayer is born....

Thanks to Buffy, the famous (and infamous) Slayer that Nina's father died protecting, Nina is not only the newest Chosen One—she's the last Slayer ever. Period.

As Nina hones her skills at the Watcher's Academy, the boarding school for Watchers-in-training and where she grew up, there's plenty to keep her occupied: her cute Watcher who she may or may not still have a crush on, a monster fighting ring, a demon who eats happiness, a shadowy figure that keeps popping up in Nina's dreams . . .

But it's not until bodies start turning up that Nina's new powers will truly be tested—because someone she loves might be next.

One thing is clear: Being Chosen is easy. Making choices is hard.

Read on for a sneak peek at Kiersten White's highly anticipated addition to the Buffyverse!

Of all the awful things demons do, keeping Latin alive when it deserves to be a dead language might be the worst.

To say nothing of ancient Sumerian. And ancient Sumerian translated into Latin? Diabolic. My tongue trips over pronunciation as I painstakingly work through the page in front of me. I used to love my time in the library, surrounded by the work of generations of previous Watchers. But ever since the most recent time the world almost ended—sixty-two days ago, to be exact—I can barely sit still. I fidget. Tap my pencil. Bounce my toes against the floor. I want to go for a run. I don't know why the anxiety has hit me differently this time, after all the horror and tragedy I've seen before. There *is* one possible reason that tugs at my brain, but . . .

"That can't be right." I peer at my own writing. "The shadowed one will rise and the world will tickle before him?"

"I do hate being tickled," Rhys says, leaning back and stretching. His curly brown hair has once again defied its strict part. It flops over his forehead, softening the hard line of his eyebrows, which are perpetually drawn close to his glasses in thought or concern. After we finish this morning's lessons, I'll tidy up my small medical center, and Rhys will train for combat with Artemis.

I shake out my hands, needing to move *something*. Maybe I really will go for a run. No one would miss me. Or maybe I'll ask if I can join combat training. They've never let me, but I haven't asked in years. I really want to hit something, and I don't know why, and it scares me.

It could be the demonic prophecies of doom I've been reading all morning, though. I scratch out my botched translation. "As far as apocalypses go, tickling's not the worst way to die."

Imogen clears her throat, but her indulgent smile softens the severity. "Can we get back to your translation, Nina? And, Rhys, I want a full report on half-human, half-demon taxonomy."

Rhys ducks his head, blushing. He's the only one here who's in line to be a full Watcher, which means he can join the Council one day. Someday he'll be in charge, part of the governing body of the Council. He wears that weight in everything he does. He's the first one in the library and the last one out, and he trains almost as much as Artemis.

Watchers were meant to guide Slayers—the Chosen Ones specially endowed to fight demons—but over the centuries we evolved to be more hands-on. Watchers have to make the hard decisions, and sometimes the hard decisions include weapons. Swords. Spells. Knives.

Guns, in my father's case.

Not all of us train, though. We all take our education seriously, but there's slightly less pressure for me. I'm just the castle medic, which doesn't rate high on the importance scale. Learning how to take lives beats knowing how to save them.

But being the medic doesn't get me out of Prophecies of Doom 101. I push away the Latin Sumerian Tickle Apocalypse. "Imogen," I whine. "Can I get something a little less difficult? Please?"

She gives me a long-suffering sigh. Imogen wasn't supposed to be a teacher. But she's all we've got now, on account of the regular teachers being blown up. She teaches for a few hours every morning, and the rest of her time is spent managing the Littles.

Her blond ponytail swings limply as she stands and searches the far bookshelf. I hold back a triumphant smile. Imogen is always nicer to me than to anyone else. Actually, everyone here is. I try not to take advantage, but if they're going to treat me like the castle pet just because I'm not all with the stabby stab, at least I should get some perks.

The shelf Imogen is searching is technically off-limits, but since Buffy—the Slayer who single-handedly destroyed almost our entire organization—broke all magic on earth a couple months ago, it doesn't matter anymore. The books that used to pose threats such as demonic possession or summoning ancient hellgods or giving you, like, a *really* bad paper cut are now as benign as any other book.

But that doesn't make them any easier to translate.

"Magic *is* still broken, right?" I ask as Imogen runs her fingers down the spine of a book that once killed an entire roomful of Watchers in the fifteenth century. It's been two months without a drop of magical energy. For an organization that was built on magic, it hasn't been an easy adjustment. I wasn't taught to use magic, but I have a very healthy respect-for-slash-terror-of it. So it's creepy seeing Imogen treat that particular tome like anything else on the shelf.

"Fresh out of batteries and no one can find the right size." Rhys scowls at his text as though insulted by the demon he's reading about. "When Buffy breaks something, she breaks it good. Personally, I think that if confronted with the Seed of Wonder—the source of all magic on earth, a genuine mystical miracle—I might opt to, say, study it. Research. Really think through my options. There had to be another way to avert that particular apocalypse."

"Buffy sees, Buffy destroys," I mutter. Her name feels almost like a swear word on my tongue. We don't say it aloud in my family. Then again, we don't say much in my family at all, besides "Have you seen my best dagger?" and "Where are our stake-carving supplies?" and "Hello, my twin daughters, it is I, your mother, and I love one of you better than the other and chose to save the good twin first when a fire was about to kill you both."

Okay, not that last one. Because again: We don't talk much. Living under the same roof isn't as cozy as it sounds when that roof covers a massive castle.

"Think of all we could have learned," Rhys says mournfully, "if I had had even an hour with the Seed of Wonder. . . ."

"In her defense, the world was ending," Imogen says.

"In her not defense, she was the reason the world was ending," I counter. "And now magic is dead."

Imogen shrugs. "No more hellmouths or portals. No more demons popping in for vacations and sightseeing."

I snort. "Foodie tours of Planet Human are canceled. Sorry, demonic dimensions. Of course, it also means no current tourists can get back to their home-sweet-hellholes."

Rhys scowls, pulling off his glasses and polishing them. "You're joking about the disruption and destruction of all the research we've compiled on demonic traveling, portals, dimensions, gateways, and hellmouths. None of it is current anymore. Even if I wanted to understand how things have changed, I couldn't."

"See? Buffy hurts everyone. Poor Rhys. No books on this subject." I pat his head.

Imogen tosses a huge volume on the table. "And yet your homework still isn't done. Try this one." A poof of dust blows outward from the book; I flinch away and cover my nose.

She grimaces. "Sorry."

"No, it's fine. I actually haven't had an asthma attack in a while." It's fine that my asthma mysteriously disappeared the same day Buffy destroyed magic, the world almost ended, and I got showered in interdimensional demonic goo. Totally fine. Has nothing to do with the demon. Neither does the fact that I'm desperate to go running or start training or do anything with my body besides snuggle up and read, which used to be its primary occupation.

I pull down my sweater sleeve over my hand and carefully wipe the leather cover. "'The Apocalypses of . . . Arcturius the Farsighted'? Sounds like the dude just needed a better prescription for glasses."

Rhys leans close, peering curiously. "I haven't read that volume." He sounds jealous.

Notes have been scrawled in the margins, the handwriting changing as it moves through the centuries. On the last few pages there are orange fingerprints, like someone was reading while eating Cheetos. The Watchers before me have made their own notes, commenting and filling in details. Seeing their work overwhelms me with a sense of responsibility. It's not every sixteen-year-old girl who can trace her family's calling back through the centuries of helping Slayers, fighting demons, and otherwise saving the world.

I find a good entry. "Did you know that in 1910, one of the Merryweathers prevented an octopus uprising? A leviathan demon gave them sentience and they were going to overthrow us! Merryweather doesn't give many details. It appears they defeated them with . . ." I squint. "Lemon. And butter. I think this is a recipe."

Imogen taps on the book. "Just translate the last ten prophecies, how about?"

I get to work. Rhys occasionally asks Imogen questions, and by the time our class period is almost over, he has what looks like half the extensive shelves piled on our groaning table. In years past, Rhys and I wouldn't have studied together. He'd have been in classes with the other future Council hopefuls. But there are so few of us now, we've had to relax some of the structure and tradition. Not all of it, though. Without tradition, what would we be? Just a bunch of weirdos hiding in a castle studying the things that no one else wants to know about. Which I guess is what we are *with* tradition too. But knowing I'm part of a millennia-long battle against the forces of evil (and apparently octopuses) makes it much more meaningful.

Buffy and the Slayers might have turned their backs on the Watchers, rejecting our guidance and counsel, but we haven't turned our backs on the world. Normal people can go on living, oblivious and happy, because of *our* hard work. And I'm proud of that. Even when it means I have to translate dumb prophecies, and even if I've wondered more and more the last few years if the *way* the Watchers and Slayers fight evil isn't always right.

The library door slams open and my twin sister, Artemis, walks in. She takes a deep breath and scowls, crossing past me and tugging open the ancient window. It groans in protest, but, as with all things, Artemis accomplishes her goal. She pulls out one of my inhalers from her pocket and sets it on the table beside me. Everything in this castle runs because of Artemis. She is a force of nature. An angry but efficient force of nature.

"Hello to you, too," I say with a smile.

She tugs my hair. We both have red waves, though hers are always pulled back into a brutal ponytail. I have a lot more time for moisturizing than she does. Her face is like looking in a mirror—if that mirror were a prophecy of who I'd be in another life. Her freckles are darker from spending so much time outside. Her gray eyes more intense, her jawline somehow stronger. Her shoulders are straighter, her arms are more defined, and her posture is less snuggly and more I-will-destroy-you-if-it-comes-to-that.

In short, Artemis is the strong twin. The powerful twin. The chosen twin. And I am . . .

The one who got left behind.

I don't just mean the fire, either. The moment when my mother was forced to choose to save one of us from the terrifying flames—and chose Artemis—was definitely life changing. But even after that, even after I managed to survive, my mother kept choosing her. Artemis was chosen for testing and training. Artemis was given responsibilities and duties and a vital role in Watcher society. And I was left behind on the fringes. I only sort of matter now because so many of us are dead. Artemis always would have mattered. And the truth is, I get it.

I was born into Watcher society, but Artemis *deserves* to be here.

She sits next to me, pulling out her notebook and opening it to today's to-do list. It's in microscopic handwriting and goes past the first page and onto at least one more. No one in this castle does more than Artemis. "Listen," she says, "I might have hurt Jade."

I look up from where I'm almost finished with this book. Every other prophecy had margin notes detailing how that particular apocalypse was averted. I idly wonder what it means that this is the last prophecy. Did Arcturius the Farsighted finally get glasses, or was this apocalypse so apocalypse-y that he couldn't see past it? It also has no Watcher notes. And Watchers are meticulous. If it doesn't have notes, that means it hasn't been averted yet.

But my own castle emergencies are far more pressing. "And by 'might have hurt Jade,' you mean . . ."

Artemis shrugs. "Definitely did."

On cue, Jade limps in. She picks up her tirade midargument. "—and just because magic is broken, doesn't mean that I should be Artemis's punching bag! I know my father worked in special ops, but I don't want to. I was good at magic! I am not good at this!"

"No one is, next to Artemis," Rhys says. His voice is quiet and without judgment, but we all freeze. It's one of the things we don't talk about. How Artemis is inarguably the best, and yet she's the assistant and Rhys is the official golden boy.

Watchers excel at research, record keeping, and not talking about things. The entire organization is ever-so-British. Though technically Artemis and I are American. We lived in California and then Arizona before coming here. Rhys, Jade, and Imogen—who all grew up in London—still laugh when I treat rain like a novelty. It's been eight years in England and Ireland, but I *adore* rain and green and all things non-desert.

Jade flops down on the other side of me, hauling her ankle up onto my lap. I rotate it for range of movement.

"That one translates as 'Slayer,'" Artemis says, peering over my shoulder. She crosses out where I had mistranslated a word as "killer." Same difference.

Jade yelps. "Ouch!"

"Sorry. Nothing is broken, but it's swelling already. I think it's a mild sprain." I glance at Artemis and she looks away, guessing my thoughts as she so often can. She knows I'm going to tell her there is no reason to train this hard. To hurt each other. Instead of rehashing our usual debate, I point to my translation. "What about this word?"

"Protector," Artemis says.

"That's cheating," Imogen trills from where she's reshelving.

"It doesn't count as cheating. We're practically the same person!" No one calls me on the lie. Artemis shouldn't have to do my homework on top of everything else, but she helps without being asked. It's how we work.

"Any word from Mom?" I ask as casually as I can manage, probing around the topic even more gently than I'm probing Jade's ankle.

"Nothing new since Tuesday. She should finish up South America in the next few days, though." Artemis planned our mother's whole scouting mission. I haven't heard so much as a word from her since she left seven weeks ago, but Artemis merits regular updates.

"Can you focus?" Jade snaps. She was on assignment in Scotland keeping tabs on Buffy and her Slayer army antics. It didn't do us much good. Buffy still managed to trigger an almost-apocalypse. Now that Jade's back at the castle without any magic, she's not happy about it, and she lets us know.

Frequently.

"Rhys," I say, mindful that Artemis would do it in a heartbeat, but her to-do list is already super full and I don't want to add to it, "can you go to my clinic and get my sprain pack?"

Rhys stands. He shouldn't have to run my errands. He ranks far above me in pecking order, but he puts friendship before hierarchy. He's my favorite in the castle besides Artemis. Not that there's a tremendous amount of competition. Rhys, Jade, and Artemis are the only other teens. Imogen is in her early twenties. The three Littles are still preschoolers. And the Council—all four of them—aren't exactly BFF material. "Where is it?" he asks.

"It's right next to the stitches pack, behind the concussions pack."

"I'll be right back."

He saunters away. The medical clinic is actually a large supply closet in the opposite wing that I've claimed as my own. The training room is amazing, naturally. We prioritize hitting, not healing. While we're waiting for Rhys, I elevate Jade's ankle by propping it on top of books that used to contain the blackest spells imaginable but now are used as paperweights.

George Smythe, the youngest of the Littles, bursts into the library. He buries his face in Imogen's skirt and tugs on her long sleeves. "Imo. Come play."

Imogen puts him on her hip. During teaching hours, Ruth Zabuto is in charge of the Littles, but she is as old as sin and far less pleasant. I don't blame George for preferring Imogen.

"Are you done?" she asks me.

I hold up my paper triumphantly. "Got it!"

Child of Slayer
Child of Watcher
The two become one
The one becomes two
Girls of fire
Protector and Hunter
One to mend the world
And one to tear it asunder

"There's a postscript, like Arcturius can't help but comment on his own creepy-ass prophecy. 'When all else ends, when hope perishes alongside wonder, her darkness shall rise and all shall be eaten.'"

Imogen snorts. "Devoured. Not eaten."

"In my defense, I'm hungry. Did I get the rest?"

She nods. "With help."

"Well, even with Artemis's help, it doesn't make sense. And it doesn't have any calamari recipes." I tuck my papers back into the book.

Rhys returns with the supplies just as the other two Littles break into the library and swarm Imogen. She's the busiest person in the castle, other than Artemis, who has already left to prepare lunch for everyone. Sometimes I wish my sister belonged as much to me as she does to everyone else.

Rhys strides toward me with the sprain pack. Little George runs at his legs, and Rhys trips just before he gets to me. The pack flies out of his hands. Without thinking I lunge and save the kit in midair with one hand, the whole motion feeling surprisingly effortless for my usually uncoordinated self.

"Good catch," Rhys says. I'd be offended by his surprise if I weren't experiencing another ripple of anxiety. It *was* a good catch. Way too good for me.

"Yeah, lucky," I say, letting out an awkward laugh. I break the ice pack and wrap it into place around Jade's ankle. "Twenty minutes on, an hour off. I'll rewrap you when the ice comes off. That will help with the swelling. And rest it as much as possible."

"Not a problem." Jade leans back with her eyes closed. She's substituted all the time she used to spend on magic with sleeping.

I know it's been rough on her—it's been rough on everyone, having the entire world change, yet again. But we do what Watchers do: We keep going.

My phone beeps. We avoid contact with the outside world. Paranoia is a permanent result of having all your friends and family blown up. But one person has this number and he's the highlight of our tenure here in the forest outside a sleepy Irish coastal town. "Cillian's almost here with the supplies."

Rhys perks up. "Do you need help?"

"Yes. I don't know how I'd manage without you. It's absolutely essential that you come out with me and flirt with your boyfriend while I check over the boxes."

The great hall of the castle, always chilly, is lit with the late-afternoon sun. The stained-glass windows project squares of blue, red, and green. I fondly pat the massive oak door as I step out into the crisp autumn air. The castle is drafty, with questionable plumbing and dire electrical problems. Most of the windows don't open, and those that do leak. Half of the rooms are in disrepair, the entire dorm wing is more a repository for junk than a living space, and we can't even go in the section where the tower used to be because it isn't safe.

But this castle saved our lives and preserved what few of us are left. And so I love it.

Out in the meadow—which has finally recovered from having a castle magically dropped into the middle of it two years ago—old Bradford Smythe, my great-uncle, is sword fighting with horrible Wanda Wyndam-Pryce. Though sword *bickering* would be more accurate, since they pause between each block and strike to debate proper stance. The mystery of the Littles escaping is solved. Ruth Zabuto is dead asleep.

I watch her across the meadow to make sure her chest is moving and she's only dead asleep, not *dead* dead. She lets out a snore loud enough for me to hear from this distance. Reassured, I follow Rhys to the path outside the castle grounds. I can still hear Wanda and Bradford arguing.

Cillian is on a scooter, boxes strapped to either side. He lifts a hand and waves brightly. His mom used to run the sole magic store in the whole area. Most people have no idea that magic is—was—a real thing. But his mom was a decently talented and knowledgeable witch. And, best of all, one who could keep her mouth shut. Cillian and his mother are the only people alive who know there are still Watchers in existence. That we didn't all die when we were supposed to.

We haven't told them much about who we are or what we do. It's safest that way. And they've never asked questions, because we were also their best customers until Buffy killed magic. But even now, Cillian still makes all our nonmagical supply deliveries. Weirdly, online retailers don't accept "Hidden Castle in the Middle of the Woods Outside Shancoom, Ireland" as a proper address.

Cillian stops his scooter in front of us. "What's the story?"

"I—"

There's a flash of movement behind Cillian. A snarl rips apart the air as darkness leaps toward him.

My brain turns off.

My body reacts.

I jump, meeting it midair. We slam into each other. The ground meets us, hard, and we roll. I grab jaws straining for my throat, hot saliva burning where it falls on me.

Then I twist and snap, and the thing falls silent, still, a dead weight on top of me.

I shove it aside and scramble to my feet. My heart is racing, eyes scanning for any other threats, legs ready to leap back into action.

That's when I hear the screaming. It sounds so far away. Maybe it was happening the whole time? I shake my head, trying to force the world back into focus. And I realize there's a creature—a dead creature, a creature I somehow killed—at my feet. I stagger backward, using my shirt to rub away the hot sticky mess of its drool still on my neck.

"Artemis!" Bradford Smythe runs up. "Artemis, are you all right?" He hurries past me, bending down to examine the thing. It looks like hell's version of a dog, which is accurate, because I'm almost certain it's a hellhound. Black, mottled skin. Patchy fur more like moldy growths. Fangs and claws and single-minded, deadly intentions.

But not anymore. Because I killed it.

I *killed* it?

Demon, a voice in my head whispers. And it's not talking about the hellhound.

"Nina," Rhys says, in as much shock as me.

Bradford Smythe looks up in confusion. "What?"

"Not Artemis. That was Nina. . . . Nina killed it."

Everyone stares at me like I, too, have sprouted fangs and claws. I don't know what just happened. How it happened. Why it happened. I've never done anything like that before.

I feel sick and also—elated? That can't be right. My hands are trembling, but I don't feel like I need to lie down. I feel like I could run ten miles. Like I could jump straight over the castle. Like I could fight a hundred more—

"I think I need to throw up," I say, blinking at the dead thing. I'm not a killer. I'm a healer. I fix things. That's what I do.

"That was impossible." Rhys studies me like I'm one of his textbooks, like he can't translate what he's seeing.

He's right. I can't do what I just did.

Bradford Smythe seems less surprised. His shoulders slump as he pulls off his glasses and polishes them with resignation. Why isn't he shocked, now that he knows it wasn't Artemis? The look he gives me is one of pity and regret. "We need to call your mother."

"How could there be a hellhound in Shancoom?" Wanda Wyndam-Pryce's tone, along with her pinched and furious expression, seems to indicate that it was my fault. Like I signed up to provide doggy day care and accidentally checked the "Unholy Hellbeast" column.

I can't stop staring at it, there, on the ground, dead.

Dead.

How did I do that?

Bradford Smythe smooths his walrus mustache. "It is troubling. Shancoom has always had natural mystical protections. It's part of why we picked this location."

"No mystical protection left." Ruth Zabuto retreats further into her cocoon of scarves and shawls. "Can't you feel it? Everything is gone. Only evil is left."

"What are you all doing?" Artemis demands, hurrying up to us. She takes in the hellhound and, before we can explain, throws herself between me and the dead demon. Her first instinct is always to protect me. "Lockdown! Everyone into the castle. Go!"

Rhys startles, and the older Watchers—three-fourths of what's left of the once illustrious and powerful Council—have the sense to look scared. If there's one threat, there might be more. They should have known that. Artemis didn't have to think about it. Rhys grabs Cillian and pulls him along.

Cillian frowns. "The castle's off-limits to me, innit? What was that thing?"

"Go!" Artemis jogs backward, scanning the trees for more threats. Sticking close to me. She's the one with training. The one who can handle this sort of thing.

Crack went its neck.

I hurry along the path to the castle doors. I should be terrified that there are more of those things out there, but it doesn't *feel* like there are. Which worries me. How would I know that?

Once we're inside, Artemis bars the door, barking out orders. "Jade and Imogen will guard the Littles in the dorm wing. Bradford, go tell them. Rhys, take Cillian and Nina. Barricade yourselves in the library. There's a secret room behind the far shelf with a window for escape if we lose the castle."

"There's a secret room?" I ask, at the same time Rhys says, with genuine hurt, "There are more books I didn't know about?"

Cillian steps toward the door. "Barricade? Losing the castle? Bloody hell, what is this?"

Artemis holds up an arm to block his way out. It's not lost on me that Rhys was assigned to protect Cillian, the innocent civilian, *and* me. She has no idea I killed the hellhound myself, and I don't know how to tell her. It feels like it happened to someone else. I'm . . . embarrassed. And terrified. Because if it felt like something else took over, that means all the weirdness in my body I've been ignoring the last couple months is definitely, super, for-sure real.

Artemis opens a dusty old chest beside the door and passes out weapons. Wanda Wyndam-Pryce recoils from a large crossbow. Artemis glares up at her. "Would you prefer a wooden switch?"

"Watch your tone," Wanda snaps. I don't understand the exchange, but Wanda takes the crossbow and hurries away. Rhys gets a sword. Bradford Smythe takes another crossbow. Ancient Ruth Zabuto pulls a wicked-looking knife from a sheath on her thigh beneath her swirling, layered skirts.

"What about—" I start.

"Library!" Artemis barks. "Now!"

Bradford Smythe shoots me a heavy, mournful look. He seems like he has something to say. I half expect him to pull a hard candy out of his suit pocket and give it to me with a pat on the head. That's about the extent of our interactions over the last several years. There's never any reason for the Council to talk to me. After all, my mom is on the Council, and she never needs me. Why should any of the rest of them?

Rhys grabs Cillian's hand to tug him along, and I run after them to the library. Jade is gone, hopefully back to her room, where Bradford Smythe can find her easily. Rhys locates a lever on the far shelf and it swings open to reveal a cramped, dusty room. We shut ourselves in.

"Explanations," Cillian says, panting. "What was that thing? And why are we locked inside the castle? And am I finally allowed to ask how the hell you lot moved a castle here in the first place? Because I have been working mightily to pretend otherwise, but I've lived in Shancoom my entire life, and I'm certain if we had always had a castle in the forest, I would have known about it. And, Nina, what—what—*how* did you do that out there?"

His gaze on me is searching and incredulous. We've been

friends since before he and Rhys started dating. He's more freaked out about what I *did* to the hellhound than the fact that there was a hellhound. I stare at the well-worn floor planks, polished by generations of my people walking here, learning here, planning here. Resting here.

The castle was never our main headquarters. It used to be a retreat for Watchers. But two years ago, way before the Seed of Wonder fiasco, the old Council and nearly every member of the Watcher society got blown up by fanatic followers of an ancient entity known as the First Evil. And it all happened because Buffy threw the balance of good and evil so out of whack that it left an opening for the First to wriggle through.

The First sent out its acolytes to murder everyone who could fight it. That meant all the potential future Slayers it could find—girls who were born with the possibility to someday take up the mantle of Slayer when the previous one died. It also meant all the Watchers. Even after Buffy rejected us, the First knew we were a threat. Buffy ended up defeating it and saving the world.

But she didn't save a single Watcher.

Those of us who survived were either out on assignment in deep cover—only Bradford Smythe and Wanda Wyndam-Pryce's daughter, Honora—or here on a field trip. Rhys Zabuto, Jade Weatherby, Artemis, Imogen Post, the Littles, and myself. My mother, Ruth Zabuto, and Wanda Wyndam-Pryce brought us to see what we could look forward to someday, to get some fresh air, and to undergo a few ritual cleansings to prepare for magical training.

I wasn't going to do those. No magical training for me, just like no physical training. I was supposed to watch the Littles while Imogen went through it. Back in those days she took care of them part-time. They wouldn't let Imogen train to be a full Watcher, because her mother, Gwendolyn Post, had betrayed the Watchers and tricked the Slayers into giving her a weapon of unimaginable power. It had always nagged at me that Imogen was held accountable for something she hadn't even done. We were here because of our parents, sure, but that didn't mean we *were* them—or even who they wanted us to be. I knew that better than anyone.

But Ruth bent the rules for Imogen because she wanted everyone who could to have basic spell training, and the best place for it was our seat of ancient power. So our heritage saved our lives. The castle protected us from being blown up along with the rest of our people.

"We should be out there with them." I place my hand against the shelf sealing us in. I don't say what I really mean, which is that *Rhys* should be out there with them. He's the one who got picked to train as a future Council member. But we both know why Artemis is running the defense and Rhys is hiding here with us.

First, Artemis is more skilled than he is. She always has been.

And second, Artemis put Rhys in here to protect me. Bradford Smythe had called me Artemis out there. He assumed that I was her. Because *I* couldn't do something like I did. It's impossible. I've never trained, never fought.

Never been allowed to and never wanted to.

Rhys stares at me as if I were a stranger. "The way you moved out there. What you did. You looked like a . . ."

Cillian interrupts us. "Again, what the hell? Would someone please explain this to me? What was that thing out there?"

I lean against the shelves, grateful to have to explain things to Cillian so I don't have to think too hard about what I did. What Rhys might have been about to say. "It was a demon."

"A what now?" Cillian rubs his hair, buzzed close to the scalp. His mother is British-Nigerian, and his father grew up in Shancoom. Cillian is the first person since Leo Silvera I've had a crush on, and it lasted all of three minutes before I realized he was not and could never be into me. Lucky Rhys.

But still better than my last crush, which ended in such a humiliating disaster that I haven't managed to work up another viable candidate in the last three years. Maybe in another three years I'll finally get over my Leo Silvera mortification.

But I doubt it. Of all the trauma in my life—and I've had plenty—hearing my lovesick poetry read aloud to my crush remains among the worst. Gods, the *least* Honora Wyndam-Pryce could have done was also kill me on the spot. But she has zero capacity for mercy.

No one knows if Leo Silvera and his mother are still alive, as they haven't been heard from in years. In Watcher society, that means they're more than likely dead. The Giles line is gone now, along with most of the Zabuto, Crowley, Travers, Sirk, and Post. Causes of death, respectively: neck broken by former ally, demon, demon, exploded, exploded, and arm-cut-off-while-being-struck-by-lightning. That last one was Imogen's mom. Poor Imogen. I'm glad she's here to give me perspective. My mom actually *could* be worse.

Regardless, there are so few of us left. I hope that, somewhere out there, the Silveras are still alive.

Just as fervently as I hope I never have to see them again.

I don't know why all this terror has made me think of Leo. Wait. No. It makes perfect sense that heightened, terrible emotions trigger my memories of him.

"A demon," I repeat, trying to refocus. "There are a lot of different types. Some of them are transplants from hell dimensions. Some of them are part demon, part human. True demons don't usually exist on this plane, but sometimes they can infect people. Like vampires."

"Vampires?" Cillian squeaks as he turns to Rhys. "Those are real. Vampires are real. I thought—I knew about magic, obviously, but I thought you were just some divvy cult. You never mentioned *vampires*. That seems like pretty critical information you could have given me sometime in the year we've been dating. 'Hey, Cillian, you've got nice lips and also did you know there are demons and vampires in the world?'"

Rhys barricades the bookshelf door with a table. He looks mildly abashed. "I didn't want to talk business with you. I like that you aren't part of this. And I kind of assumed you knew, what with your mother being a witch and all."

"That was crystals and chanting and shite! Some light levitation! None of this. Exactly how many demons are there in the world?"

"Too many to count? Thousands. Maybe tens of thousands. And it depends on how you classify them."

Cillian leans back so abruptly in his chair he tips over, landing roughly on the ground. "Tens of thousands? Why isn't the government doing anything about it?"

"Which government?"

"Ours! Nina's! Anyone's! Surely someone is taking initiative."

"Sometimes they do. But demons are good at being secret." I move to tug on my hair but freeze. I grabbed a hellhound's jaws with these hands, snapped its life away. Shuddering, I tuck them into my pockets and let Rhys fill in the rest. Demons have been around forever. Portals, hellmouths, and magic allow them to hop in for visits from their dimensions. Hard to track. Hard to fight.

"That's where we come in," Rhys says. "Our group has been

working since the darkest of dark ages to help protect humanity. We know all the prophecies, the demons, the looming apocalypses. But even from the start, we couldn't do it alone. We—they—imbued a girl with demonic powers so she'd become the Slayer and hunt demons."

Cillian raises an eyebrow. "So these ancient blokes thought, hey, let's pick just *one* girl to keep humanity safe? What kind of stook plan was that?"

"Those are our ancient ancestors you're criticizing," Rhys says, mildly hurt.

But I've gotta admit, I'm with Cillian on this one. Except that's why there were Watchers, too. We didn't give Slayers that responsibility and then abandon them.

They abandoned *us*. Buffy led the charge, as always. She was the first Slayer in our entire history who rejected our guidance. Our knowledge. Our help. Like we were holding her back instead of supporting her.

My head is spinning. I keep feeling the crack of the neck. "But then Buffy, the most recent Slayer—"

Rhys interrupts me. "The most recent-ish. All Slayers started out as Potentials. When the current Slayer died, the next one was called. So there was only ever one. Most Potentials never became Slayers. Anyway, Buffy died once—"

"Twice," I correct.

"Irrelevant to the current explanation," Rhys huffs. "She died, so another Slayer, Kendra, was called, but then Buffy was resuscitated, so there were two Slayers, but then Kendra died, and the Slayer after her was—"

"Give me the Wikipedia version, for God's sake," Cillian says.

While Rhys tells the story, I climb up on a chair in front of the high window and peer out at the trees. I don't want to listen to what Rhys is saying. I already know it. Two years ago when Buffy was fighting the First Evil, she was going to lose. So she did what she always does: She broke something. This time it was the binding of the Slayer power. The rules that had been in place, that had worked since the beginning of time, were eliminated.

Suddenly every girl with the potential to become a Slayer *did* become a Slayer, or would become a Slayer when she was old enough.

She let the Watchers die, and then she flooded the earth with almost two thousand new Slayers. And then she got around a thousand of them killed in battle, because of course she did. There's a reason there was only supposed to be one Slayer and a whole organization of Watchers. And having all those new Slayers didn't tip the balance in favor of good. It did the opposite. Demons content to slurk through the night, doing their demon-y things? Suddenly felt threatened. The more Buffy pushes, the more the darkness pushes back. And it pushed back so hard, the world almost ended.

I give up on the window. There's nothing out there. I don't know how I know, but I do. And I feel sick with dread at what all these new abilities and senses might mean. For sixty-freaking-two days I've been able to ignore them. But I can't anymore.

Rhys has caught up to Buffy's most recent terrible exploits in his explanation. "Do you remember a couple months back when the world almost ended?"

"The world almost *ended*?" Cillian asks, aghast.

"Oh, right." Rhys rubs his forehead. Maybe this is the real reason we don't talk about this stuff to anyone who isn't a Watcher. It's *complicated*. "The world almost ended because another dimension was taking over ours."

"Sixty-two days ago," I whisper. And we had to sit here in our castle, watching it unfold, because if we revealed ourselves, odds were we'd die in the crossfire. I hated it. Artemis about went mad. But what bothers me the most is, even without our help, it worked out. Sort of. "In order to prevent the end of the world, Buffy destroyed the Seed of Wonder that fed all magic on earth."

Cillian whistles low and soft. "I thought it was just . . . one of those things. Like we lost the magic Wi-Fi signal or something."

"Didn't you notice that day the sky burst open and there were earthquakes and tsunamis and stuff?" I ask.

He shrugs. "Global warming."

Rhys has gotten lost in the spines on the bookshelves. It's hard for him to focus, looking at all these books he didn't know we had. So I continue. "Right. Global warming, and also transdimensional global threat. And all of this—the broken magic, the new Slayers, the almost end of the world—it's all because of Buffy."

Cillian snorts. "Sorry, I just. I can't get over her name. *Buffy.*"

I fold my arms, glaring. "What, she has a girly name, so she can't destroy the world?"

Cillian holds up his hands defensively. "That's not what I'm saying."

"She was a cheerleader before she became a Slayer," Rhys says.

Cillian bursts out laughing.

I don't want to defend Buffy—ever—but I'm annoyed anyway. "Have you seen a cheerleading competition? Each and every one of those girls could take you, even without mystical Slayer powers."

"Is that how you killed the demon thingy out there, then? You've trained as a cheerleader?"

I feel the crack all over again. "That's not the point. I don't even like Buffy. All she ever does is react. She never thinks through the consequences, and my family keeps paying the price." I take a deep breath to steady myself. "And the whole world too. Because this last time, she also broke it. No more magic. No more connections to other worlds. And no more new Slayers. Ever. She blew the door wide open, and then she slammed it shut."

"She needs to make up her mind," Cillian says. "Make more Slayers! End the Slayers. Break the world! Save the world."

Rhys takes over my chair at the high window, looking out. "To be fair, a lot of people have tried to destroy the world over the years. It's a whole thing."

"Huh. Who knew?"

"We did," Rhys says.

"Fair enough." Cillian grabs my hand and makes me sit next to him. "So, what's your story, Nina? This Buffy. It's personal, innit?"

I close my eyes, words that have been drilled into my brain since birth swimming into focus. *Into every generation a Slayer is born: one girl in all the world, a Chosen One. She alone will wield the strength and skill to fight the vampires, demons, and forces of darkness; to stop the spread of their evil and the swell of their number. She is the Slayer.*

There's a painful lump in my throat when I speak. "Every Slayer used to get a Watcher. And Buffy got the best." I open my eyes and smile. "My dad was her first Watcher."

When Merrick Jamison-Smythe found her, she had no idea who she was or what was coming for her. My dad had worked his whole life training Slayers, teaching them, helping them. And he watched those he trained before her die. So when faced with a choice between allowing himself to be used against Buffy or dying, he chose the Chosen One.

Enter the Buffyverse with the ultimate reading for the ultimate fans.

EBOOK EDITION ALSO AVAILABLE

Simon Pulse
simonandschuster.com/teen